Murder by Chance

To Wendy—
Enjoy!

Murder by Chance

Pat Dennis

FORTY PRESS

This book is a work of fiction. The names, characters, places and incidents are products of the writer's imagination or have been used fictitiously and are not to be construed as real. Any resemblance to persons, living or dead, actual events, locales or organizations is entirely coincidental.

Murder By Chance

Forty Press, LLC
427 Van Buren Street
Anoka, MN 55303
www.fortypress.com

Library of Congress Cataloging-in-Publications Data
Library of Congress Control Number: 2012955116

Dennis, Pat

Murder By Chance/Pat Dennis

ISBN 978-1-938473-04-3

First Edition: March 2013

10 9 8 7 6 5 4 3 2 1

For Elizabeth Andrejasich Gibes
(the other writer in the family)

Chapter 1

Asking a group of seniors to walk toward the light is like sending a vampire into a gaggle of nuns. It is never a good idea. But Betty Chance had little choice.

From Chicago to northern Minnesota, Take A Chance Tours had battled January's tempestuous weather. Betty's tour bus was four hours behind schedule when it pulled up to its final destination: Moose Bay Resort and Casino.

Blanketed by three feet of powdery snow, with drifts reaching over six feet, the only path to the hotel entrance was a narrowly-shoveled sidewalk. Even the sparkling neon lights surrounding the hotel's rotating doors were shrouded by the blizzard-like conditions.

It was nearly midnight.

"Okay folks, we're at Moose Bay!" Betty lifted her chubby arms and waved her fingers in the air in celebration. "Woo-hoo!" she chirped.

The forty-four tired and surly passengers sat silent. Not one of them followed her lead. Instead, the group of mostly senior citizens stared glumly out the frosted windows as they clutched tightly at the purses or small bags they carried. A few pulled their thick winter caps farther down over their ears. Others tightened woolen neck scarves.

Betty winced. Her riders were acting as if they'd arrived at the North Pole. Everyone was in a bad mood.

Betty knew she had to play the cheerleader—a plus-sized, fifty-five-year-old cheerleader, to be sure—but a cheerleader nonetheless. She knew she could do "perky" as well as anyone. And that this time her job depended on it.

She brushed her feather-cut, salt and pepper bangs to the side. Her goal of hosting the best gambling junkets in the Midwest was in peril. She needed to lift her clients' mood. Fast.

She sang out, "It's party time!"

Silence.

Her eyes darted up and down the aisle of the luxury motor coach.

"Woo-hoo!"

Nothing.

Ice on a distant lake cracked. Betty wished she were standing on it.

Having read in one of her how-to marketing books that it takes three repetitions for a message to stick, she inhaled deeply and belted out one last "Woo-Hoo!" as she flashed a gleaming white smile and unfurled an enthusiastic thumbs-up gesture.

Nada.

Betty gave up, announcing in a defeated monotone, "When you exit the bus, please walk toward the ligh…entrance…at the end of the walkway. This is the closest we can get. I've been assured the sidewalk is not icy. If you want to start gambling immediately, I'll have the staff put your luggage in your rooms. And thank you again for betting on Take A Chance Tours."

She turned and scurried off the coach, snagging the sleeve of her Calvin Klein jacket on the doorframe. "Damn," she sighed, snaking a finger into the rip of her favorite eight-dollar find.

Betty purchased most of her clothes from consignment shops or thrift stores. She loved finding a vintage treasure buried within a mound of discards for a fraction of its original cost. Being frugal was more than a choice, however. It was a necessity.

As she stood at the bottom of the steps examining the tear, she noticed the bus sway slightly. She froze. It swayed again. Betty leaned into the stairwell and motioned frantically to her driver. "Tillie," she called in a loud whisper, "get out while you can!"

The curvaceous redhead looked at her quizzically.

"Now!" Betty said, her eyes widening.

Tillie McFinn scrambled out of her seat and down the metal stairs.

"Good Lord, Betty, you're acting like my life's in danger."

"Trust me," she said, pulling Tillie away from the door,"it is."

As co-owner of the two-year-old Take A Chance Tours, it was Betty's seventy-eighth time as a tour host. Early on, she learned to never underestimate a gambler's determination to reach the casino floor, no matter what their age. The opportunity to play penny slots, dabble in three-card poker and chow down at an all-you-can-eat-buffet could turn a slow moving octogenarian into an Olympic sprinter. On steroids.

Passengers that were docile only a few moments earlier were now pushing against each other as they tried to get off the bus as quickly as possible. Betty could hear the rustling of coats and the shuffling of shoes and boots parading down the sardine-packed aisle as the bus rocked with their movements. She could now feel an air of expectation coming from her passengers as they finally realized that a casino was only yards away. And a winning jackpot within reach.

"You could at least offer a lady your hand!" Hannah Forester snipped as the stacked heels of her sensible shoes landed on the top step.

Betty positioned her manicured hand to assist, but Hannah ignored it, reaching out to Tillie instead. Betty realized her repeat client was livid because she hadn't won a bingo game on the bus. Although the prize was a measly three dollars a game, Hannah wanted it. Of course, Hannah wanted everything.

"Humph!" Hannah sniffed, "Paying three hundred and twenty-nine dollars of my late husband's hard earned money to receive this kind of treatment?"

Despite Tillie's help, Hannah tottered a bit as her feet hit the concrete. Betty knew Hannah's unsteadiness wasn't due simply to age. For in a battle of scents, Jack Daniels will always defeat any store-bought fragrance that stood in its path.

"Hannah," Betty said firmly, "Safety is far more important to us than schedule." Betty let that thought sink in before she added the facts: "Tillie was forced to drive slowly *due to the weather*."

The crowd standing behind Hannah was growing. Betty could tell they were anxious to get off the bus and onto the casino floor. But Hannah wasn't appeased. With a flip of her red wool scarf, she sputtered, "I don't have that many years left on this earth to spend one moment more than necessary on a bus."

So, get off the friggin' thing, Betty wanted to scream. Instead she bit her tongue and reached deep into her pocket. She pulled out a booklet and held it out to Hannah.

"It better have buffet coupons in it, Buffet Betty!" Hannah said contemptuously, snatching the booklet from Betty's hand and stomping off toward the hotel.

Betty prayed silently, *God, if you let anyone win a jackpot on this trip, could it be Hannah?* A hundred-buck jackpot would transform the Dragon Lady of Calumet City into Mother Theresa—if only for a moment; one, glorious moment!

In truth, although Hannah's normal demeanor was that of a malcontent, Betty didn't mind trying to please her. Business was finally looking good. And so was Betty's personal life.

Two years ago, she thought her life ruined. Her husband, a Chicago homicide detective, had left her—and left her in debt. After twenty-seven years of marriage he had dumped her for an older, fatter woman—the rich one who could cover his gambling debts.

At fifty-three, she found herself divorced, unemployed, and not only financially underwater, but drowning. It was unfair. It was her husband's compulsive gambling that destroyed their savings account, after all, not anything she did. Betty had spent her entire marriage being the 'good wife' who was faithful, cut coupons, held garage sales, and kept both furniture and clothes far too long. But she'd trusted her husband completely. She now understood that she had naively believed every lie he ever told her. But why wouldn't she? She'd been madly in love with him from the first moment she saw him in his policeman's uniform.

Although she hadn't realized there was something wrong from day one in her marriage, her body had been signaling her all along. Every single pound she gained during her stint as Mrs. Chance was a cry for comfort and protection.

After the divorce, Betty spent the next six months crying, cursing, and buying chocolate by the carton. By the time her favorite stretchy, size 1X pajamas couldn't be pulled up over her hips she realized she'd moved out of Pleasantly Plumpville and became the latest resident of Fatland. She never forgot the one moment that convinced her it was time for a change.

She'd just finished off a bag of Keebler's when the doorbell rang. She hoisted herself off the couch and moved toward the door. For a moment, she'd wondered if she'd forgotten she'd ordered a pizza for dinner. It had almost become a daily habit. But it wasn't a teenage boy holding up a Supreme who stood at her door. It was a Girl Scout clutching a box of Thin Mints. Betty smiled down at the child and watched as the girl's eyes flew open and her smile grew wide.

"Can I help you?" Betty asked.

The girl's eyes traveled up and down Betty's body in amazement before blurting out, "I bet you'll order a hundred boxes!"

Betty never thought she could feel so good about slamming a door in a ten-year-old's face.

Yet it was that moment that Betty decided to finally change her life. In order to do so, she realized, she too would have to change.

Later, when asked how she did it, she realized her answer sounded like the start of an old joke..."*A therapist, a minister and a librarian walked into my life and . . .*"

The therapist instructed her to start a combination food and exercise journal.

The minister suggested she keep an Attitude-of-Gratitude diary.

The librarian said "been there, done that," bought Betty a *Thank God I'm Single Again* t-shirt, and gave her a list of recommended audio books on positive thinking. She also urged her to keep a daily log of her rage. She assured Betty that the first day she forgot to write down her anger would be the day she had moved on with her life. Gloria worked for the Chicago Public Library and Betty knew better than to question a librarian.

The very next day she loaded up her MP3 player with the suggested audio books and hit the road. Literally. She could only make it around a single block in her Southside Chicago neighborhood. But even that short distance was filled with temptation. Frankie's Sausage Emporium, Uchanski's Bakery and the most evil of all: Theresa's Chocolate Rescue. They called out to her each time she passed.

Still, Betty was determined. She focused her eyes straight ahead and squeezed her nostrils as she scurried past her favorite haunts.

Her first few days of walking turned into weeks and then months. It was during those many solitary walks that the idea of owning a tour company specializing in gambling junkets popped into her head. Twelve months later, she was earning a living doing something she loved and was one-third of her way out of debt.

Her entire life had turned around for the better. Betty had more friends now than she did when she married. Her ex had never wanted to socialize, blaming his anti-social behavior on the stress of his job. She had no idea he spent what little spare time he had at the track, or worse, with another woman. Yet, when she lost her marriage she found something she loved even more: time. And she used it to do what she hadn't done for years: focus on herself.

She forced herself to go to a hair salon. True, it was only Great Clips, but she got the "works," and for the first time even splurged on some of the hair products. She joined a gym and attended Zumba classes. Betty even purchased sexy underwear. For a change, she didn't even check the price tag before she placed them on the counter. All she cared about was they were lacey and red, something the old Betty would never have considered. The old Betty preferred stiff white cotton that looked like it could last an eternity. The new Betty wanted something that looked like it wouldn't make it through a one-night stand.

Betty had even lost ten pounds since her divorce. That meant only forty more pounds to go. She understood her goal weight of one hundred and fifty was still heavy to many, but to her it was this side of paradise.

A thin, wobbly voice broke her reverie: "Could I take your hand, Miss Betty?" It was Mr. Ogawa, one of her new riders.

"Mr. Ogawa, I'm so sorry. My mind was drifting." She smiled at the gentle man who'd informed her earlier that he was not on a vacation, but a quest.

"Thank you, Miss Betty," he said, stepping off the bus.

"This is the Fun Book I told you about, Mr. Ogawa" she said, handing him the coupon booklet. It was Ogawa's first time visiting a casino. Learning to gamble was number thirty-six on the checklist he called *88 Things to Do Before I Die*. Each *thing* represented a year of his life.

"Oh, thank you very much," he cooed, with a wink. "I'm all into fun you know."

She continued to hand each passenger a booklet as they climbed off the bus. Some took it without a word while others mentioned they were glad the driver had been cautious. Only a few grumbled about their late arrival.

"Can I go to my room? I'm too tired to gamble," the seventy-some-year-old Mrs. Kotval said, shifting her "I Saw Siegfried and Roy at the Mirage" canvas tote bag from one side to the other. She adjusted her pink spangled Circus-Circus visor and checked her watch, a cheap Gucci knock-off bought on the streets of Vegas for fifteen bucks.

Betty responded, "Of course you can. Just wait for me on one of the sofas near the front desk. I'll get your key for you."

No one else made that request. Betty knew that ninety percent of her passengers would be gambling within minutes, no matter how late their arrival.

To be sure, if sleep seemed evasive Betty herself would plop down in front of a video slot machine before long. Easy access to gambling was one of the perks of the business for her, as well as an area of caution. She understood her personal tendency toward addiction. And if it looked like she was slipping, she'd remember how often she'd uttered the words "*I'll take a half a dozen Krispy Kremes, please*."

If she wasn't cautious, an uncontrollable penchant for slot machines could easily become her next uncontrolled passion. Fun size candy bars quickly stopped being fun when she noticed seventeen of them in the bottom of her purse. She gave up on extreme couponing when she found herself driving twenty-one miles to save twenty-five cents on a can of beans. But gaining a few pounds due to lack of self-control, or wasting three bucks worth of gas to save a quarter was not comparable to what could be lost to a gambling addiction.

So far, she'd been conservative with her gambling. In order to continue working in the gaming industry, she'd have to remain that way. But then, she'd always been a cheapskate. Even with her vices. She'd rather eat a bag of M&Ms than a pound of Godiva. Betty didn't crave fancy French restaurants or their pricey menus. The local diner featuring Mac & Cheese was just fine with her. Losing twenty bucks after an entire night of church basement bingo was her kind of entertainment; not gambling away thousands playing high stakes poker.

After the last of the passengers appeared to have disembarked, Tillie motioned toward the inside of the bus. "I'll check to see if everyone's off," she said, as her short, petite, 36-year-old body bounded up the steps. Inside, she lifted her zirconia bejeweled hand to her forehead and peered toward the back of the bus. "I don't see anyone."

"That can't be right," Betty replied, waving a single booklet. The casino's marketing department had sent her exactly forty-four Fun Books, one for each passenger. "There's one left."

"Then we must have a sleeper," Tillie said, lifting up on her tiptoes and craning her neck as she looked across the high seats.

It wasn't unusual to discover a rider snuggled into the plush seats of the rented luxury bus. The passenger would be snoring away, oblivious to the fact that the group had arrived at its destination.

Betty charged back up the steps. She too looked out across the padded headrests. She didn't see a single soul.

She began to walk down the narrow aisle carefully checking out the twenty-three rows of seats. Except for the odd candy bar wrapper, or tossed aside magazine, everything appeared normal. She could even smell the scent of an orange that one of her passengers had eaten earlier. It wasn't until she and Tillie were standing next to the washroom, that a different scent made her gag.

"Do you smell that?" Betty asked, as her vivid imagination began its warm-up stretches.

Tillie sniffed. "Yeah, it's weird. Kind of like that pricey rotting cheese…covered with dollar-store perfume."

Betty stared at the large double back seat just below the tinted rear window. A lone newspaper lay spread out on a seat cushion. Even in the dark, Betty could see it was written in a foreign language. There was nothing else. No containers were left unopened or rancid liquid spilled on the seat. Across the aisle from the seat, was the washroom. It was a room so small that, unless it was urgent, most passengers refused to enter it.

She glanced at the room's closed metal door, and noticed the occupied sign was lit. Her eyes continued downward until she saw a small puddle of liquid that had seeped out from underneath the door. The color was golden with a rose tint. The watery substance had a fluorescent glow.

Betty and Tillie exchanged nervous looks.

"Hello?" she said, tapping loudly, hoping an aged client would open the door. Or at least give an irritated "Occupied!"

When there was no response, she pounded on the door.

"Hello, anyone in there?" she yelled. Again she waited for a response. None came.

She jiggled the knob. The door was locked.

"This isn't good," Betty said and pointed to the locked key box, located on the side of the door. A spare key to the restroom was hidden inside. "Tillie, will you open it?"

Tillie nodded and, stepping around the wet carpet, punched in the combination to the lock. The key box door slid open. She reached inside and grabbed the thin brass key.

Betty thought it ironic that earlier in the day she'd told Tillie a potential problem in traveling with seniors is that, at any moment, any one of them could die suddenly. Though it hadn't happened to her yet, a few months ago a senior citizen had died of sudden heart failure while traveling with Tours by Tina. Not only did a human life end, Tina's ridership declined by thirty percent for the rest of the year.

Now, it looked to her as if her small talk to Tillie was nothing less than a premonition.

Tillie slid the key into the restroom keyhole. The latch clicked and she opened the door. A silver box catapulted toward her, its thick pink liquid content splashing all over her face and torso. "What the . . .?" she gasped and instinctively shut the door.

A toilet paper roll careened down the aisle.

Tillie touched the goop on her face with her fingers. She slowly drew her fingertips to her nose. "It's soap!" she announced, clearly relieved. Then she pointed: "Look, the liquid soap container was ripped off the wall!"

"Open the door again," Betty commanded, gearing herself for whatever was lurking in the tiny room. A scenario of possibilities raced through her mind. Someone could have suffered a fatal cardiac attack. Or perhaps they were still alive, but too sick to unlock the door. Or maybe the person inside committed suicide because they realized that Take A Chance's destination—a casino—was the last place they needed to be.

Tillie slowly reopened the door, inch by inch, blocking Betty's view with her arms. The driver's shoulders slumped downward before she muttered, "My god!"

"What?" Betty demanded.

Tillie swallowed hard. "Remember how you said you worried about your seniors dying suddenly from natural causes?"

"Yes?" Betty replied in a small voice.

Tillie used her thumb to gesture toward the interior of the restroom.

"I can assure you…" Tillie said "…this ain't natural."

Betty squeezed herself around the metal door and stepped in front of Tillie.

An enormous male outfitted in a jogging suit filled the cubicle. His three hundred and fifty pound body was slumped face-first against the outside wall of the bus. The gray velour clothing covering his massive rump, thighs, and back gave the appearance of an overstuffed armchair crammed into the tiny space.

Tillie was right about one thing. There was nothing natural about this man's death. Not with a butcher knife buried in his back.

Chapter 2

Betty stood next to the parked tour bus. She closed her eyes hard, squeezed for a hopeful moment, and then snapped them open. *Damn! She wasn't having a nightmare. This was real.*

She shivered in the frigid air, buttoned up her jacket and turned her collar up around her neck. She rubbed her hands together for warmth and noticed her breath was forming little clouds of frost. She watched as the paramedics pushed the gurney toward the ambulance. The EMTs weren't bothering with IV's. She'd overheard an officer tell them the moment they arrived that the body was ready to be bagged and tagged.

"I can't believe this, Tillie," Betty said, burrowing her hands deep into her jacket. It was the fifteenth tour the two women had worked together. By the seventh, they had become close friends.

"I can't believe *him*," Tillie said, pointing to the law enforcement officer that stepped out of their tour bus. "He kind of looks like the sheriff in that cartoon flick, if the sheriff was sexy, that is."

"*Toy Story*?" Betty asked.

Tillie nodded, her eyes remaining fixed on the officer.

Betty agreed that the short, muscular young man bore a striking resemblance to the animated character of Sheriff Woody. His wavy reddish brown hair flopped around on his head in the strong wind. His eyes were small brown pupils surrounded by a sea of white. His face was long and his prominent chin square and strong. His skin was as pale as sweet cream.

"You think a man who looks like a cartoon is sexy?" Betty asked.

"I think all men are sexy, animated or not," Tillie responded. "How old do you think he is?"

"It's hard to say. Could be like Dick Clark was and look twenty years younger than he actually is," Betty responded.

"Well, then he's got to be thirty-four because he looks fourteen to me." Tillie said. But before wrapping her arms tighter around her body, she unzipped her jacket to reveal a bit of cleavage.

Betty applied the brakes: "Oh, no you don't, Tillie. This is not the time to flirt. Not only could it hurt our business, it might hurt the investigation. The sheriff has to have his eyes on the crime, not your spectacular boobs."

Reluctantly, Tillie zipped back up.

The Sheriff stomped over. He said crisply, "I'm Sheriff Severson. Let's go inside to talk, ladies." He pointed toward the building and abruptly walked toward it.

His dismissive attitude didn't bother Betty. She understood policemen. Not only had she spent decades being married to one, she'd been born into a family of Chicago cops. Homicide investigations were as familiar to her as cookies at Christmas.

Betty and Tillie followed the sheriff inside. As they entered the lavish hotel lobby, squeals of joy and moans of disappointment escaped from the casino floor. Even at one thirty in the morning with death at its door, Moose Bay was a maze of people racing to find their fortune.

Betty noticed Mrs. Kotval waiting patiently on one of the overstuffed, burgundy leather sofas. Tall ferns and a brass coffee table enveloped her. The Beatles' *We All Live in a Yellow Submarine* was playing softly overhead. Mrs. Kotval's white, Velcro-strapped sneakers tapped reflexively on the travertine marble floor to the beat of the music.

"Sheriff, will you excuse me for just one minute?" Betty asked, bee-lining for her client before he could answer.

She placed her arm gently on the woman's shoulder. "I assumed the hotel staff had taken care of you, Mrs. Kotval. I was sure you had your room key by now."

"Oh, I do, dear. It's true I was tired earlier, but now I don't want to go to bed. I want to see what's going on with the…" she whispered, "murder." She beamed: "I feel like Angela Lansbury! Did you know *Murder She Wrote* is one of my favorite TV shows?" she asked gleefully.

Betty pursed her lips. It seemed pointless to mention that a real murder was hardly comparable to a fictional one. Anyway, her client seemed to be in a jolly good mood about the whole thing and she didn't want to spoil it. Take A Chance Tours had at least one satisfied customer.

In fact, Betty wished she could take the murder as lightly as Mrs. Kotval did. But she'd seen too many murder investigations gone wrong where innocent people end up on death row. It made her anxious. The fact that the investigation was being led by what looked like a man-child didn't make her any less so.

"Okey-doke, have a good night," Betty said before following Severson and Tillie to a small conference room. Two other local policemen were already inside the room. The door shut behind them. For the first time, Betty was away from the noise of ambulance sirens and screeching patrol cars. The sheriff motioned for Betty and Tillie to sit at the large oak table.

As she slid into her chair, the thought crossed Betty's mind that her tour company was DOA, just like the bus victim. Bad publicity would mean fewer riders. Casinos might decline to work with her. Take A Chance Tours would have to shut its doors.

The sheriff removed his fur-lined bomber jacket and hung it on the back of a chair. As he did, Betty noticed the pint-sized sheriff's massive biceps. They looked like they would burst through his khaki sleeves at any moment. In her experience, there were two kinds of cops. The ones who treated their bodies like they were a weapon for survival that needed to be fine-tuned at all times. And the others who thought their bodies were nothing more than over-sized dumpsters for junk food.

Tillie poked Betty in the side and whispered, "His shirt is tighter than mine!" She sighed. "He's not a toy sheriff. He's a boy toy sheriff."

Severson turned around. "Did you say something to me?"

Tillie shook her head. "Nope, just girl talk."

The sheriff gave her a stern look and said, "I don't think this is a time for chitchat." He walked to the head of the table and sat down.

"We understand, Sheriff," Betty responded gently. She leaned forward as if to share a confidence: "I was married to a police lieutenant for twenty-seven years." She smiled.

In the past, when Betty identified herself as a policeman's wife, it usually worked to her advantage. Only three weeks earlier, a smile and mention of her son Codey was rewarded with a warning instead of a four hundred dollar speeding ticket.

Severson's shoulders stiffened and his eyes turned into stone-cold versions of *I give a crap about that, because?*

Betty slumped back into her chair.

"I'll need to speak with each of your passengers," he said.

Betty remarked quietly, "It's so late, Sheriff. Can you possibly do it in the morning? Most of my clients are senior citizens. Mr. Farsi was actually one of our youngest riders."

"The victim?" he asked. Betty nodded.

"What can you tell me about him?"

"Not much, unfortunately." Betty reached down and picked up the leather tote bag she carried. Inside was a trip list of the passengers' names, gambling and hotel preferences, a short bio and emergency numbers. It was the same information she'd faxed to the casino the day before their arrival. "This was Farsi's first time traveling with Take A Chance."

Severson leaned back in his chair, clasping his hands behind his head. His biceps were tight against his shirtsleeves, as if he were the Incredible Hulk on the verge of exploding out of his clothes.

Tillie gasped as Betty stepped lightly on her foot underneath the table to stop her. Betty meant for the tap to be a warning to behave. Betty knew the last time Tillie got close to a set of biceps like that she behaved so outrageously flirtatious, she was almost arrested for solicitation.

Severson continued. "Do you know why he chose your company?"

Betty answered, "Because we're the best?"

She laughed. Severson didn't.

Betty cleared her throat. "I'm not sure. This particular junket is The Boomer Blast but it's open to anyone, of any age. We advertise it in senior magazines, on our website, and a few oldies-but-goodies stations in the Chicago area."

"The group you're hosting isn't a specific organization or club?" Severson asked.

"Not this time," she responded.

"Was Farsi traveling with anyone?"

"I don't think so, but I'm not sure. It was the first day of the tour so I hadn't gotten to know the new passengers very well." She added proudly, "I try to eat at least one meal with each new client or at least gamble next to them."

The Sheriff stared at her for a moment. "So, you're a gambler?" he asked with disdain. The sound of his voice suggested the adjective "degenerate" should be tossed in as well. "Well…I…" Betty began to backpedal.

"*Buffet Betty* a gambler?" A voice interrupted from behind. Tom Songbird, head of casino security, stood in the doorway, a lopsided grin on his already craggy face. "Why, she drops thousands every time she visits."

Betty turned around and smiled—probably more than she should, considering the circumstances. In his mid-thirties, Tom referred to himself as lean but never mean. Right now, he seemed as friendly as ever and to her that was a good sign, especially since she managed to deliver a stiff to his tribe's doorstep.

She looked at the sheriff and explained, "The thousands he's talking about are thousands of pennies. Tom likes to tease me because I'm too much of a coward to be a high-roller."

"But she's brave enough to be a terrific low-roller!" Tom laughed.

"Buffet Betty? Is that your nickname?" Severson inquired, not to be sidetracked.

"My pen name," Betty clarified. "I write a little online blog about casino buffets."

"It's hardly 'little'," Songbird contradicted. "Buffet Betty's Blog is famous. I'm sure she gets tens of thousands of hits every day."

Betty agreed. "Oh, I do. In fact, blogging is what led me to the casino tour industry. I wrote about casino buffets for years. Just for fun. Eventually, my blog became popular. When I realized I needed more income after my divorce, I decided to . . ."

"...do what she loved and the money would follow," Tillie interrupted. "She's told me that story a dozen times since I've known her. Of course, if I did what I love doing for money, you'd have to arrest me, Sheriff." Tillie shot the sheriff a wickedly flirtatious smile.

Severson didn't laugh. Nor did he seem amused. He didn't seem to be anything but granite. Betty thought if he played poker wearing that face, no one could beat him. His expression didn't provide a clue as to what he was thinking.

Maybe the Sheriff isn't such a young fool after all, she thought.

Sheriff Severson turned to Tom. "You have anything for me?"

"I called my friend in the FBI," Tom answered. "He can't locate any information on an Alexander Farsi." He turned to Betty. "The emergency contact number Farsi had given you was a pre-paid cell phone. There's no way to trace the owner. And the company Farsi supposedly worked for? The one he listed on his form? No such company. At least not that the FBI can find."

The sheriff gave Betty a quick look of total disbelief and demanded, "Don't tell me that Take A Chance doesn't check the backgrounds of their riders? Or their ID's?"

Betty squared her shoulders, preparing herself for a fight if need be. "There's no reason to check. We're not traveling out of the country. Each client pays for the trip weeks ahead, using a credit card, check, or sometimes cash. We've never had a problem."

"Not having had a problem is no excuse for not preparing for one," Severson lectured. "Anyone in transportation has to be extra cautious these days. Remember 9/11?" he asked condescendingly.

Betty tightened. Of course she remembered 9/11. But she also remembered a little thing called constitutional rights. She didn't think it was possible, but the sheriff made her feel even more uncomfortable. She'd heard stories about getting on the wrong side of the good old boys up north. There was no telling what could happen to her, Tillie, or even her passengers if any of them did. She nodded like a good student.

The sheriff seemed satisfied. He asked, "How did Farsi pay for his trip? Did he use cash? Credit card?"

Betty answered honestly, "I don't know."

"Then find out, please," his tone betraying his growing impatience. "If he used a credit card or a check, I want the account number."

"I'll have that information for you ASAP," Betty replied, trying to sound cooperative—and professional. "I'll call my niece and business partner Lori in the morning. She handles the company's finances."

Severson gave a slight roll of the eyes as he turned his attention to Tillie and asked, "You didn't see anything suspicious happening at the back of the bus from your rearview mirror?"

Tillie shifted uncomfortably in her chair. "I didn't see anything at all."

"You're telling me you didn't notice Farsi going into the toilet? He was kind of hard to miss," the sheriff said. "He must have taken up the entire aisle."

Tillie chuckled thinking he made a joke.

He hadn't.

"It was dark," she answered nervously. "Sometimes, I can see the outlines of bodies moving about, but that's about it."

Betty intervened. "We turn the interior lights down after dusk. The lights were turned off completely after our stop in Tyler Falls."

Severson's eyes narrowed. "Tyler Falls is only an hour from here. Why'd you bother stopping when you were already late? Something doesn't add up with your story," he stated.

Betty's discomfort quickly turned into anger. The sheriff was obviously suggesting they were hiding something. She spat out, "I felt both Tillie and the passengers needed a break to stretch their legs because of the road conditions. I was the one who insisted that Tillie pull into the truck stop."

"Did Farsi get off the bus when you stopped? Did he go inside the truck stop?" Severson asked in a singsong voice that suggested the idiots in front of him wouldn't have noticed anyway.

Betty clenched her teeth before admitting, "I can't say for sure."

The sheriff shot a glance at Tillie. "Did you "stretch your legs" as well?"

"Sure did. Plus I bought a cup of Joe for the road!" Tillie responded, then realized it was irrelevant information.

The sheriff asked the next question, as if he already knew Tillie's answer: "Did you manage to *lock* the bus when you went into the truck stop?"

Tillie's face turned red and for the first time she was completely flustered. "I don't remember if I did. So, I guess the answer is... maybe?"

"Didn't you count the passengers when you left the truck stop to make sure they all got back on?" he demanded.

"We did," Betty sputtered, realizing what she was about to admit. "Well, not actually *count* because it looked to me like everyone was in their seats. And I knew for sure none of our passengers were still inside the truck stop."

Severson looked into Betty's eyes for a moment. "Exactly how..." he began to ask, his lids blinking rapidly like valves allowing his frustration to escape, "...did you 'know for sure'?"

Betty could tell he expected her response would simply continue the downward spiral. She wished her answer could change that but she knew better. "Because," she answered honestly, "I was the last one out of the truck stop. None of my passengers were inside when I left. I assumed they all were back at the bus."

Severson turned to Tillie and asked accusingly, "Are you sure the only thing you did in Tyler Falls was buy coffee?"

Betty fumed. While she recognized that they may not have been as vigilant as they perhaps should have been, she was proud of the company she built—the company she *had* to build after her law-enforcement husband ("Defend and Protect", indeed!) left her to fend for herself. She was proud of the hard work she and Tillie put in each and every trip. She would not let Sheriff Severson bully her into thinking they were incompetent—or worse.

Betty interrupted, "Why are you asking her that, Sheriff?"

"For two reasons." He paused, letting their imaginations run a little. "One, if the EMTs are correct, Farsi was killed an hour before you arrived at the casino, which, coincidentally" (he nodded toward

Tillie without looking at her) "was right about the time Ms. McFinn was supposedly buying her latte."

Tillie exhaled. Her last bit of cheerfulness dissipated. Her chin dropped to her chest.

"And the second reason?" Betty asked, trying to contain her anger.

"I don't trust her and neither should you," said Severson.

"And why's that, Sheriff?"

"Because," he said, leaning forward and folding his hands on the table, "your driver's an ex-con."

Chapter 3

Betty grumbled to herself as she opened the door to her hotel room, still furious at Sheriff Severson's attitude toward Tillie.

She walked to the bed and fell backwards on top of it. She wasn't going to sleep. The sheriff had made her too angry to sleep. Not only was he rude and accusatory, there was no need for him to remind her of her friend's background. Tillie had revealed all of it the first day they met.

Betty recalled how Tillie strolled into the office of Take A Chance Tours, smelling of Aqua Net hairspray and menthol cigarettes. Her tight denim skirt ended three inches from the top of her knee-high black leather boots. The short, faux fur jacket she sported was as shockingly pink as her lip-gloss. Numerous tattoos were easily visible. Betty guessed that another dozen were hidden beneath her ensemble.

She stopped in the middle of the room, her feet planted shoulder-width. As she placed her hands hard on her hips, her bracelets slid down her arms coming to a screeching halt at her wrists. She looked like she was prepping herself for battle, as if defending herself was an everyday occurrence. Though she was small in stature, an Amazonian warrior would look timid in comparison.

"Who's in charge of this juke joint?" Tillie asked loudly.

Well, thought Betty, this office is hardly a "joint." But when Tillie flashed her big, winning smile, she knew the brash woman in front of her was just being friendly.

Betty stood up and reached out her hand.

"I'm Betty Chance, the owner."

"Chance? As in 'no chance in hell'?" Tillie asked, unleashing that smile again.

Betty resisted the urge to roll her eyes. Since marrying into the Chance family, she'd heard that particular phrase a million times.

But at least this warrior princess hadn't used the one she dreaded the most: fat chance.

"It's not as uncommon of a name as you might think," Betty replied. "And you are…?"

"I'm your new driver," Tillie said, shaking Betty's hand firmly. "I've just been hired by Chicago Bus & Truck."

Tillie's eyes roamed the room until they caught Betty's expectant look.

"What?" Tillie asked.

"And you are…?" Betty asked.

"Oh, sorry," she said laughing, "The name's Tillie. Tillie McFinn."

"Well, Tillie, it's wonderful to meet you."

Betty sat.

"Welcome aboard!" she said and motioned for Tillie to follow suit. She did.

"You didn't have to come in to meet with me in person," Betty said. "I trust the company to hire the best."

"It's better we get acquainted beforehand," Tillie replied, crossing her legs.

"I suppose you're right since we'll be spending a lot of time together."

"Yeah…time," Tillie smiled nervously.

Her top leg began bouncing up and down as if a toddler were aboard. Tillie was one hundred and twenty-five pounds of nuclear energy compressed into a five-foot-two-inch frame.

"Well, I like to get everything out in the open before a working relationship is established," she said.

Out in the open? Betty leaned back in her leather chair. Whatever Tillie was going to tell her it was guaranteed to be interesting.

"First of all," Tillie continued earnestly, "I'm a real good driver. I've driven professionally for over seven years. I've never had an accident or a ticket."

"Yes, I know," Betty began, "You come highly recommended and…"

"Plus, I go to Mass once a week," Tillie continued anxiously, "sometimes even twice!"

"Well, that's great," Betty said, wondering if Tillie had ingested seventeen gallons of Starbucks prior to her arrival. She'd never met anyone who was so apologetic and high-strung at the same time. "But you really didn't have to come all this way...."

"Yes, I did!" Tillie said with such force that it stopped the conversation.

Betty straightened a pen on her desk.

"Like I said," Tillie resumed, softening her voice, "I don't like surprises and neither do most people." Her leg stopped its galloping. She took a deep breath and looked Betty in the eye. "At least not when it comes to finding out the person they work with served a little time." Tillie fell silent. And waited.

Well, well, Betty thought, the one-woman fun factory in front of her had been in prison.

She feigned ignorance. "Time?"

Tillie let out a slow breath. "I did ten years in the Dwight Correctional Center for armed robbery. I was released seven years ago this June."

"*Armed* robbery?" Betty asked, now feeling a twinge of worry.

"If it helps, it was *only* a tiny gun, and I was *only* nineteen at the time," Tillie said. "But, a gun is a gun; and robbery is robbery."

Betty asked, "And who did you rob, if you don't mind my asking?"

"A stupid convenience store." Tillie rolled her eyes as she had done so many times since the night she walked through the door of the dimly lit establishment of narrow aisles, crammed shelves, and three-day old pastries. "And to top it off, it happened on the worst night of any girl's life."

Betty lifted one eyebrow quizzically.

"Her best friend's wedding," Tillie responded. "Not only was my BFF leaving me to live with some dweeb in What-the-F, Ohio, but I was PMS-ing big time, craving chocolate and desperately needing a tampon."

"You were sent to prison for shoplifting Tampax and candy?" Betty asked skeptically.

"Well, there's a bit more to it. My mistake was stopping at the wrong store after the reception. I was kind of stoned and a little tipsy from wedding toasts and…"

"*Kind* of stoned?" Betty asked doubtfully.

Tillie admitted, "Okay, really stoned, but I had an excuse. It was my job as the maid-of-honor to look like I was celebrating when I wasn't," Tillie paused as if remembering something incredibly horrible. Her shoulders shuddered and she added, "…and don't even get me started on the dress I was forced to wear. Let me just say that day-glow orange is never a good color choice, no matter what the season."

Betty bit her lip to refrain from laughing. She'd been to one to many autumn weddings where the bridesmaids' ensemble had the sex appeal of a traffic cone with ruffles.

Tillie continued. "My driver for the evening was the best man, the groom's brother. As soon as I got in the car, he tells me not to worry. That he's packing heat in case someone tries to hijack the car."

"I assume he too was from What-the-F, Ohio?" Betty asked.

Tillie nodded. "I thought he was just a small town kid who'd come into the big scary city for a family wedding. I demanded he hand me the gun immediately or I wouldn't let him give me a ride home."

"Bad idea?"

"Big time bad idea. Right after I slipped the 38mm into my rhinestone clutch bag, I insisted we stop at the nearest minimart. Like I said, I needed a fresh tamp and I was jonesing for a Snickers. So when he pulls into the parking lot, I get out alone and head into the store in my full length taffeta nightmare. I managed to cram myself and my puffy skirt down the skinny aisles. When I came to the sanitary needs section, I opened my bag. Naturally, I had to pull the gun out of the bag to get to my money."

"Naturally," Betty concurred.

Tillie continued. "The cashier immediately held his hands up in the air like I was there to rob the place. Suddenly, I could hear police sirens in the distance. I assumed the cashier set off the security alarm because he saw the gun."

"What happened next?"

"I panicked. The only thing I understood completely was that I still needed Tampax. So I grabbed a box and shoved it in my purse. What I shouldn't have done was spend four minutes trying to find the Snickers. You know, it used to be easy. You wanted a Snickers, you grabbed a Snickers. Now they have Snickers Caramel, Snickers Dark Chocolate, Snickers Lite, Snickers Everything-But-The-Kitchen-Sink. Just give me a friggin' Snickers!" Tillie took a breath. "Any-ways, that gave the police cars enough time to arrive."

"Cars?" Betty asked. It was hard enough to get a cop car to arrive at a crime scene, much less plural. The convenience store must have been in one of the worst neighborhoods in Chicago.

"Three of them," Tillie answered. "They screeched up the moment I stepped out of the front door. It was then I saw my supposed date speeding away, leaving me to face the Chicago police on my own. My temper got the best of me. Suddenly the whole evening flashed before my eyes. My best friend leaving me to face adulthood alone, the amazingly stupid dress I was wearing, a wedding band that only played ABBA, and then some jerk was deserting me and heading to Ohio, just like my BBF. It was all too much to take."

"What did you do?"

"I lifted the gun and aimed it directly at his car. I took a shot and one of his back tires exploded. Fortunately, I knew enough to drop the gun and hit the ground in surrender. I didn't want to die in a shoot–out with the cops."

"And they gave you ten years for that?" Betty asked skeptically.

Tillie said, "They gave me ten years for choosing the wrong man to hang out with. Something I've managed to do all of my life. That small town rube was also a big time felon, wanted in two different states. The gun I had in my hands had been used in the killing of a highway patrolman. Bottom line, the judge threw the book at me for a first time offense.

Betty totally understood what happened. When it came to murdering anyone in law enforcement, tears often blurred judgment.

Tillie added, "But I do know it was my fault. I shouldn't have put the gun in my purse. I shouldn't have gotten that stoned and drunk.

I should not have taken the Tampax or the six candy bars. See, the thing with me and shooting out tires? That's got nothing to do with me being a criminal. It's got something to do with my having a short fuse. My shrink told me it's genetic, something I inherited."

Betty's eyebrow arched up in confusion. "Genetic?" she asked.

Tillie's chime-like laughter filled the room. "Can't you tell by my red hair? I've got one hundred percent Irish-whiskified DNA on my daddy's side." She mimicked an Irish brogue, "McFinn, don't ya know!"

Betty placed her hands over her lips, trying to hide her smile, and considered the situation. She appreciated the fact that Tillie wanted to be honest about her past and wondered how many people refused to hire her once they found out she'd been in prison. Betty believed people could change. She sensed that the thirty-some-year-old woman in front of her was a far cry from the gun-wielding kid of the past. She thought of Tillie's joke: "As in no chance in hell?" But Betty believed in second chances, having been forced into one herself. She decided to live up to her name, and that of her company, and take a chance.

"Well, then," Betty smiled, "we're bound to get along."

"You think?" Tillie replied, clearly relieved.

"Because," Betty added, "I'm half Irish too!"

Tillie's grin could have circled the moon.

"Then for sure we'll get along!" Tillie said. She added mischievously, "Or maybe just get into a whole lot of trouble."

A year later, lying on a hotel bed in Moose Bay, Betty wondered if trouble would once again become Tillie's middle name. After all, the sheriff had just suggested Tillie was his prime suspect.

Betty sat up and looked around the hotel room. Her luggage had been sitting unopened for hours. Normally, she would have been in the room almost as long as her bags. She would have updated her blog and checked her email. And since it was 3:07 A.M., she'd be sound asleep and not riding the rollercoaster of emotions she was feeling.

She knew she should call her son Codey before he left work for home. Like his dad, he was a Chicago cop. There was a good chance that by now he would have heard of a murder on a tour bus originating from the Windy City. Codey worked the third watch—the late shift—in Chicago's nightclub district. Unlike his father, who investigated homicides, Codey had chosen vice.

She decided to wait until morning. She was emotionally exhausted.

She vacillated between wrath and overwhelming sadness. Farsi's death wasn't her fault but she felt guilty nonetheless. If she hadn't started Take A Chance Tours, the man would be alive and Tillie wouldn't be getting the third-degree from a small-town sheriff.

But what could she do? Find an office job? She'd fought dyslexia since birth. Her typing speed was only forty words per minute, unless you counted the mistakes—then her average was near zero. Typing was one of the few things she couldn't conquer. Another one was waitressing. She gave up after three days of short-changing the restaurant through her own mistakes. She pondered working as a Wal-Mart greeter like her friend Vicki but soon realized that standing on her feet all day, while remaining cheery, was not something she could carry off for more than a week. Not with her bunions, weight, and passion for high heels. Maybe she should have waited for her online blog to grow and eventually support her. True, her blog only earned around sixty dollars a month. Tops. But the income from it was growing daily—by pennies.

Betty decided if she couldn't sleep, she might as well do one thing she was good at, tackle her blog. She was too tired to bend down so she kicked off her shoes.

Usually, she posted an entry on Buffet Betty's Blog as soon as the tour arrived at its destination. A few of her insomniac readers would certainly have noticed by now she hadn't written a thing. In fact, they'd probably already commented in the response section. They'd be asking if she'd arrived yet or, teasing her that she'd forgotten her dedicated fans, if she was sitting mesmerized in front of a penny slot.

Tonight's posting would be a challenge. Normally, she'd type in a few sentences that were fun and informative. *We've arrived safely at our destination! And I am now counting the hours until a breakfast of Stuffed Pecan French Toast at the Hungry Moose Buffet! Stay tuned!*

But the murder made such entries trivial. What could Buffet Betty say? *Forty-three of forty-four passengers arrived safely at Moose Bay, with only one DOA! For gamblers, that's pretty good odds! Now for something really important—let's talk Prime Rib!*

She knew she would have to come up with something. Maybe a quick shower would help to clear her mind. Afterward, she'd tackle her blog.

She undressed. A quick body check in the full-length mirror told her what she already knew. For a fifty-five-year-old, doctor-defined-obese broad, she didn't look half bad.

She referred to the extra pounds on her frame as Wrinkle Puffers. They were better than any beauty cream she could buy at Macy's. And safer than Botox. Unless someone looked real close—and no one had since her husband disappeared—not a single line was visible from across a room.

Betty entered the marble bathroom and twisted the faucet in the walk-in shower to hot. When the temperature was just right she stepped in. Water from the five adjustable heads pulsated against her body. She fiddled with the knobs, and found the setting that stung her body with needlepoint precision. It was like liquid acupuncture. Every inch of her body tingled in pleasurable pain.

Her body was tired but her mind wouldn't rest. As the water rippled down her back, she started going over what might have happened on the bus. Tillie had left the bus unlocked, allowing passengers to come and go as they pleased. But by leaving it unguarded, she had unwittingly created an opportunity for a stranger to walk on board. If there was a silver lining in that act, it was that the murderer could have been somebody other than a Take A Chance client or employee.

Perhaps Farsi's death was a simple case of a robbery gone wrong. That would explain why Farsi's ID was missing. A lot of people used disposable cell phones and the fact that Farsi owned one was hardly sinister. Even his fraudulent job history didn't bother Betty. It wasn't that unusual for a man to lie every once in a while. Heck, even thrice in a while.

Betty turned off the water just as her phone rang in the other room. She grabbed the largest towel, wrapped it partially around her, and then decided 'What the hell' and let the useless fig leaf—unless you're a size zero—cover up drop to the floor. She shuffled naked into the next room and grabbed her cell phone.

"Hello," she said, water dripping down her body and into the carpet.

"It's me. Are you okay?!" It was her niece Lori. She was also Take a Chance Tours' accountant.

"I'm fine," Betty answered, knowing immediately why her niece was calling at such an hour. Lori must have heard what happened. Her niece seemed to worry about every little thing lately. Her aunt's well-being was no exception. "Did you hear about our passenger being murdered?"

"Of course I did," Lori's answered sternly. "Please, don't lie to me when you answer the next question. Were you or Tillie in any danger at any point? Could it have been you that was murdered?"

Betty wanted to state truthfully *maybe*, but she knew better. She said, "As far as I know, we were in absolutely no danger. I don't think the killing was a random event. The murderer was after Farsi and no one else."

She could hear Lori breathe a sigh of relief.

"By the way, how did you hear about what happened?" Betty asked and did a head toss of her wet hair. Droplets sprayed across her bare shoulders. She rolled her eyes upward in a failed attempt to see the wet trickle pestering her forehead. She walked over to the oak wardrobe and opened it. Betty grabbed the complimentary white terry cloth robe from inside and slipped it on, passing the cell phone from one hand to the other as she did. She was pleased the robe almost came together in the center when she pulled it tight. Last time she was at Moose Bay, it didn't.

"Are you kidding?" Lori responded. "The murder is being featured on every single cable news network, including CNN!"

"Oh, great," Betty groaned.

"Seems like an I-reporter on YouTube heard about it on his scanner and alerted the stations."

"Great," Betty groaned again.

Lori continued, "But I heard about it first from Hannah."

"Hannah?" asked Betty in surprise, and plopped down into an armchair.

"Yeah," said Lori, "She's already asked for a refund."

"Hannah called you at home?" Betty was slightly irritated that Hannah hadn't said something to her first. "How did she get your number?"

"I'm listed, remember?" Lori could tell Betty was going into her mother-protector mode so she made a pre-emptive strike: "Aunt Betty, you and I talked about that and decided it wasn't a big deal. Besides, she's the only client who calls me."

"She's called before?" Betty said exasperated.

"I didn't want to bother you about it; there was no need to," Lori said confidently.

"Actually," she said, her tone changing, "I think it's kind of funny. At the beginning of every trip, usually after she tallies up her first day losses, she calls and asks for a refund. But after the trip is over, she never brings it up again." Lori laughed, "Until next time!"

"You should've told me that she…"

Lori interrupted her "—No I shouldn't have. You hear enough complaints on the job as it is. I can bat a few of them for you. As your accountant, my job is to keep the business end of the company going. I figure Hannah's always going to be griping."

"Unless she's ahead," quipped Betty, some of the tension disappearing from her voice.

"Probably even then," countered Lori.

"That's true," Betty conceded. "But this time, she might deserve a refund."

"Maybe," said Lori.

"Maybe they all do," Betty added, sounding defeated.

"Not if we call it the Murder Mystery Tour!" Lori joked and then gasped. "Oh my God, I can't believe I said that. I'm sorry. It's too early to make jokes, isn't it?"

"Probably," Betty answered.

She reached over and turned on her laptop which was sitting on the table next to her.

"Do you think it will affect Take A Chance?" Lori asked.

Betty decided to downplay her response. "If anything else happens as a result of this trip, like a lawsuit . . ."

"—or more bad publicity," Lori injected.

"...We could lose the business," Betty added solemnly. For the first time, Betty regretted letting Lori invest in Take A Chance Tours.

When Lori's mother, Betty's sister, died, Lori had inherited two-hundred-thousand dollars. She told her aunt she wanted in on the action. She immediately invested $50,000 in Betty's new enterprise, in exchange for becoming an equal partner. When she turned over the check to her aunt, she'd jokingly used the phrase "Let it ride". Yet Lori insisted it wasn't a gamble at all. She was convinced the two of them could turn the fifty grand into a travel company worth millions within a decade.

Betty knew Lori had always felt the two of them could accomplish anything, even capture lightning bugs on the moon, if need be. Or at least that's what Betty began to tell her niece when Lori was only two-years old. From the first time Betty laid eyes on her as in infant, Lori captured her heart. She'd kept it prisoner ever since. All Lori had to do was smile at her aunt, and Betty's heart would melt.

Betty made sure she did everything she could to make her niece a part of her life. She treated her as lovingly as she did her son Codey. If possible, she always included Lori in their family activities. When she and Larry took their son to Disneyworld, they insisted that Lori come along as well. Every weekend, Betty made sure that Lori spent some "you and me" time with her. From simply sitting at the kitchen table playing the board game Chutes and Ladders, to later in life when they shopped for Lori's prom dress, their moments together shined.

Betty was there for her in the bad times as well. She wiped away Lori's tears when her father walked off. She let her niece rage in anger in her kitchen while tossing cups and plates as she screamed at the unfairness of her mother's cancer. Later, when Betty's sister died, she held the 15 year-old, disturbingly silent Lori in her arms for hours, telling her she would be okay. That her mom was watching over both of them.

Lori moved in with her aunt. There was never any question that Lori would do anything else. After college she moved out knowing she could move back at any time. Betty's home had become Lori's home. It always would be. It only made sense that Betty's new business would be a family business, if Lori wanted it that way.

Lori interrupted her thoughts and brought her back to the moment. She asked, "Do you have any idea who might have killed Farsi?"

"Farsi wasn't his name," Betty informed her as the laptop's screen lit up. "According to the FBI, Alexander Farsi from Chicago doesn't exist. Neither does Argylite Chemicals."

"What's that?" asked Lori.

"The company he claimed to have worked for."

"Wow!" said Lori, "you mean everything he said was a lie?"

"I'm afraid so."

"Can't they identify him with finger prints or DNA?" asked Lori.

"Only if he'd ever been arrested or worked for the government." Betty typed in her username and password. She thought she was being very clever when she initially set up *password* as the username and *username* as the password. But, according to her cop son Codey, a 4th grader could figure it out in thirty seconds. She'd never bothered to come up with anything else.

Lori had avoided the question but now asked "Do you think the killer was one of our passengers?"

"I was afraid of that at first," Betty sighed. "But if the murder occurred in Tyler Falls, the killer could have come on board and left without any of us noticing."

"That's what Hannah's complaining about, by the way," Lori added.

"That she could have been murdered?" Betty asked, as she clicked onto the Internet and accepted the hotel's wireless access agreement.

"No, that the bus stopped in Tyler Falls," Lori answered. "If it hadn't, she says, she'd be a multi-millionaire now."

"What is she talking about?" Betty barked. Sometimes, her clients tested her patience.

"Don't you know?" Lori asked. "A progressive slot hit a half-hour before you arrived. Someone won $13,000,000 on a machine there at Moose Bay."

"And Hannah thinks it should have been her?" Betty asked.

"She says it was *her* machine that paid out. Go figure." Lori chuckled.

"Cripes," Betty said, as she logged in to her website, "What else can go wrong?"

"Maybe I should join you at Moose Bay," Lori suggested.

"No, I'm fine, stay in Chicago. I'll keep you informed about what's going on. Love you," Betty said, and hung up.

Betty's eyes drifted toward her webpage displayed on her laptop. She used her finger to quickly scroll down to the comment section from her readers. Even without her posting about the deadly event, her fans were already posting about the homicide.

Even without her posting about the deadly event, her fans were already posting about the homicide. She used her finger to quickly scroll down to the comment section. She recognized most of the names. They were her regular passengers who also read her blog, or the many readers who never left their home but managed to "virtually" travel and eat with her across the country. These armchair travelers were kindred spirits who loved buffets, road trips and gambling as much as she did. Her readers were a constant support and inspiration to her. But there were also the unwelcomed trolls who posted thoughtless and cruel comments, even at the saddest of times.

"Hey what's this about a guy being murdered on your tour? Are you okay?" – retread77

"I just saw on Fox News that people are being killed on your tours. Do you think its terrorists?" – patriotic44

"I always get killed at a casino – usually by a dollar slot machine." – vegas4evr

"Hey jerk, now is not time to make jokes. Somebody's dead." – retiredhippie

"Betty be careful! I love your tours!" – cubsrule

"Of course someone died. It was seafood buffet night." – lenowannbe74

"Betty, are you alright?" – grannygambls

"Not if she had the seafood buffet. Sorry, I couldn't resist." – lenowannbe74

Betty wanted to reply—*I was OKAY before I saw the POSTS*—but didn't. Instead she wrote, "*Thank you for your concerns about the tragedy on our tour bus. For full information as to what happened, click on any of the many news links provided by our readers. FYI, Moose Bay is one of my favorite casinos and is home to a wonderful buffet. I am completely confident that the rest of the tour will not only be safe, but also fun for our clients.*

As she hit the send key she realized it was the first time she'd lied to her readers. She wasn't sure that she and her passengers were safe at all.

Chapter 4

A little after dawn, Lori checked her reflection in the airport's bathroom mirror. Her appearance reminded her again how different she was from her mother. If it were up to her, she would have been born a brunette like her mom or her Aunt Betty. She always thought that dark-haired women appeared not only more exotic but also more intelligent than blondes. Brunettes did not look "movie star dumb" like the first man she dated said she did. Apparently, it was meant as a compliment.

Lori flipped her hair around a bit, just enough to test its bounce appeal. Good enough, she decided. If fate had deemed she was meant to look like she couldn't add one plus zero, she might as well look the part.

Grabbing the handle on her Louis Vuitton luggage, she wheeled it out the door toward the ticket counter. It didn't bother her in the least that she was disobeying her aunt's instructions to stay put in Chicago.

Although Betty told Lori she didn't need her, there was always the chance she would. And Lori wanted to be there if she did. Lori needed something too: a break. She had to get away from Chicago and her day-to-day—no, make that night-to-night—activities. Perhaps breathing in a bit of frigid, fresh air would give her a chance to clear her thoughts.

Struggling as she pulled the wheeled cargo down the marble floor, she realized she'd packed too many clothes, as usual. Inside the case were half a dozen cocktail dresses, each one a sophisticated eye-catching number that revealed very little, but promised so much more.

There were also three Donna Karan business suits, five pair of designer jeans and dress pants, six silk tops, and Ann Roth shoes. The only outrageous apparel she carried with her was a gift from Tillie, a silver lamé bikini that could double as Christmas tree tinsel in an emergency.

She hadn't told her aunt of her travel plans because she would have tried to stop her. But their company never had a client murdered while in their care. If necessary, Lori could spend part of the time sweet-talking the casino heads, convincing them that it would be advantageous to continue a relationship with Take A Chance Tours.

According to Tom Songbird, half of the male staff at Moose Bay had a crush on her. So if a sly smile and imported stilettos would help mend a business relationship, so be it. She had little choice: she was nearly bankrupt.

Everything Lori had left was riding on Take A Chance bringing in a profit until the next fiscal quarter. The extra money would help her shield the losses she'd carefully hidden from her aunt. With any luck, and a small amount of creative accounting, the company could stay afloat.

But luck hadn't been her friend for a long, long time.

Before Take A Chance Tours was established, Lori had never gambled. She'd never bought a lottery ticket or played bingo at her Catholic church. Even community raffles seemed a silly waste of money that could have been more wisely spent on facials or in a bookstore. There wasn't one thing about gambling that attracted her. Until she tried it for the very first time.

During their first month of operation, Take A Chance was offered a familiarization trip to one of the largest casinos in the Midwest. "Fams" were a continued and treasured perk of working in the travel industry. The entire cost of a familiarization trip was covered by the gaming establishment trying to impress the travel agencies or tour operators. Employees were provided free travel, hotel, food and three hundred dollars in chips to wager. There were only three Take A Chance employees at the time: Betty, Lori, and Gloria, their part-time, recently-retired public librarian.

Once the trio arrived at a casino, Gloria cashed in her chips, squirreling away the proceeds in the bottom of her purse. She then headed back to the hotel room to watch Animal Planet on the Discovery

Channel before opening up the latest Alex Kava thriller to read.

Meanwhile, Betty turned her chips into dollar bills and headed toward the penny slot machines. After three hours of gambling, she walked away twelve bucks and one free buffet ahead. Twelve bucks wasn't a lot to most people, but for Betty it was a new used-something from her favorite thrift store. Life didn't get any better than that.

As for Lori, she sauntered up and down the aisles for a while, wowing nearly every male in the place. Her beauty even stopped a few of the gamblers in their tracks, though they had more of a chance getting lucky at the tables than they did with her.

Finally, Lori sat down at a three-card-poker table, a game she was assured was easy to learn, play, and win.

She lost ten dollars on her first hand, but won her second and third. By her tenth win in a row, Lori started to believe there was no way for her to lose. When she walked away from her first poker game two hours later she was eight hundred dollars ahead.

One week later, she sat at her desk inwardly fighting an overwhelming urge to drive to the nearest casino. Finally, when her anxiety was so intense that it was hard to breathe, she feigned a headache and raced out the door, straight to the Indiana border where riverboat casinos beckoned from the other side.

It took less than a year to go through the rest of her inheritance.

After that, it was only one month before she dipped into the company funds.

Fortunately, no one knew of her little vice, not even her aunt. As Chief Financial Officer, Lori was in control of the company finances. It was easy for her to raid the cash box or write checks to her personal account. After all, there was no one looking over her shoulders.

As she reached the airport's ticket line, exciting yet frightening thoughts about letting herself take yet another financial risk started to jet-ski across her mind. Maybe she should gamble a dollar or two at Moose Bay. What harm could it do? Hitting a jackpot could be the answer to all her woes.

Besides, there was no way she'd risk more than, say, twenty bucks. Or forty. If she'd put off having her hair styled for a month, she'd save two hundred dollars right there. If she did that, she rationalized, then she actually wouldn't be losing any money if she chose to gamble. Not a dime. So actually, it wouldn't be like gambling at all!

And that meant she could actually wager a hundred and still be even and . . .

"May I help you?" the female voice sounded, dislodging her ruminations.

She stepped up to the front of the queue and laid her ID and MasterCard on the counter.

The agent entered the information into the computer. "You're booked on Flight 271 to Minneapolis, Miss Barnes. From there you'll take the Northern Wind Charter and arrive at the Moose Bay airport at 9:37 A.M."

"Thank you," Lori answered, taking back her ID and charge card—the only one with available credit. She didn't bother to confirm the price of the trip she'd booked an hour earlier online. She couldn't afford it anyway.

Except for the fifty grand she'd invested in Take A Chance Tours, she'd lost every dime she had. Plus, she'd recently taken out $19,000 for an "advance on her salary" from Take A Chance. She wouldn't see another paycheck for five months.

The agent asked, "Miss Barnes? Is there anything else? Would you care to purchase a flight back?"

"No, thank you," Lori responded, and headed toward the security checkpoint. She didn't need a round trip ticket since she'd ride back on the Take A Chance motor coach. Her aunt always kept one seat available.

Lori placed her bag onto the security conveyer belt. She stepped up to the TSA agent and lifted her arms as his wand navigated her body. As she stepped backwards, she instinctively felt someone staring at her.

She did a quick turn around and found herself looking into the puppy dog eyes of a thirty-something-year-old man. He looked as if he were her devoted pet, one who was waiting to be fed, petted, pampered, and controlled. His black business suit was cut so well, Lori recognized it as custom made. His yellow silk tie glistened against a pristine white shirt. His watch contained more gold than her jewelry box.

She didn't know his name, but it didn't matter. She'd already decided his nickname would be Mr. Gorgeous.

She half-smiled at the look he was giving her. It suggested she'd never again have to open a door, pull out her own chair, or pump gas if he were with her. He'd do everything for her that she'd ever need done.

Men were like that around Lori. There was always a man waiting on the sidelines or standing nearby wanting to help, pleading to be of service. Her mom told her once that being beautiful made life too easy for Lori.

You won't know what to do once life gets hard, her mother had warned. The minute she started her first panic attack, she realized her mom had been right all along.

Mr. Gorgeous stepped behind her and asked hopefully, "Are you heading to Minneapolis?"

"Just to catch another plane," she answered and walked away knowing his eyes were following her every move. To taunt him even more, she adjusted her normally slow, seductive wiggle to rapid.

Lori chuckled bitterly to herself. She easily attracted most men and quite a few women. Everyone wanted to be near her, except for the one woman she really wanted—Lady Luck. Long legs and green eyes didn't mesmerize Lady Luck. Nor did she care that fate took Lori's mom away from her when she was just a teenager. Or that Lori's father had disappeared without a word when she was eleven years old. Or even that Lori was a survivor of childhood leukemia. Lady Luck didn't give a damn that Lori often woke up in the middle of the night, sweating through her clothes, awoken by the recurring nightmare of cancer genes eating her alive. Nightmares reminding her that neither DNA, nor luck, were in her favor. Lori knew her beauty was an inheritance that would eventually disappear, just like the money from her mother's estate had. To Lori, everything ended far too quickly. There was even the chance that Aunt Betty would just vanish, just like her mom and dad. And then what would she be left with? Nothing. Except herself. And to Lori, that wasn't good enough.

Chapter 5

This sure beats breakfast at Denny's!" Tillie cooed above the din of table chatter and clanking silverware. At 7:45 A.M. the 300-seat Hungry Moose Buffet was packed with salivating patrons. The casino's patrons were either in line at one of eight different food stations, or happily chowing down at their table.

Betty grinned. "Sure does. They've actually managed to out-Vegas Vegas."

She pointed upward to dozens of handcrafted chandeliers lighting the room. Each one featured twelve small Tiffany lanterns with stained glass panels suspended from bronze twigs and leaves.

The ceiling was painted to look like a blue sky, filled with cumulous clouds that moved slowly across the horizon. The visual feat was accomplished by a series of clear ceiling tiles that allowed 3-D images to be projected upon them. In the evening, the blue would slowly change to black until night glistened above with thousands of twinkling LED stars.

"Is the food as good as the place looks?" Tillie asked, her green eyes roaming over the hand-painted Native American scenes on the walls.

Betty nodded. "Yep. I gave it five popped buttons."

When Betty made the decision to rate restaurants, she decided to forgo the traditional "five star" or even "five fork" rating systems. Instead, popping buttons from the strain of too much food made more sense to her. One popped button meant the food was barely edible. Five popped buttons meant not only would your pants fall down from eating too much, you wouldn't even care.

Betty saw that many of the diners were whispering to each other while staring at Tillie. Almost everyone, it seemed, was checking out the driver's off-duty ensemble. Black spandex Capri pants seemed painted onto Tillie's thighs, while a skin-tight, polyester top of black and white tiger stripes covered just enough of her voluptuous torso to remain decent. On her feet were open-toed, red high-heels. Glossy black and white, wooden giraffe earrings dangled from her earlobes. Her ample cleavage threatened to escape her shirt's deep V-neck. A portion of an entire American flag, tattooed on Tillie's right breast, could be seen waving patriotically with each breath she took.

If Tillie were working the Strip in Vegas—say as a drag queen imitating Dolly Parton—her outfit wouldn't be noticed. But in northern Minnesota, a casino patron's normal attire was a tribute to everything flannel. The men donned their best plaid while women wore pastel sweat suits with embroidered images of bunnies hopping playfully across their heaving bosoms.

"Follow me," a short, round hostess smiled and led the two women to a table in the middle of the room.

Betty pulled up a chair, while Tillie asked "Would you mind ordering coffee for me? I've got to grab some grub. I'm starving."

"No problem." Betty smiled. She watched Tillie sashay her way to the Egg Cetera station, the name of which was proclaimed from a dangling neon sign. Throughout the day, the signs would change with the crowds, evolving from a breakfast buffet to lunch to dinner. It was a metamorphosis barely perceptible to the human eye, requiring slow-motion photography for its intricacies to be observed.

Tillie stood in line, waiting for the omelet chef to ask her what she wanted. Her choice of ingredients ranged from freshly diced Roma tomatoes to chunks of Maine lobster and medallions of range-fed bison. Next to the station stood a variety of other egg dishes such as spinach quiche, frittatas, and various egg casseroles.

Betty's favorite food station was titled "Southern Comfort". Hot baking powder biscuits, peppery gravy, and two-inch thick sausage patties called to her as soon as she stepped foot inside the buffet. She momentarily fixated on the tantalizing scent of smoked maple-flavored bacon wafting through the room. She envisioned trays of thick slices butted up against vats of steaming grits or steel cut oats.

A carving chef waited patiently behind the counter, willing to slice off a hunk of ham the size of an eighteen-wheeler.

A server appeared at the table and asked, "What would you like to drink?"

"Coffee for two, please," Betty answered.

She needed caffeine. She could barely keep her eyes open. She hadn't slept in twenty-four hours. Plus, she was trying to project an upbeat, positive attitude for her tour group. She couldn't let anyone see the concern and fear she was actually feeling.

Tillie came back to the table, carrying a plateful of goodies. A Pepper Jack & Cheddar cheese omelet covered a third of her plate. The rest of the plate was overflowing with hash browns, fresh fruit, and miniature Stuffed Pecan French toast sticks drowning in pure maple syrup. As she sat down, she asked, "Aren't you going to eat before you start scheduling passengers for the sheriff to interview?"

Betty nodded as the server filled their cups to the brim with steaming coffee. She stirred in a dollop of cream, took a sip and then looked around the restaurant. She could see at least ten of her clients having breakfast. Mr. Ogawa was one of them. Unless the sheriff had a hole in his head, Mr. Ogawa would be off the hook as soon as he said hello.

Betty took a big gulp and announced, "I'll talk to a few clients on my way to Southern Comfort."

Tillie forked another pile of hash browns and said, "Let me know if you need help."

Standing up, Betty pulled a small notebook and pen out of her purse and headed toward Ogawa's table.

"Good morning," she said, and produced the biggest smile she could muster. Except for Mr. Ogawa, no one smiled back. At any moment she expected to hear a barrage of complaints from her clients. She was certain their sullen mood was because of the murder. Instead, true to a gambler's nature, she quickly found out their anger was related to their missed fortune. It wasn't only Hannah who felt the jackpot should have been theirs.

"You heard about the jackpot for thirteen mil?" Harold Turner asked right before a mound of catsup-drenched hash browns disappeared into his open mouth.

"I did," Betty said, trying to sound upbeat. "I guess that was one lucky player."

"Luck has nothing to do with it," Turner said, as a few of the potatoes escaped through the side of his mouth. He didn't notice. "Those machines never pay off," he continued, "I don't care if they're supposedly linked to Vegas or not."

Multi-linked progressive slots were linked with other machines in casinos spread across the country. The headquarters for the company running the nation-wide games was located in Las Vegas. By pressing the spin button, a player could hope to hit the same jackpot as one who was playing the same progressive machine two thousand miles away.

Turner scoffed. "Who's got that kind of money to pay out nowadays? I'll bet you 3-to-1 the casino says the win isn't legit."

Betty had heard the same gripe about wins being legitimate before. Rumors were spread throughout the gaming world about local casinos using bogus excuses to refuse big jackpot payouts. It didn't help that every slot machine was tagged with a sign reading, *Machine Malfunctions Voids All Pays.*

"Mr. Turner, Moose Bay is a very reputable casino," Betty explained. "In fact, it was voted one of the . . ."

Turner interrupted her, "Has the jackpot winner been paid, yet?"

"I have no idea," Betty answered honestly, assuming the man had been paid, but sometimes with a payout that large it's delayed until the win is verified.

"And who knows who would have won it if we hadn't been late?" Mildred Pudlowski said, her razor-sharp lips forming a pout. "I could've been the one playing that machine."

Betty sighed. There would be no choice but to repeatedly apologize on this trip, though being late seemed to be a trifling matter compared to what Mr. Farsi suffered. She said, "Again, I'm sorry we arrived late. But to be honest, considering the weather, I'd still insist the driver take a break. The roads were very icy."

Mr. Ogawa reached up and touched her arm. "There's no need to apologize, Miss Betty. We arrived safely and that's what counts. If I've learned one thing in my eighty-eight years, it's that no one can predict the future."

Mildred rested her fork and admitted, "That's for sure. In fact, I'm getting so old I can't even remember my past, much less figure out what's going to happen next. Well, I suppose it doesn't really matter who won the money. If I had, I'd probably just end up putting it back into the machines."

Betty grinned. "If I remember correctly, Mildred, you only play penny slots. It would take you a while."

"Oh, if I won the big one, I'd move up to nickel slots in a heartbeat." She pointed at her table companions. "I'd even pick-up the breakfast tab. Maybe even lunch!"

The entire table burst out in laughter, except for Turner who continued to scowl. Nothing seemed to make him happy. He acted as if he was looking for a fight.

"I'm going to grab a bite to eat. If each of you could stop at my table on the way out, I'd appreciate it," Betty said, and left without waiting for a response. She didn't want to take the chance anyone would refuse, especially Turner.

On her way to Southern Comfort, Betty stopped by another table of six passengers and asked them to do the same. When she finally reached the station, she grabbed a large plate but filled it with tiny portions: a half of a biscuit, a tablespoon of gravy and a single turkey sausage link. She'd stop by one more station to try something new to review on her blog. But it, too, would be no more than a mouthful. Just because she wrote about food, didn't mean she had to eat an entire portion to know how something tasted.

She didn't want to pack on any additional pounds. Not when it took her as long as it did to lose ten. She cruised over to the next station, Griddle Me This, and wistfully looked at the variety of pancakes, Belgian waffles and French toast. She chose one small silver dollar pancake, and a miniature chocolate covered waffle.

She reached for a giant-sized blueberry & mango pancake, paused, and muttered out loud, "You have enough, girl." She turned back to her table, shutting her eyes as she passed trays of jelly-filled donuts, custard filled Danish, and still-warm-from-the-oven almond croissants.

By the time Betty made it back to the table, Tillie's plate was clean.

"Is that all you're eating?" Tillie asked, pointing to Betty's plate.

Betty grinned. "I have enough," she said, using her favorite phrase before reminding herself one more time, *I have enough.* For her, it was a string of words that kept her centered and on track, whether she was talking about money, food, family or friends. Betty always tried to remember that, in so many ways, her life was abundant.

After her husband deserted her, any comfort she could find came with accepting the fact that she was so blessed, and even without Larry, she had enough. She had enough money to subsist, enough friends with shoulders to cry on, and enough family to be with during the holidays. She had enough.

Of course, there were times when she wanted more, but having all she needed was all that really mattered. As long as she kept an attitude of gratitude, Betty knew she could handle anything that came her way.

Then she saw it coming.

The tiny, angry, vintage steamroller was heading in her direction.

Anything that came her way, she reminded herself. Or anyone.

Hannah stopped abruptly in front of Betty and began to tap the tiled floor with the tip of her metal cane. In Hannah's hands, the cane was more than an aid to the elderly. It made her look like the high commander of a senior citizens' SWAT team.

"Good morning, Hannah." Betty smiled sweetly while preparing herself to be verbally pounced upon. She swallowed hard before uttering her next words, "Would you care to join Tillie and I?"

Tillie jumped up immediately. "I'm through eating. I have an appointment at the spa for a manicure." She raced out of the buffet as quickly as she could, considering the shoes she wore. As she did, her swaying hips knocked into more than one table along the way.

Betty didn't blame her. If she could have done the same, she would have. But her job called for her to sit and listen to whatever venom Hannah would spew forth.

Hannah sat down across from her. She rested her cane against the table and snapped, "I called Lori this morning to complain. As far as I'm concerned, she's the only good thing about Take A Chance."

"Lori *is* wonderful," Betty agreed. "She told me you called. Hannah, I promise that you'll get a full refund."

"Refund? I don't want a refund. I want my thirteen million."

"Hannah, a jackpot belongs to whoever wins it, not who wants to win it. If that were the case then everyone here would . . ."

Hannah interrupted, "Everyone *here* knows that it was *my* machine that hit the big one. I play that machine every time I'm here. I only leave it to eat or sleep, and at my age I don't do either very long."

"Look, we'll give you back your money for the trip, and I'll personally cover all your meals."

Hannah just glared, her rheumy eyes taking on the sharpness of a sniper. "I could cover my *own* meals, if you'll give me my jackpot."

Betty took in a sharp breath to calm herself before responding. "Hannah, you do realize I have bigger problems than you not winning a jackpot? You do remember one of my clients was murdered?"

"He deserved it," Hannah said, frowning.

Betty felt as if someone had slapped her in the face. "What do you mean he *deserved* it?"

Hannah shrugged. "He was grumpy. He wouldn't talk to anybody on the bus. He even refused a stick of sugar-free gum when I offered it to him." Hannah paused before adding, "I don't offer gum to just anyone. The way he refused, you'd think I was being a flirt."

Betty's demeanor changed and she pulled her lips together, tightly. She knew better than to laugh out loud. Did seventy-one year old Hannah really think a man *deserved* to die because he refused her token of friendship? Even more astounding was the chance that Hannah was offering more than just a Chiclet to a man who was more than a decade younger than she.

Betty shook her head in wonder. Homo sapiens, especially the older ones, never failed to surprise her. Nearly every male under the age of ninety acted as if their aging body were a Halloween costume that could be discarded at any given moment if the right opportunity presented itself. Then again, Betty decided, it was good that an older woman could see herself in the same, misguided light.

Hannah grabbed her cane and held it midair. “I’ve already called my son, the attorney. He told me I could sue if I wanted.” She turned around swiftly and scurried away, pushing servers and customers out of her way with her cane as she headed toward Ogawa’s table.

Betty’s mood shifted into a downward spin. If Hannah’s litigious son was anything like his mother, Take A Chance Tours was driving straight into bankruptcy.

Chapter 6

Tom Songbird repeated the M-word again as he and Betty waited for the sheriff to arrive. It was 9:00 A.M. "Money! We're going to lose a lot of money."

For a change, Tom wasn't the cool, calm and witty stud in the room. Instead, he was openly worried about the casino losing money. His tribe would also lose money in the process. For Tom, family and friends were all that mattered. If he was acting like a nervous nelly for a change, Betty knew his concerns were serious.

Tom tapped the conference table rapidly with the tips of his perfectly manicured fingernails. He once told Betty he spent a small fortune every week at his hair stylist. Plus, he'd willingly hand over a week's pay for the perfect pair of shoes. Tom represented his tribe to the people he encountered while on duty. He was determined to be treated with respect, and not merely brushed off as if he were some low level security mall cop.

He and Betty were waiting inside the conference room they had been in the night before. Betty nicknamed it Interrogation Central. Songbird continued, "There's no way around it. Gamblers are suspicious. And murder is not good for business." He tapped again.

The scent of Tom's aftershave drifted toward Betty. She recognized it as Burberry Sport for Men, a pricey little item that her ex-husband started wearing after he met his sugar-mommy. Before that, the only fragrance Larry wore was Old Spice.

Betty leaned over and asked, "Is this the first murder at Moose Bay?"

Tom nodded. "There's been a few deaths before, but they've all been natural."

Betty asked, "Describe natural."

Tom sipped the last bit of coffee in his cup before answering. "The usual. Heart attacks, strokes, the sort of thing that happens when seventy percent your clientele is older. We've never even had a suicide here."

"That's pretty amazing" Betty said, remembering the frightening statistics of towns that allow legalized gambling. Las Vegas alone boosts twice the national average for suicide. And these days there were mini Las Vegas's popping up all over the country.

Tom added, "My staff is trained to keep an eye out for anything suspicious or disturbing. We take suicide prevention very seriously. There's nothing worse than gambling gone bad."

"With your clean history, having a murder delivered to your front door must have been shocking," Betty admitted.

Tom answered honestly. "Not just to me, but to our employees as well. Everyone's concerned about the effect it will have on business. Even when a ninety-nine-year-old dies in their sleep in one of our hotel rooms, it makes the papers. A drop in business always follows, at least for a few days."

"Well, I would have to think that someone wining thirteen million is bound to help the casino. That big of a jackpot will receive nation-wide publicity."

Tom said, "The progressive win is my other problem. The news about it could turn out to be bad. There's something not right about that win."

She understood his anguish. A suspicious win could be just the spoiled icing on the cake the casino didn't need. Like any gaming establishment, Moose Bay wouldn't pay a large sum of money until the win was validated. If the win turned out to be a malfunction or—high-tech robbery—not a penny would change hands.

"Of course, the winner's already threatened us with a lawsuit," he said.

Betty grabbed the black carafe sitting in the middle of the table and refilled both their cups with coffee. It was going to be a very long day. She asked, "What do you think happened—a malfunction? Did someone hack into the system?"

"No idea. It's just…something's off." Songbird slowly scratched his head. "The win registered but the system's microchip set off a warning at the same time. That's very odd."

The suspected tampering wasn't good news, especially if other players found out about Moose Bay's hesitation to hand over a check. Gamblers wouldn't care about the legalities of a win. The only thing they'd remember was that Moose Bay refused to pay.

Betty stirred a stream of cream into her cup and asked, "Have you let the press know what's going on?"

"Not yet," Songbird replied, "not until we can say one way or the other what we're going to do."

"You can bet the alleged winner will definitely let them know," Betty said before advising, "It will look better if it came from you first."

Songbird nodded his head in agreement. "We have our guys working on it, as well as at the other end, in Nevada. We've notified the gaming company that developed the software to look into possible tampering."

He fiddled nervously with his watch and continued, "And if it gets out, every wise-guy with a computer will decide they can figure out a way to cheat Moose Bay out of millions. Eventually, one of them will."

Betty nodded. One bad act usually led to another. "Speaking of news, either good or bad, I haven't seen any media types poking around." If the crime had occurred in Chicago, Betty knew dozens of camera crews would be following their every move by now.

"Oh, they're here, all right," Tom said. "They started arriving twenty minutes after that I-Reporter put it on You Tube. Since it's tribal land, I can keep them from coming onto the casino's campus. But half a dozen news trucks are currently parked outside the entrance, which is off-reservation."

It crossed Betty's mind that the two incidents—the homicide and the alleged mega jackpot malfunction—might be connected. Having two major crimes linked to the same place, and occurring in such a short time span, could hardly be considered coincidental.

"Did you tell Severson there's something wrong with the progressive win?" Betty asked.

Tom shook his head. "No, and I'd like to keep it that way for as long as possible. Let's keep him focused on Farsi's death until I have more facts."

The subject seemed to be finished for the moment, so Betty asked a question about which she'd been very curious. "How did Severson become the town sheriff at such a young age?"

"The same way everything is done in this town—connections. His father was the sheriff before him. He was killed by a sixteen year-old punk during an attempted robbery at a convenience store."

"That's horrible," Betty responded. Her heart ached every time she heard of one of the good guys being killed by one of the bad. It reminded her that every single law enforcement officer's life was on the line daily, including her son's. Yet, the fact that Severson's father was killed easily explained his contempt for Tillie's convenience-store escapade.

Tom continued, "I guess most people felt sorry for the kid, so they voted for him. None of us thought he would actually get elected. He was only twenty-three years old at the time."

"What kind of Sheriff has he been?" Betty asked, suspecting once the kid was sworn in it would have been next to impossible to get rid of him, even if inept.

Tom's answer surprised her. "Not that bad, but don't forget where we're located. Usually the biggest thing that happens is someone steals an outboard motor."

The door to the conference room opened and a casino worker entered, pushing a cart filled with trays of pastries.

Betty gave Tom a quizzical look.

Tom explained. "The sheriff requested we provide treats for the passengers he's interviewing. He said people would open up to him more easily if they're on a sugar high. Between you and me? I think he just wants free donuts."

The two laughed like old friends. They both needed to.

Betty pulled away from the table and stood up. She walked to the window that looked out over the casino's parking lot. As far as she could see, every parking space was taken. Business was always good at a casino and as the economy worsened, business only improved. After all, losing a retirement fund at a casino was way more fun than losing it on Wall Street.

Betty turned around. "Do you think Severson has the skill to discover who killed Farsi?"

"Honestly? I don't know. This is the first murder investigation he's led."

"His first?" Betty asked just as the door burst open.

"Whose first?" the sheriff asked, entering the room. His deputy followed closely behind.

Tom immediately came to her rescue. "I was telling Betty about my nephew's first date," he lied.

"Hmm," Severson muttered and then carefully positioned the files he was carrying at the end of the table. Reaching into his briefcase he pulled out a large legal pad and three pens. He laid them neatly in front of him. Next, he removed a small tape recorder from his case and set it on the table. He looked like a schoolboy who'd just taken *Let's Investigate!* out of the local library.

With his thumb, Tom gestured towards the voice recorder. "Sheriff, you don't need to use that."

Severson puffed up his chest, obviously upset at being challenged. "Of course I have to use a tape recorder. Every law enforcement manual insists that I . . ."

"That's not what I mean, Sheriff. This is a casino. Look up at the ceiling."

Severson glanced up. Positioned overhead were several eyes-in-the-skies.

Tom continued, "Our cameras provide digital audio recordings, as well as visual. There's not one square inch of this facility that isn't being captured by our security department."

The sheriff hesitated before responding. "Turn off your surveillance system for this room. I'm not sure of the legalities of having the casino record the interviews. Everything has to be by the book. I can't take a chance of having this case thrown out on a technicality."

Tom nodded. He hadn't thought of that. "The system can certainly pinpoint any camera," Tom said as he turned for the door. "I'll have them shut this one off—just let me know when we can turn it back on." He gave Betty a wave and disappeared through the door.

Betty slid a piece of paper in front of the sheriff. "This is the list of clients I've scheduled so far. You asked me to schedule them in ten-minute increments."

The sheriff scanned the information. "There are only eight listed."

"I'll locate more while you're interviewing the first eight."

"You didn't think I was going to interview everyone myself, did you? I don't have time for that. Two other officers will be interviewing suspects at the same time I do."

Betty bristled. There was no reason for the sheriff to refer to her elderly clients as suspects.

"Should I schedule three interviews at one time then? One for each of you?" she asked through gritted teeth.

Severson nodded.

"Okay, I'll try. But, you should know that most of my clients have purchased an Early Bird Bingo packet, so they'll be reluctant to . . ."

Betty stopped speaking when Severson flung his pen across the room.

He glared at her and said, "Mrs. Chance, I am trying to solve a murder. I don't care if your passengers are scheduled to play Texas Hold'em with the Pope, my investigation comes first!"

"I understand," she answered solemnly.

The sheriff turned on the voice recorder before adding, "There's one more thing. You're going to have to arrange for transportation back to Chicago for your passengers. The Take A Chance bus is officially a crime scene. It's staying in Minnesota until the BCA releases it."

"When will that be?" Betty asked, knowing that any investigation by the Bureau of Criminal Apprehension could take months.

"Last time I checked, there was an eight week backlog."

Betty sputtered, "Sheriff, I have to pay for the bus every single day I have it."

He smirked. "Don't you have insurance?"

To be honest, Betty didn't know if the insurance would cover any of the events of the last twenty-four hours. Lori made all of the decisions when it came to insurance, or any financial matter.

In a stern voice Severson said, "It could be worse."

"How?" Betty wanted to know.

"I could keep every client of yours locked up in the town's jail, if I wanted. As far as I'm concerned, everyone on your tour is connected to Farsi's murder until proven otherwise. That means everyone, from the eighty-year-olds with sticker-decorated walkers, to…well, you."

Betty knew the sheriff was bluffing but she began to despise the man. If he treated her this rudely, no telling how he would treat her clients. He'd more than likely alienate every person he encountered, making it impossible to catch the killer.

It came to her in a flash. If anyone were going to catch the murderer, it would have to be her. And she needed to do it before someone else was found dead. Or even, she thought satisfyingly, arrested for slapping a gun toting, boy toy sheriff.

Chapter 7

Betty pushed open the exit door and stormed out of the conference room in a fury. As she hustled down the hallway, her heels made loud clicking sounds on the highly polished oak floor.

"Betty, wait up," Tom yelled, following closely behind her.

She kept walking, her breathing labored and her lips tightly pursed. She didn't have a history of panic attacks, but she felt one coming on. An inexperienced rookie was threatening both her and Take A Chance Tours.

Betty finally stopped moving when she felt Tom's hand on her shoulder.

"I saw you bolt out of the room. What happened?" Tom asked.

Betty sighed. "I don't know, Tom," she said, "Maybe everything's hitting me all at once."

He gave her shoulder a comforting squeeze then let his hand drop to his side. "You've had a rough time, no doubt," he said.

She responded, "First the murder, then the bus being declared a crime scene, not having slept in over 24 hours, and now the sheriff threatening to toss all of my clients into jail . . "

Tom burst out laughing. "Have you seen this town's jail? The holding cell's the size of a clown car. Your clients would have to take turns."

Betty smiled. "I guess I just don't like being bullied, especially by a punk kid."

Tom nodded in agreement. "Severson can be a jerk, but I think his heart's in the right place."

"What place is that?" she asked. "The Senior Prom?"

Tom laughed. Betty reminded him of his own mom, always waiting to serve up either a wisecrack or a slice of warm apple pie. He'd felt a kinship with her since the first day they'd met. Two peas in a crazy pod.

"If you need help getting a bus to take your people back to Chicago, I can make a few calls."

"Thanks, but I'll contact Lori. She should be able to get another bus here by the time we need to leave."

"Say, why don't I give your people tickets for Boris the Baffler tonight?" Tom offered. "The guy's a great showman. I think he can actually read minds."

She gave him a grateful thumbs-up. Her clients loved anything free.

"Take your mind off all this stuff for a while, Betty," Tom said affectionately.

"That would be wonderful. Thank you," she said and gently touched his arm.

The duo walked to the end of the hallway together, and reached the entrance to the casino. The electronic-sounding mimic of coins crashing onto metal assaulted Betty from all directions.

She glanced at her wristwatch. "I still have to schedule more clients for interviews."

"I could have their names called over the intercom," Tom suggested.

Betty shook her head. "I don't think they'd appreciate that. I'll ask Tillie to give me a hand. Thanks for everything, Tom," she said. Considering the trouble she'd brought to his door, the head of security could have taken a very different attitude than that of a friend.

"The tickets will be at the box office," Tom assured her as he walked away.

Betty headed toward the brown velvet settee against the wall in the hallway. She needed to make a few calls and once she entered the gaming area, it would be too difficult to talk on her cell phone. She sat down and pushed 2 on her speed dial.

Her office phone rang. A high-pitched nasal voice answered, "Good Morning, Take A Chance Tours."

Surprised, Betty asked, "Isn't this your day off, Gloria? Is Lori sick again?" The fact that Lori wasn't in the office again concerned Betty. She'd been taking more time off than usual, lately. Betty was afraid there could be something medically wrong with her niece. Something Lori hadn't shared. If so, that could explain why she'd been acting so secretive.

"Lori's on her way to Moose Bay," Gloria answered.

Although her niece was told to stay put in Chicago, Lori usually did what Lori wanted. Now that she knew, she wasn't all that surprised.

"Is she driving up?" Betty asked.

"She's decided to fly. She should be arriving pretty soon."

Betty was glad. It would feel good to have Lori around for support.

"Have the phones been busy this morning?" Betty asked.

"I've already taken six cancellations," Gloria told her.

Lori's theory had proven correct. News was instantaneous, especially if it was bad.

"Any of them give you a reason for canceling?"

"A few mentioned the murder," Gloria replied, "but the others didn't offer an explanation."

"You'll probably have more calls," Betty warned.

"Actually, I have two on hold right now" Gloria informed her.

Crap!

"After you've helped them, check with the Minnesota charter companies. See if you can arrange a bus to take us back to Chicago."

"But, I've never . . ."

"Gloria, it'll be easy. You're a smart woman. I'll call you in a few hours to see what you've found out. But take care of the customers on hold first."

The second she hung up, Betty regretted doing so. She'd forgotten to tell Gloria not to talk to any reporters who might call. Not only was her occasional employee extremely talkative, she excelled in exaggeration. Gloria claimed her flair for creative chatter was the result of reading too many books while working as a librarian. There was no telling what would end up on the ten o'clock news if Gloria were involved.

Still, with all her chattiness, Gloria was one of Betty's favorite people. If it weren't for Gloria, Betty would never have listened to the audio books on positive thinking that changed her life.

Betty hit 6 on her speed dial. It took ten rings before Tillie answered.

Tillie said, "Sorry, I didn't answer right away. I saw your name on the ID, but I was in the middle of putting out a cigarette."

Betty noticed Tillie walking toward her while talking to her on her cell.

Tillie grinned at her, waved, and continued speaking. "I lied earlier about having an appointment. I just wanted to get away from Hannah."

Tillie clicked off her phone when she was within a foot of the settee.

Betty shrugged. "I can't say I blame you. By the way, her son's a lawyer."

Tillie burst out laughing. "Ain't that the icing on the pie? Did she threaten to sue?"

"Her son told her she might have a case."

"A case of Jack Daniels," Tillie quipped. "He sounds as nutty as she is. Know what really amazes me?"

"What?"

"That I'm not married to him. I'm just one big old refrigerator magnet to lunatic women and their damaged offspring."

Betty grinned as she stood up and handed Tillie a list of the passenger's names. "Can you help me locate a few of these folks? I penciled in an approximate time for the interview next to their names."

Tillie asked, "What if they refuse to show?"

"They can't," Betty said. "According to the sheriff, everyone's a suspect."

Tillie stared at the long list. "Crap on a Spanish cracker! My name's numero uno. The sheriff might as well string the noose around my neck right now."

"Don't worry," Betty reassured her. "He's interviewing everyone, including me. I wouldn't be surprised if he tries to interrogate Farsi."

"You think Baby Butt Severson knows what he's doing?"

Betty hesitated. "You know I never want to speak badly about anyone in law enforcement…"

"But…?" Tillie teased.

"But nothing," Betty said resolutely.

"That's because you're from a family of cops. Me? I'm from a family on COPS."

Betty chuckled.

"Personally, I think the sheriff's a blooming idiot," Tillie continued, "and I don't mind saying so."

Betty couldn't have agreed more but wouldn't verbalize it. "Can you mention to our riders that we have free tickets to the showroom tonight?"

Tillie's face lit up. "Boris the Baffler? The mentalist guy? Cool!" Unable to resist, she said "Hey, I've got an idea. Let's ask him to channel the murderer's name. And when he does, voila!" She added with pride, "Voila is French, you know."

Betty pointed toward the first carousel of dollar slot machines in the middle of the casino's aisle. "There's Arnie Holstein. He's first on your list."

"Okey-doke," Tillie said, stood up, and adjusted the V-neck of her top to its lowest position. Betty watched Tillie wiggle her way through the crowd. A smile spread across Arnie's face as Tillie approached. Ten seconds later he frowned. That's one down, Betty thought.

Getting passengers to agree to be anywhere at any given time was always a difficult task. Gamblers tended to get lost in both time and fantasy. It was nearly impossible to get them to leave a winning machine or table. She knew of one bride-to-be who missed her own wedding because she was "on a roll".

Betty surveyed the gaming area that stretched in front of her with its twenty-five hundred machines. The machines ranged from very basic video poker to electronic slots featuring fairies, monsters, celebrities and popular television shows from the sixties. Ninety percent had morphed from the old-fashioned three-cherries-in-a-row to high-tech high-resolution digital images featuring up to two hundred and forty-three possible wins.

The slots at Moose Bay were ticket-in, ticket-out slots. Inserting a coin into a machine was history. All of the machines—even the ones called "penny slots"—accepted only paper currency or paper tickets.

Betty walked toward the first machine where one of her regular clients sat. Twenty lines of animated forest creatures were flashing by on the slot machine screen in front of Bernice Lang's eyes. She was ahead two hundred and thirty-four dollars.

"Looks like you're doing pretty good," Betty said, placing her hand on her client's shoulders.

Bernice sat mesmerized by the spinning screen in front of her. "I'm doing okay."

Betty said gently, "The sheriff would like to schedule a meeting with each of the passengers."

Bernice hit the play button like a judge pounding out a guilty plea with his gavel. "I don't know a thing about the murder or that Farsi guy."

"It's just a formality," Betty comforted.

"I don't want to leave this machine. I'm winning. Someone else will start playing it as soon as I get up."

"I'm afraid you'll have to. Can you be at Conference Room B at ten-thirty?"

"Fine, but if I end up losing money on my next machine, you'll owe me one of those buffet coupons you carry around."

Betty unzipped her purse and pulled out a vinyl coupon carrier.

"This is the best I can do for now," Betty said handing a fifty-percent off coupon to Bernice. "But you'll be glad to know the casino is giving us tickets for Boris the Baffler."

"You can give my ticket away. I don't want it," Bernice snapped.

Betty was surprised. "Are you sure? I hear he's wonderful."

"Mind readers scare me. I don't want anyone to know what I'm thinking. What if I have a dirty thought during the show? No thanks."

"Well, I don't think he can actually read . . ."

"Even if he can't, he's still creepy. Just take a close gander at him." Bernice pointed to a poster hanging on the wall.

"I will," Betty promised. "Remember, Conference Room B..."

"Yeah, yeah. Ten-thirty," Bernice barked irritably, not taking her eyes off the screen.

To show her client she always kept her word, Betty immediately walked over to the life size poster of the entertainer.

Standing six inches in front of his photo, Betty found it impossible to tell his age. Airbrushing had blurred decades from his face. Boris could be in his twenties or edging toward his sixties.

His hair was not only a brassy bleached blond but was cut into a 80s mullet that screamed Euro Trash. His muscular body strained against his skintight white silk jumpsuit. Starburst patterns of red, black, green and clear rhinestones adorned an ensemble that would make Liberace's ghost green with envy.

Unlike most casino headliner's publicity photos, The Baffler was not surrounded by a bevy of barely-dressed babes. Instead, three men in security uniforms encircled him, holding tightly onto their night-sticks, while Boris held his hands cuffed over his head.

Blazoned across the top of the poster were the words, "Even the Casino Is Afraid of His Powers!"

How hokey, can you get? Betty thought, happy in knowing no one could actually read another person's mind.

Chapter 8

Betty believed there were two types of homicide detectives: those who talked about their work when they got home, and those who didn't. Her husband Larry had been a talker.

In the beginning of their marriage the two of them would sit together at night in their pine-paneled den. She'd sip her way through a half glass of Cabernet while Larry downed three or four brews.

She'd tell him briefly about their son or the volunteer work she did that day. He would belch out sighs of boredom.

All Larry wanted to do was discuss his work. Betty attributed his self-absorption to stress. Later, in therapy, her psychiatrist referred to him as a megalomaniac, a polite way of saying "The guy's an asshole!"

Now, when people asked why her marriage ended she'd repeat an old joke she once heard: she and her husband divorced over religious differences; he thought he was God, and she didn't.

Yet, though he didn't want to listen to her stories, Larry bragged about her ability to analyze a crime. Of course he never told her personally how proud he was of her talent. She'd only heard about it at the precinct's annual holiday party. Two of Larry's subordinates whispered loudly over beers that Betty was the brains behind the beast. One of them actually said it was too bad Larry wasn't a stay-at-home-cop and Betty the working detective.

But she never told Larry what she'd heard. She knew he'd crucify the two men if she did. Larry didn't take kindly to criticism or praise. Nor was it easy for him to compliment anyone, even his own son. He'd grown up in a family that believed in discipline, not rewards. As always, she forgave Larry for his faults, convinced he would eventually change into the husband she convinced herself he could be.

After all, she was only the way she was because of her own family.

Betty knew her uncanny skill at analysis was partially due to having a law enforcement dad. The other reason was her family's habit of playing mind games, the good kind. Puzzles, math problems, crosswords, board games, and chess were all part of her daily life while growing up.

She'd thought about being an officer herself, but when she fell for Detective Chance, she decided otherwise. Having two cops as parents doubled the chance for a child to become an orphan. Betty didn't like the odds.

Still, her family's obsession with games of strategy taught her that life could not only be fun, but tricky. If one searched long enough, and hard enough, there was usually a solution to any problem.

Betty hoped she'd passed on that little bit of wisdom to her son. She hit 1 on her speed dial. Codey answered on the third ring.

"Hey Kiddo, doing the crossword?" she teased, knowing full well he wasn't. Codey was in his office, doing the one thing cops hated most. Paperwork.

Her son's response didn't replicate the warmth in her voice. He answered gruffly, "I've left you four messages that you haven't returned," he said testily.

"I'm sorry, Codey," she began before being interrupted.

"Don't you know how worried I am about you?"

"I'm fine," she reassured him. "I've told you before, you don't have to worry about me. I can take care of myself."

When it came to protecting his mom, Codey was a bear. It was sweet, Betty thought, but unnecessary.

Frustrated, Codey lectured: "Mom, this isn't about your being able to change a flat tire or shovel snow off your roof. You're involved in a murder."

Betty put on her best mom's-still-in-charge voice. "And that's why I'm calling you son, to see if you know anything, or may have heard anything while on duty. Or if you do hear something, let me know ASAP. Okay?"

"The Chicago Police Department is 400 miles away from Moose Bay! What do you expect us to hear? Who the murderer was? His motive? Where he bought the weapon? And maybe what he had for lunch? You're the one who should know these things. You're the one driving around northern Minnesota with a corpse in your bus."

"Bathroom of the bus actually," she corrected him, not bothering to tell him he really shouldn't talk to his mother in that tone of voice. She knew his heart was in the right place. She would mention it later, once the killer had been arrested.

"Did the police say how long he'd been dead?" Codey asked with exasperation.

"A while I guess," Betty answered, preparing herself for a barrage of 'moms!' "Since Tyler Falls."

"Wait a minute," Codey said. Betty could tell by the silence that he was googling the distance between Moose Bay and Tyler Falls. After a few seconds he yelled, "That's over an hour's drive away. Don't tell me you didn't notice that someone was in the can for that long?"

"Seniors take a long time in the bathroom," she explained. "It's one of the things that you get used to as a tour host."

If she were video chatting with him, Betty knew she'd see her him shaking his head in disbelief.

After a brief pause, Codey asked, "How is the passenger that found the body? I know how traumatic that can be. Are they okay?"

Reluctantly, Betty admitted, "We're fine."

"Huh?"

"Tillie and me" Betty said. "We're the ones who discovered it."

"Cripes, Mom!" Codey yelled into the phone.

Betty sighed in understanding. "Codey, honey, finding a body like that made me realize again how hard your job is."

"So is yours, I guess" he said. "Do you need me to come up? I still have a few vacation days left. I can be there in a matter of hours."

Betty replied, "Thanks for the offer but I don't think the Boy Wonder would approve."

"Who?"

"The town's sheriff. Severson. He's like twenty-four years old," Betty told him.

"You're kidding? Is he any good?" Codey asked.

Betty stated, "I'm not too impressed, but in my eyes, no one's as good a cop as you or your dad."

After an uncomfortable silence Codey replied, "Yeah, dad is a pretty good detective."

Betty was glad he didn't add his usual rant--but as a husband and father he sucks.

Betty often wondered if Codey had chosen "vice" to keep an eye on his father. Turned out, her ex-husband Larry was actually one of the worst of Chicago's finest. He may have maintained fidelity to his police oath, but his marriage oath was another matter. That was another little fact she discovered after the divorce. Not only did he fall in love with another woman, but he enjoyed an occasional working girl as well.

Codey continued his inquiry. "Are you sure you don't need anything?"

Betty admitted, "Actually, I do. It's one of the reasons I called. I was wondering if you could do background checks for me."

"Mom! By 'anything', I meant like sending you a pick-me-up bouquet. You're not thinking about working the case, are you? I know you helped Dad solve homicides but I really think that . . ."

"Of course not," Betty interrupted him with a lie. "It's just that there are a few clients I know nothing about."

Over the phone, she could hear him slurp down coffee before answering.

"All right" he said. "You want me to look into the victim's background first?"

"You can't. Seems like the name he used with our company isn't real. They're running tests this morning to see if either his prints or DNA turn up anything."

"Mom, don't tell me you don't check IDs?" Codey groaned.

"You and Severson weren't partners once were you?" Betty replied. She didn't bother to answer his question because it was a moot point. From now on Take A Chance would check everyone's ID. Well, maybe not Hannah's. Even Homeland Security probably gave her a pass.

"So, if I text you a few names, will you run a search for me?" she asked.

"Yeah, I guess. Promise me you won't put yourself in any danger?" Codey begged.

"Of course not," Betty said. "Anyway, Lori's on her way here to watch out for me."

"That's good to know. Are you worried about the sheriff questioning your driver?" Codey asked.

Betty felt herself stiffen. She loved her son more than anyone in the world but sometimes he was just too conservative and judgmental. He never trusted Tillie once Betty informed him of her history.

Betty answered in a firm voice, "Tillie will be fine. She's a terrific bus driver, a great traveling companion . . ."

"And an ex-con with a temper."

Tillie stared up at the small jet in the distance. It was circling the landing strip at Moose Bay's airport. She leaned back against one of the ornate pillars that decorated the casino's entrance and pulled a pack of menthol cigarettes out of her coat pocket. Yanking a glittery plastic lighter out of her other pocket, she lit the cigarette. The first drag spread through her body, calming her.

She could have stayed inside to smoke. A casino was one of the few places left where a smoker felt welcomed, but Tillie never broke her own rules.

While in prison, Tillie wrote down a set of simple instructions that her counselor said would keep her from becoming a repeat offender. Smoking outdoors fit in perfectly with Rule #7—think of others, not just yourself.

Tillie watched the plane descend. Before going back inside, she would take the list from her pocket and read each rule three times. The guidelines had become a daily mantra. The ritual of repeating the words helped her remain centered.

As long as she followed the rules, she knew her life would be fine.

It was only when she became anxious that her brain misfired, causing her to quickly forget any promise she'd made to herself.

When you're under extreme stress you have poor impulse control her counselor had repeated over and over.

As Tillie took her final drag, she told herself she had to stop worrying that the sheriff would connect her to Farsi's murder. She couldn't allow herself to think about that, at all. If she did, her anxiety level could reach an all-time high. Then there was no telling what she'd do.

There was only one thing Tillie knew for certain: no matter what it took, she would never allow herself to be sent back to jail. Not in this lifetime.

Chapter 9

Ding-ding-ding-ding-ding sounded the nearest slot machine while small flashes of light bounced around the vast space. Accompanying the noise were thousands of other dings coming from a thousand other machines. It was a little past ten in the morning and the casino was in full swing. Every seat was taken and rows of onlookers circled the blackjack tables like paparazzi near the red carpet. Except this time, there were no million dollar photos of celebrities to be shot. There was only the chance to be near the action, and perhaps if they were lucky, join in.

Betty inhaled deeply. The years of stale cigarette smoke that permeated the carpet and walls made her feel at home. She adored the musty odor of a casino. Her addiction to nicotine remained hidden deep within her. But she was committed to stay an ex-smoker. Being in a casino was as close to lighting up again as she'd ever get.

Betty scanned the room, looking for her clients. She knew most of them on sight, but was afraid a few of the new ones might get past her. She wished she'd handed out name tags but most of her customers disliked them. Hannah, of course, complained that men used the tag as an excuse to peek at her 'you-know-whats'. Others felt it ridiculous to slap a sticky piece of paper on nice clothing. One male passenger complained that Betty should have known his name immediately, considering what he paid for the charter. Betty made the decision early on it would be wiser just to learn her passengers names and faces as quickly as possible.

After working with seniors for so long, she'd begun to realize they all looked alarmingly alike, just as all babies looked cute and cuddly, even the ugly ones. Perhaps it was nature's way of protecting the most vulnerable, to make every baby adorable, and to make every adult over the age of seventy look like they could be your beloved grandparent.

Betty headed toward Poker Alley with its rows of video poker machines. It took only a minute to discover Mrs. Kotval sitting at the quarter slots.

"Good morning," she said to her client who was playing one nickel at a time, the minimum amount allowed on the twenty line nickel machine. If Mrs. Kotval played the maximum allowed per spin, it would cost her a dollar. By betting on only a single line, she saved ninety-five cents. Of course, if any of the other nineteen lines revealed a winning sequence, it wouldn't matter. Her five cents would be casino history.

Mrs. Kotval swiveled her seat, tugging at her pale green sweatshirt embroidered with the words '*Keep my grandma off the streets! Take her to a casino!*' A photo of her granddaughter was captured in a cross stitched frame on the front.

"Hello Betty," Mrs. Kotval said with a big smile, her dentures gleaming like cultured pearls. "Know what? I'm only down two dollars and I've been gambling for three hours. Isn't that wonderful?"

Betty nodded. She loved gamblers who were realistic. The ones who looked at gaming as recreational and not an investment portfolio.

"Good for you," Betty said before explaining the reason she was there.

"Does that mean I am suspect?" Mrs. Kotval asked, hopefully. "That would be so wonderful. I could tell my grandchildren. They watch *Murder She Wrote* every time they visit. They gave me the Special Edition DVD collection for my birthday."

"Then you'll be happy to know you are indeed a suspect, Mrs. Kotval."

"Really?" Mrs. Kotval's eyes lit up.

"Everyone is," Betty admitted giving her a reassuring smile.

Betty noticed Mrs. Kotval's look of surprise turn to disappointment. She regretted having said it. Clearly, Mrs. Kotval was enjoying the suspicion.

"I can't wait to tell my family," her client beamed. "For once I'll be like those wicked women on TV. My grandkids won't call me Angela Lansbury anymore! I'll be more like Joan Collins!"

It took Betty only a few more steps to discover another rider. She leaned in close to the seventy-seven-year-old woman playing Double Bonus Video Poker, or DBVP as the die-hard gamblers referred to it. Betty said loudly, "Mrs. Browne?"

The tiny sprite exhaled a blast of cigarette smoke which rushed to join the massive thundercloud swirling overhead. The woman bent and rubbed her cigarette out in an already overflowing, red plastic ashtray.

"What can I do for you, dear?" Mrs. Browne asked absently, not turning around to see who called her name. With one hand she fiddled with her hearing aide while her other hand tapped the Max Coin button. Every hit of the button cost her a total of one dollar and twenty-five cents.

Betty continued, "I have good news and bad news. The bad news is that the sheriff wants to interview all of my passengers this morning."

"Why, that would mean stopping everyone from gambling." Mrs. Browne said and shot Betty a withered pout. "I haven't hit a straight yet this morning, much less a royal flush."

"You'll still have plenty of time for gambling," Betty assured her.

Mrs. Browne looked down at her pale, spindly hands. "Time is the one thing that most of us seniors do not have, Betty."

Betty was accustomed to her clients complaining about their age. It didn't come as a surprise. Betty whined about her own as well.

"Don't you want to hear the good news?" Betty asked.

Mrs. Browne quipped sternly, "If it's about religion, I'm not interested."

Betty chuckled. She loved that old people said whatever they wanted to, regardless of the consequences. She announced in an upbeat tone, "The entire tour's been given complimentary show tickets. You can see Boris the Baffler for free."

"But I see Boris right now, dear," Mrs. Browne responded, and proceeded to hack up an unfiltered tsunami as she pointed to the main entrance of the casino.

Betty's eyes followed the direction of Mrs. Browne's blue-veined and nicotine-stained spindly digit. She expected to see yet one more life-sized glossy advert. Instead, what she saw was far more impressive—The Baffler himself was being escorted through the casino.

His entrance was worthy of kings. Had he been sitting astride a white horse, Betty felt his appearance could not have been grander. Boris stood at the top of the steps that led to the casino floor in an unbuttoned, black lame jacket that covered a partially unbuttoned white silk shirt. The shirt's collar was stiff and turned upward. The chest hair that peaked through his clothing was covered by two gold chain necklaces that could easily tow a Ford Fiesta in winter. An extravagant rhinestone belt buckle shaped like a lightning bolt held up his pristine and pressed white silk pants. The fact that most of his fingers glittered with opulent rings was almost as interesting as the handcuffs that locked his wrists together.

An entourage of short, paunchy uniformed security guards surrounded him. Their presence only heightened Boris's stature and regal demeanor.

That guy deserves an Oscar! Betty mumbled before laughing out loud.

Suddenly, the soft rock Muzak overhead changed to the sound of heralding trumpets. Except for a few hardcore gamers, nearly every head in the casino turned to watch the procession.

Boris reached the middle of the room and stopped. Holding his cuffed hands over his head, he surveyed the room. His presence was so overwhelming that Betty noticed a few women gasping. A few others giggled. The men chuckled. One or two mumbled "gimme a break."

The entertainer swirled sideways and stared directly at a large, black haired woman sitting in front of a dollar slot machine. Betty could have sworn the woman gave him an evil glance. But then the lady's demeanor changed and she smiled widely at the mind reader.

Good God, Betty wondered, *did the entertainer use mind control off stage as well?*

"What is your name, darling?" Boris asked in a thick accent that reminded Betty of the Slavic storekeepers in her neighborhood. But there was a twinge of Russian in it as well. Perhaps even English?

Boris sounded as if he grew up moving quickly from one country to another. His voice was strong enough to reach across the room.

"Conchita Catalina Mendoza de Arroyo," the woman answered in a brisk Spanish accent. "I am here on a tour of the Americas. In Madrid, I was a famous flamenco . . ."

Boris' hand shot up immediately in a stop position. Conchita bit into her lip hard, as if it were almost impossible for her to stop her babbling.

With a flourishing bow Boris informed her, "You'll be happy to know you'll soon win a jackpot." Murmurs of amazements and scoffs of disbelief rippled through the gambling crowd.

"A jackpot?" she asked, using her arms in a bent and upward position as she snapped her fingertips, in a classic flamenco dancer stance.

"Si!" Boris growled back, his face a bit stern for the occasion Betty thought.

Conchita spun around on the stool and pressed a button of the one-arm bandit on the Wild Cherry slot machine. The reels spun and stopped. A cluster of bars, blanks appeared. Not a single cherry had materialized. Conchita hit Max Coin again and another three dollars disappeared from her seventy-six dollar credit posted on the machine. There was only one bar. On her third try and subsequent loss, Boris shrugged to the crowd and walked away.

The woman continued pushing the button on her slot machine. Boris walked only a few feet down the aisle before he stopped. He folded his arms across his chest and adopted an omnipotent smirk. He turned his head slightly and looked behind him, toward Conchita. On her next try the self-proclaimed former flamenco dancer hit a jackpot of one thousand dollars.

The crowd around her burst into yelps and applause. Boris continued his parade, the security guards in close proximity. Suddenly, a man seated at a slot machine, dressed in overalls and a flannel shirt put his hand in front of Boris.

The grizzly gambler said in a loud, irritated tone, "Help my wife win. She's never won more than five bucks in her life."

One of Boris' eyebrows shot upward in disbelief. "That's not true, Sir."

"Sure it is," he insisted.

"No it isn't. She won your heart, didn't she? That has to be worth more than five dollars," Boris told him.

Instead of a satisfied sigh, a loud grunt came out of the man's mouth. He said, "Trust me. I ain't no prize."

"Sure you are. You're a retired plumber with a good income and . . ."

The man's eyes opened wide. He asked, "Hey, how did you know that?"

Boris ignored his question and said, "And you've been married for twenty-nine years."

"My God, you can read minds!" the man sputtered.

"And you read *Playboy*," Boris paused in a dramatic fashion and then added, "for the articles, of course."

The burly man's wife's mouth dropped opened in shock, while he sputtered, "Okay, you can stop right there." Avoiding his wife's eyes, he continued, "You win. I'll buy a ticket to your damn show."

"Thank you," Boris said, and continued down the aisle. As he did, dozens of gamblers asked him to predict when they would hit a jackpot or tell them their fortune. He only nodded slightly in recognition of their requests. He spoke to no one until he reached the end of the aisle and stood directly in front of Betty.

His hazel eyes looked at her with a mischievous glint that bordered on leering. Boris was at least twenty-years younger than Betty.

She decided to be as bold as Boris. "Are you reading my mind?" she asked, giving him a look that confirmed he was.

He answered, "You're very brave, aren't you. I like that in a beautiful woman."

Betty played along. "I like that in a beautiful man."

"You'll need help getting inside your hotel room, no?" he purred, his words dripping with possibilities.

Betty was surprised when she found herself becoming flustered. Was this Euro Trash actually making a pass at her? A woman old enough to be his mother? (Well, his sister; Okay, his mother.) And shamelessly in front of a crowd? At the same time, suggesting she needed help, *his help* to get into *her* hotel room? What else would he think she needed once they were inside?

Betty laughed at the thought that she might be on the prowl. She'd read that older women hitting on younger men was the latest fad. Cougars, she'd read. Too bad she couldn't tell Boris that the only clothing she was interested in removing was good-old fashioned support hose. Even then, it would only be to soak her aching feet.

Betty responded, "Thank you, I don't need help."

"Ah, but you do," he teased seductively. "As always, you've lost your room key."

Betty immediately put her hands in her pockets to retrieve the key. Nothing. She quickly opened her purse and rummaged. Nothing. She laughed out loud. What she thought was a come-on was just a part of his act. It was true. She had lost her hotel key.

Boris started to walk past, but stopped even with her. He leaned over and whispered into her ear, "Don't worry. Your business will not suffer because of the homicide. In fact, you'll be more successful than ever."

Betty almost fell over in shock. But she was surprised even more when he added, "And yes, Liberace would be very jealous of my outfit."

Could Boris actually read minds? She'd thought the burly, *Playboy* reading ex-plumber was just a shill, someone who was paid a few bucks to act surprised. But there was no way Boris could know her thought about Liberace's ghost.

And what about the jackpot that just happened to the retired flamenco dancer? How could he have predicted that? Could this alleged mentalist actually forecast when a jackpot would be hit? Or could he somehow make a machine pay out?

Tom Songbird was right. Boris the Baffler was a great showman and his powers were beyond baffling. They were friggin' scary.

Chapter 10

It was only 11a.m. as Betty returned to her room for a fix. The room had a glass cabinet filled with items that would satisfy every impulse—at exorbitant prices. Alcohol held no interest for her. Chocolate was her drug of choice and the truffles called out to her. Their siren song was as irresistible as a Kentucky Fried Chicken drive-thru two blocks south of a fat farm.

Momentarily setting aside her frugality, she reached inside the cabinet and pulled out one of the twelve-dollar candies. When it came to chocolate, Betty had always been promiscuous. When she saw the size of the temptation that awaited her, there was no way she could have said no. It was the largest truffle she'd ever seen. Its sole purpose on this earth was to be devoured by someone like her. Betty carefully unwrapped the gold packaging, slowly peeling back the wrapping, allowing the bittersweet scent to drift upwards. She inhaled deeply as if capturing the musky scent for an eternity. Next, Betty took a moment to appreciate the sheer beauty and weight of the chocolate and raspberry cream delight that had been rolled in a layer of cocoa powder. She bent her head downwards as she lifted the god given morsel close to her lips. She opened her mouth and prepared herself for an invasion of mouth tingling pleasure. Her white teeth sank slowly into the dark, succulent globe. The candy burst onto her tongue and Betty shivered in delight. Belgium chocolate was better than sex. And the best part? She didn't have to shave her legs to experience something better than an orgasm.

She set the second chocolate morsel on top of the armoire. Once she created a spreadsheet of the murder—evidence, motives, suspects—she'd allow herself the pleasure of another truffle.

As she powered up her laptop three short knocks interrupted her.

"Room service," called the voice on the other side of the door.

Betty headed for the door but didn't bother peering through the small, brass peephole. "What are you? Some freak who knocks on women's hotel doors hoping to seduce them?" she asked.

"I'm a freak who knocks on men's hotel doors hoping to seduce them," the smooth voice said in an exaggerated whisper.

Betty yanked open the door and said, "Too bad."

The head of security stood in the hallway. "Got a few minutes?" Tom Songbird asked, his dark eyes sparkling.

"Sure," she answered, motioning for him to come inside.

Though he was twenty-some-years younger than Betty, the two had hit it off during her first visit to Moose Bay. When he met her niece Lori on the same trip they too became fast friends. If he wasn't gay, Lori swore she would have married him the first day she met him. So did Betty.

Betty returned to the square table in the room, next to her laptop. Tom sat across from her, his long legs stretched out to the side.

"What's up?" she asked, leaning back, eager to hear his response.

"I need to talk to you about a couple things. But first, I ran into Lori as she was checking in. She said she'd meet you at the buffet at noon."

"Great," Betty said.

He continued, "I find myself worrying about you. You have to be under a lot of stress right now. Are you doing okay?"

Betty pointed toward the empty candy wrapper on the desk. "I'm coping the best way I know how."

"Have you been able to work on your blog?" he asked.

She shook her head. "I did a quick post, but that was it. I'll manage to write more before the tour is over. If you're concerned, the buffet will be given another five popped buttons."

Tom shook his head. "I'm not worried. If we need to improve, we want to know. Just write the truth like you always do."

She appreciated his reaction. She'd already been banned from two casinos because she wrote the truth. But, there was no way she'd give five popped buttons for sliced turkey that could double as retreads.

Tom leaned over and spoke softly. "I promise you this will go no farther than this room, but do you have any idea what's going on? Why someone was murdered on your bus? Or who did it?"

She said, "Honestly, I haven't a clue. That's why I came back to the room. I thought I'd go over the notes I keep on our clients. To see if anything seemed unusual.

"Want another opinion for a couple of minutes?" he asked.

"Sure, you can help me with my suspect spreadsheet. A rating of ten bullets puts the suspect on the same level as Jack the Ripper. One bullet means they're as pure as Snow White."

Tom gave her a sideways grin. "Really? Snow White, pure? She was shacking up with seven men."

Betty shot back: "They were short. Add 'em up and you've got one NBA center." With a click of the mouse, Betty opened the current junket's file. Inside were individual documents on every passenger. Her eyes scanned the list of names. The cursor landed on a document. She clicked it open.

She said, "As far as Severson is concerned, everyone on the bus is a suspect. So let's start with seventy-seven-year-old Lydia Browne. Widow, chain smoker, and retired kindergarten teacher. She likes video poker and prefers restaurants to buffets. And Mrs. Browne douses her body in White Diamonds perfume."

Tom asked, "Is that the Elizabeth Taylor brand? I think my mom wears it."

Betty nodded. "I made that notation because I've had complaints. I try to sit her next to someone who won't mind being assaulted by fragrance."

"Anything else about her?" Tom asked.

Betty continued, "She walks twenty minutes a day while carrying portable, water-filled dumbbells. This is her sixth trip with us. Her astrological sign is Taurus, and I notify her two hours before any departure or she'll forget about it."

"I'd give her a rating of two," Tom said, folding his muscular arms behind his head.

Betty's eyebrows shot up in surprise. "Not a 1?"

"She's a smoker. You never know what they'll do if they run out of cigarettes. Tell me about someone who hasn't traveled with your company before."

Betty's eyes scanned down the list of names and clicked on a document. "Here's a newbie. His name is Marcus Slevitch. He's sort of an odd duck."

Tom sat forward. "How so?"

"I was in the office the day he signed up for this trip. He was barely communicative. When he paid, he just threw the wad of cash on the counter. He was very abrasive."

The security chief's brow furrowed in thought. He asked, "What else do you have on him?"

"He lives near Midway airport. He's sixty-four years old and single. He checked off Blackjack as his game of choice. He has no known allergies or medical needs, and is not on any prescription drug, which is kind of amazing considering how big he is."

"How big?" Tom asked.

"Three-fifty, maybe four hundred pounds. But he's tall so he carries it well" Betty answered, not knowing if that were even possible. But, as a plus size adult herself she felt she had to stick up for the man. If there was a global tribe of fat people, he was an honorary member of it, just like her.

Betty picked up her cell and texted Slevitch's name and address and hit send. When Codey received the message he'd check on Slevitch's background. Like Farsi, perhaps Slevitch wasn't who he claimed to be either.

Tom checked his watch and said, "I need to get back downstairs, but I have some information to share with you about Farsi."

The tone of his voice scared Betty. "Go on," she said.

Tom announced, "Severson discovered Farsi's identity."

Betty breathed a sigh of relief. "That's great news."

Tom continued, "His real name is Danya Novikov. In his twenties he was arrested for scamming casinos in Vegas. He served six months for using a monkey paw at the Stardust."

"What's a monkey paw?" Betty asked, knowing it probably had nothing to do with an actual primate.

"It's a foot long piece of bendable steel that has a claw-like end. A gambler inserts it into the payout shoot and it triggers the coin counter to release coins," Tom explained.

"Did he go straight when he was released?" Betty asked.

Tom said, "Not at all. Two years later, he was caught fishing at a dollar slot on the strip. You know what fishing is, right?"

Betty nodded. "With the older mechanical slots, someone could tape a piece of string to a coin and drop it into the slot. The coin would register as a credit and then be yanked back out. If they did it enough times, they'd build a small fortune in credits they could turn into cash."

"That's right," Tom agreed.

"I suppose he did another six months?"

"No" Tom smiled, "but he did manage to accidentally break his legs."

"You mean someone broke his legs for him," Betty said. She shook her head. "He had to be either really stupid or really lucky to think he could cheat a mob-owned casino and get away with it."

Tom shrugged. "He was both. It wasn't until the late 70s that organized crime lost control of the city to corporations. The guy could have ended up in an unmarked grave in the desert, instead of hurt in a hospital."

"I guess his luck ran out when he signed up for our tour," she noted. It wasn't a joke. Remembering the knife in her passenger's back still made her tremble.

"Is there anything else you need to tell me?" she asked, knowing the security chief was on a tight schedule.

He nodded. "There is one more thing. Well, actually, two million things."

The corners of Betty's eyelids crinkled into a look of confusion. "I don't understand."

Tom answered, "Two million dollars were hidden inside Farsi's luggage."

Chapter 11

Tillie waited until the elevator doors closed before exclaiming, "I never thought I'd be tempted to break the law again, but gheesh for two million buckaroos!"

"You're kidding aren't you?" Betty asked, as the elevator began its descent. Tom Jones' "She's a Lady" thumped through the overhead speakers and bounced around the compartment. The sleek mahogany walls were polished to perfection. A glass picture case on the back wall featured the showroom's upcoming headliners. Jay Leno would be at Moose Bay the next week. On the side walls, a slim ceiling to floor mirror accented the cubicle. Mirrored tiles dotted the ceiling. Behind the glistening glass, security cameras were capturing their every move.

Tillie shrugged her shoulders, "Maybe. But it's a good thing I didn't know Farsi had that kind of money on him. I wouldn't have been able to drive while I was sitting in his lap."

Betty laughed. "Actually, the money wasn't on him. It was in his luggage."

In an exasperated tone Tillie added, "It was underneath my butt the entire trip? I was sitting on a fortune and didn't even know it."

"I think someone else did, though," Betty said. "I'm sure that's why he was killed."

Tillie asked, "Do you remember how the casino staff put our passengers' luggage inside the lobby when we arrived?"

Betty nodded, wondering what Tillie was hinting at.

Tillie said, "The bags just sat there unguarded. Anyone could have walked off with Farsi's millions."

"That's true. For that kind of loot," Betty said, "there are people who would certainly commit murder."

The shiny brass doors opened and the two women stepped out

into the corridor. The tinny, clinking sounds of electronic coins being dropped into—and pouring out of!—machines was heard through the casino doors. A joyous "Yahoo!" and an exasperated "Oh Crap!" or two intermingled. A live band played R&B in the distance.

Betty and Tillie headed toward the buffet.

As they approached the restaurant, Betty placed her hand gently around Tillie's waist and asked, "You were kidding about breaking the law, weren't you?"

"Are you nuts? I wouldn't go back to jail for a measly two million."

Betty breathed a sigh of relief until the driver added," Now, if we were talking three mil. . ."

"Aunt Betty!" The sound of Lori's voice interrupted them. Her niece stood near the entrance, dressed in a form-fitting tailored black pantsuit. A hint of a pink lace-trimmed camisole peaked from beneath the buttoned lapel. Her long blonde hair cascaded over the jacket's shoulders.

She hugged her niece. "Thank you for coming."

Lori embraced her back. "No problem. Is there anything new I should know about?"

"About two million new things," Tillie taunted, as they joined the diner's queue.

By the time they were seated at their table, Betty and Tillie shared everything they knew about the homicide.

As the server filled their cups with coffee, Betty said, "Tillie and I have decided to still call the victim by his fake name, Farsi."

Tillie added, "Farsi rolls off the tongue better than Novikowicky-wacky or whatever his name really was."

Lori said, "So, if Farsi served time for tampering with slots, it's hardly unusual that he ended up on a gaming tour."

"I agree," Betty answered.

Lori's eyes shifted toward the food station. She asked, "Could we start eating soon? I'm famished."

The three immediately stood up and headed in different directions. Lori ran straight to the dessert bar where dozens of fruit tartlets were being offered at *Dessert First*. Lori could eat eight of them and never gain a pound. Tillie travelled *Around The World in 80 Bites*, loading up on bits and pieces of global entrees along the way.

Betty trudged to the *It's So Easy Being Green* food station. She was feeling the effects of being sleep deprived and knew that one too many carbs would knock her out. To help keep her eyes open, she'd munch on green lettuces and crisp veggies. Maybe she'd even write about her choice on her blog. She'd title it *Low Carbs and Casino Highs.*

She headed back to the table, setting down her plate of organic spring mix and fresh broccoli. Tillie and Lori were already seated. Lori's plate held two fruit tartlets and a half-consumed slice of blueberry cheesecake. In front of Tillie were five mounds of international goodies.

As she spun strands of pesto laden pasta round and round on her fork, Tillie said "Lori, wait till you get a look at Sheriff Severson. You'll wonder why he's not at band camp."

"He is kind of young," Betty helpfully explained.

"Kind of?" Tillie shot back. "He should be a Cub Scout, not the town sheriff."

Betty reminded her, "Like it or not, Severson is who we have to deal with." She glanced down at her plate. She felt her resolve to restrict her calories weakening.

Tillie asked, "Why hasn't the FBI been called in? I drove across two state borders getting here. On *Matlock*, when state lines were crossed the FBI was always brought in to investigate."

Betty took a swig of coffee. "I don't think they would be interested unless Farsi was connected to terrorism, forgery, or some other federal crime."

A glimmer of insight registered on Tillie's face. "Maybe the money's fake! Maybe Farsi planned on using counterfeit bills to gamble with on the slots?"

"$2,000,000 on slots?" Betty questioned.

Tillie reminded her, "Not everyone plays the penny machines like you do. What's the highest limit machine here?"

"There are several ten dollar machines in the high roller area, as well as two twenty-five dollar ones," Betty answered.

"Twenty-five dollars at one time?" Lori asked, while her fork balanced a thick wedge of cheesecake.

Betty nodded. "Twice that much if you play the max."

"Gheesh! Wait a minute," Tillie grabbed her purse and started rummaging through it. She pulled out a bottle of sparkly fingernail polish, one compact, three lipsticks, a manicure set, and a sewing kit. She placed them all on the table. Finally she found what she had been looking for, a small hand calculator.

Tillie said, "A slot player makes a bet every four seconds. That's fifteen bets a minute." She started playing with the buttons on the calculator. "Gosh, that's nine hundred bets every sixty minutes! At fifty dollars a bet, that's forty-five thousand dollars an hour. Farsi could go through $2,000,000 in less than forty-five hours of gambling."

A wicked smile crossed Lori's face. "True, but he'd probably score a free buffet out of the deal."

The trio couldn't stop laughing. Betty put her hand over her mouth. "I can't believe I laughed at a joke about Farsi in public. I hope no one heard us."

Betty looked around. No one was paying any attention, except for a lone man standing at the buffet entrance. His eyes were directed straight at Lori.

"Lori, I think you have an admirer." Betty gestured subtly toward the impeccably groomed man. He looked as out of place at an all-you-can-eat buffet as a G Q model buying hair gel at Wal-Mart.

"Actually, she has two admirers," Tillie said pointing without any subtlety at Sheriff Severson, who stood only twenty feet from their table. He was holding a plastic tray piled high with food.

Each noticed the other gazing longingly at Lori. They glared at each other.

Tillie asked, "What is this, a stand-off at the OK Corral? They look like they're positioning themselves for battle."

"They are," Betty said. She was familiar with the idea of men fighting over her stunningly beautiful niece. "Lori, do you know the guy in the doorway?"

"He's just someone I met at the airport," Lori answered nonchalantly, though her eyes sparkled. "Actually, he just looks like every other gorgeous man out there. In fact, that's what I nicknamed him—Mr. Gorgeous."

"He's more than that." Betty explained. "I've seen him win poker tournaments on television. I just can't remember his name right now."

Tillie added, "I think the name Lori gave him fits him perfectly—Mr. Gorgeous. Lori, if you haven't already guessed, the other gawking fool is Tiny Town's Sheriff Severson."

At that precise moment, the sheriff managed to knock his silverware off his tray. It clanged loudly as it hit the tiled floor.

Mr. Gorgeous winked at Lori before walking out of the buffet. Meanwhile, Sheriff Severson bent over to pick up the fork he dropped and a cake plate slid off his tray. He managed to catch it in the air. Half the room broke into applause. The sheriff's face turned beet red as he walked to Betty's table.

"Would you care to join us?" Betty asked.

"No, I'm heading back to the interrogation room. Gotta keep working," he said, before asking, "Is this your daughter? She sort of looks like you, except a lot younger."

Tillie cleared her throat.

Betty replied, "This is my niece, Sheriff. Lori Barnes."

"I'm Sheriff Severson," he said, his voice deepening right before it cracked.

"I thought you might be," Lori acknowledged, a sly smile turning her full lips upward.

"Okay, well—then—goodbye," he said, and sped away.

When he was out of earshot, Lori whispered, "Oh, my."

"My feelings exactly," Tillie added, "Except I'd add 'what an ass' to the end of that phrase."

"Still, he is kind of cute," Lori added. She shifted to focus on her aunt. "Aunt Betty, I know how you like to solve any problem that comes your way, but you do not have to find out who killed Farsi, even if he was one of our passengers. That's what the police are for."

Betty answered, "I realize that. But as long as the case remains unsolved, I'm terrified one of our other riders will be hurt." Or, more concerning, she thought to herself, one of them could actually be the murderer.

Tillie added, "Betty does have a point. If the murderer's still out there, who knows who'll be their next victim? It could even be one of us."

Lori's eyes widened. "Are you really scared there's going to be another murder?"

Betty answered honestly. "I think we definitely should be afraid, if only to remember to be cautious."

Tillie said, "The killer could be anyone in this room. Or it could be an international hit man."

Betty asked, "Why do you think Farsi's death may have global implications?"

Tillie answered, "Oh, I haven't decided anything. Yet. I never make rash decisions."

Betty and Lori exchanged looks.

"I just said it *could be* international," Tillie added defensively. "But I do know it doesn't have anything to do with extraterrestrials."

Betty looked bemused. She was fully aware of Tillie's obsession with anything from beyond.

Lori asked, "Are you talking about aliens from outer space?"

"Of course," Tillie answered, "but there's not a shred of evidence that ETs harm humans. Although the probing thing they do is not very nice."

Betty interjected, "So if you don't think the killer is from Mars, what are you thinking?"

Tillie answered, "Canadians. The border is only a few hundred miles north of the town Farsi was stabbed in. The murderer could have come straight down from Canada and then gone back up again. According to the radio shows I listen to, terrorists border-hop all the time, just to practice for the Big One."

"What Big One?" Lori asked, although she should have known better.

"The attempted overthrow of the United States of A. But you have nothing to worry about," Tillie comforted. "They will not succeed."

Without a hint of judgment in her voice, Lori asked gently, "Do you listen to a lot of talk radio while you drive?"

Tillie answered, "Yep, that's what got me interested in ETs, terrorists, remote viewing, and the fact that for only thirty dollars a month there are vitamins that are guaranteed to add seventy-five years to your life."

Betty interrupted, "But Tillie, Minnesota is probably fifteen hundred miles north of Mexico. The murderer, or terrorists for that matter, could easily come up from Mexico instead of coming down from Canada."

"See what I mean? International possibilities!" Tillie sat back proudly.

"I'm going with a crime of passion," Lori decided. "Farsi was probably killed by a jealous husband. In romance novels, stabbing is always a crime of passion."

Betty added, "Statistics do indicate that if you're going to be murdered, a relative is going to do it."

"And that's why I avoid family reunions," Tillie smirked. "But I'm not forgetting that any old nutcase hanging around the truck stop could have done it as well. Or it could have been a lover's triangle like Lori suggested. Farsi wasn't the best-looking man but, as they say, all dogs are grey in the dark."

"Doesn't the saying go, *all cats are . . .*" but before Betty could finish her question, an eardrum piercing series of siren blasts screeched, warning everyone to immediately evacuate. The building was on fire.

Chapter 12

Maybe it's just a drill!" Tillie said over the blasting siren and scurry of workers and guests.

Lori added "I don't smell any smoke."

The fearful look on the faces of the staff assured Betty it wasn't a drill. The buffet workers were instructing everyone to leave the restaurant. The crowd reacted with a mix of irritation and fear. There were only two customers who dropped their forks and raced out of the room.

A feeling of dread enveloped Betty. There was no way she couldn't take the alarm seriously, even if it ended up being a prank. She didn't think she could endure losing another client, especially to a fire.

"We need to take care of our people," she told Tillie and Lori, while scanning the room for Take A Chance passengers. She could see at least four tables that were filled with her clients.

"Well, at least nothing else could possibly go wrong on this trip," Tillie announced, standing up.

If only, Betty thought, pushing herself up from the table. She didn't want to remind Tillie that trouble usually arrived in threes.

Betty pointed toward Hannah's table. "Tillie, guide Hannah and her companions out. I'll escort Ogawa's group and the table next to him." She turned to Lori. "Do you recognize the guy in the far corner?"

Lori grabbed her tote bag from the floor. "Yeah, I remember him," Lori said, pointing to Slevitch who was sitting alone. He was still eating his meal as if nothing was happening.

Each of the women headed toward their designated table. They scrambled through the crowd heading to the exit. There was no sign of the panic that is usually portrayed in movies when sirens go off unexpectedly. Most of the people walked at a normal pace chattering or laughing that the alarm was sure to be false.

Betty maneuvered her way around tables while inhaling deeply in an effort to smell signs of an actual fire. The only smoky scent she could detect came from *Mama Bear's Barbecue*. The aroma of smoked hickory and burnt pork was wonderful, but hardly threatening.

When she reached Ogawa, she placed one hand on his shoulder. "We need you to leave now. Will all of you follow me, please?" she asked, and motioned for those at the next table to follow as well.

"Is something wrong?" shouted an elderly gentleman seated to the left of Ogawa. He began fiddling with his hearing aide.

"For Pete's sake," a woman next to him screamed into his ear as she scooped up another chunk of Pecan Pie ala Mode. "Turn up your hearing aide, Alfred. Can't you hear the sirens?"

"Sirens? What sirens?" he asked in a panic. "Are the Germans dropping bombs again? Damn Hitler!"

"Yes, damn Hitler, Mr. Yoder," Betty shouted over the continuing whir, giving him her hand as she helped him stand up. "Now let's go."

Mr. Ogawa stood as well. He folded his napkin and placed it carefully on the table before he spoke. "Thank you, Miss Betty. Thank you!"

"There's no need to thank me, Mr. Ogawa," Betty shouted over the continuing noise.

"But there is, Miss Betty. There is. This trip helped me cross another thing off my list of things to do before I die."

"What's that?" She asked as she tried to get the elderly group to pick up their pace.

Mr. Ogawa beamed, "Why, number eighty-seven on my list, Miss Betty—to experience a natural disaster. There's nothing unnatural about fire, is there?"

Unless it's arson, Betty thought.

Thirty minutes later the all-clear notice was given. Betty and Tillie stood in the far corner of the hotel lobby packed with fidgeting gamblers and hotel guests. Betty had no idea where Lori was.

Unfortunately, Hannah was easy to spot. She was walking toward them. Hannah's eyes were frozen slits of pettiness as she stopped in front of them. She announced, "That was a complete waste of time. This place isn't burning down. I'm starting to believe you're in cahoots with the casino to stop me from winning my jackpot!"

Betty reminded her, "Hannah, you were at the buffet when the alarm sounded, not sitting at a slot."

"And just where do you think I'd be right now if the alarm hadn't sounded? Probably hitting the big one at the Double Diamonds machine, that's where!" Hannah crooked an index finger pointing directly at Betty. She turned and pushed her way through the crowd in what Betty could only think of as the ultimate hissy fit.

Tillie asked, "Do you think that woman's ever happy?"

"Only when she's telling everyone how unhappy she is," Betty explained. "Did you know Hannah only travels with Take A Chance Tours? I think we're the only people Hannah has left, besides her son. Maybe that's why she's so crabby."

"Or maybe she's so crabby because she has no family willing to travel with her," Tillie retorted.

A voice came over the intercom. "Moose Bay would like to apologize to its guests for any inconvenience. We assure you it is completely safe to return to what you were doing. The alarm turned out to be false."

Betty heard a few utterances of *Thank god*, or *I told you so* as the rabble dispersed. She did notice a couple of dollars being passed between men. Even the chance of the casino burning to the ground was an opportunity for the most die-hard of gamblers.

A round of applause broke out in the hotel corridor. A parade of young fireman with axes on their shoulders and sporting fireman's helmets jauntily walked through the crowd.

"M-hmm," Tillie said, fluttering her eyelids as she used her hand to fan her face. "If there isn't a fire, then why am I feeling so hot and sweaty, like I should be taking off all my clothes?"

Betty agreed. "Firemen are very sexy."

"You got that right. I mean there are men and then there are—*fire* men." Tillie let out a quick wolf whistle. One of the hunkiest men turned around and gave Tillie a quick wink in return. "I can't believe a real, live firefighter flirted back at me," Tillie said in a breathless whisper. "Maybe I can convince him to rescue me before I melt from desire."

"I think it's a little too late for that," Betty teased.

Tom Songbird made his way over to the two women. He looked concerned.

"Where's Lori?" he asked, glancing around.

Betty answered, "We separated earlier to gather up clients. I'm sure she's around here somewhere. Do you need to speak with her?"

He hesitated. "I'll call her on her cell. But first, I've something to tell you."

Tom's hand gripped Betty's shoulders. Her stomach did a flip-flop, as if warning her of the turbulence that lay ahead.

Visions of a second victim with a knife sticking out of its back flashed before her eyes. Finally she asked, "Was someone hurt again?"

Before he could answer, Tillie interrupted. "You've found another body in a locked room, didn't you? Just like Farsi?"

Tom shook his head. "We didn't find a body, but there's something almost as terrifying."

"What?" Betty asked, her stomach deciding to do one more cartwheel.

"Another bathroom crime scene. And your business card was laying smack dab in the middle of it."

"Was her card covered in blood?" Tillie asked, wide-eyed.

"Like red icing on a devil's food cake."

Lori watched as Slevitch slouched away from her. Like her aunt suggested, she'd guided him out of the buffet when the alarms sounded. He followed her lead, but didn't say a word. He only grumbled incoherently and acted as if he were irritated at her insistence to flee. As soon as the all-clear was given, Slevitch left without saying a goodbye or thanks. She accepted his demeanor as normal for a gambler whose moods probably depended upon the status of their bankroll. Lori began looking for Betty and Tillie as she gazed out over the dispersing crowd.

She felt a strong grip on her elbow. Without looking at who was behind her, she allowed herself to be led out of the lobby. The scent of cologne told her all she needed to know. Her guide was Mr. Gorgeous.

"You're not worried the casino might be wrong, and the fire may actually be real?" she teased as he led her toward the high stakes poker room.

He stepped in front of her and stopped. His face registered a mock frown. "A little extra heat is the least of my concerns. What I'm worried about is luck."

"As in bad?" she asked coyly, her eyes taking on a look of interest.

"Exactly," he admitted. "Usually, I don't give luck a second thought. Poker is a game of skill. But nothing's gone well for me since you shot me down at the airport. I can't afford to act like a teenage boy suffering his first crush. I'm at Moose Bay on business. I play for a living. My name is Tony."

For the first time it registered with Lori who the man was. She suddenly realized she'd read about him while thumbing through the gaming industry magazines at the office.

"You're Tony Gillette?" she asked. Gillette was regarded as one of the best poker players in the world.

He shrugged as if it were no big deal. "Yes."

"You've been on the *Galactic Series of Poker*. How many championships have you won? Three?" she asked, finally understanding why the legendary player was in northern Minnesota. Songbird had told her that a nationally televised championship poker game was scheduled at Moose Bay within a few days.

"Four," Gillette corrected and led her into the high limits room where, according to one review she'd read, the "big boys played the big games". Though she'd been at Moose Bay often, she'd never ventured inside the room. She stayed at the five dollar tables in the middle of a thousand machines. The noise surrounding those tables was energizing, fun, and deafening. The penny players at the machines would hoot and holler every time they won fifty cents. The high rollers in this room, however, where the minimum play was often three digits, earned the right to both privacy and a display of opulence that honestly took her breath away.

Brass sconces lit up the thirty-foot walls made of imported walnut. A stained glass dome of ebony hand-cut pieces, framed in pewter, resembled a map of the stars. The big dipper was directly above her head. The black shards were embedded with tens of thousands of tiny, flashing fiber optics that were so bright Lori thought she was actually looking at a star-studded sky. It was only an illusion. But if she wanted to see the real thing? Well, that could happen at a flick of a switch. The dome ceiling would slide open, allowing the high rollers the pleasure of the night sky.

Twelve dark wood, oval tables were meticulously arranged around the luxurious room, each one with padded leather arm rests. High, plush leather swivel-chairs promised comfort for as long as a player could afford to remain in the game. Throughout the room, stunning cocktail waitresses provided impeccable service, retrieving top shelf drinks or anything else the player wanted from the room's private, s-shaped, solid brass bar.

Tony guided her to the center table where the dealer waited patiently. It appeared to be his private table, a fringe benefit available only to the highest of rollers.

"What was it like to win your first tournament?" Lori asked, remembering how thrilled she felt the first time she played for fun.

He smiled. "It felt good, but not as good as when I played poker for the first time. I walked away with a thousand bucks in my pocket. I only had twenty bucks to my name when I started playing."

A cocktail waitress, dressed in a black and red silk bustier edged next to them.

"Beverages?" she asked.

Tony declined. Lori ordered Perrier on the rocks.

"You won a thousand dollars the first time you played poker? That's pretty impressive," Lori said, knowing that he must have been very young at the time. Perhaps he'd even been the same age as she was when she discovered the game.

"Not really," he laughed, sliding three stacks of poker chips in front of her. "I had an edge. I was the only sober player at the table."

Lori laughed.

She stared at the black chips in front of her. A shiver danced up her spine as she fingered one of the stacks.

"Do you know how to play?" Tony asked.

"A little," she lied as her heart raced. Each chip was worth one hundred dollars.

"I keep half your winnings," he grinned.

"No problem," she answered, forgetting momentarily about Take A Chance Tours, her clients, and everything else in her life.

"If you win, that is." Mr. Gorgeous winked.

"And if I lose?" Lori asked, gently stroking her chips. "What will I owe you then?"

He grinned. "Something other than money."

"Pray tell" she teased, while pushing three chips out in front of her "What could I possibly give you?"

His grin disappeared. He answered solemnly, "I'm not sure, yet."

Chapter 13

As soon as Tom pressed the tenth-floor button, Tillie commanded: "Hold this." The doors closed.

She shoved a make-up bag and a can of hairspray into Tom's hands as the elevator rose upward. Tillie continued searching her purse. Finally, she yanked a tattered paperback novel from deep inside. Tom dropped the items he was holding back into her purse.

She handed him the book and said, "This is why I thought you found another body in another locked room. Murder is my hobby, or at least reading about it is."

Betty interjected, "You probably know this Tom, but in a locked room mystery there's no apparent way for the killer to enter the crime scene, or leave it."

"Kind of like what happened to Farsi in your bus," Tom said. The elevator pinged. As the brass doors opened, the three stepped out onto the hotel's multi-colored carpeting and headed down the corridor.

Tillie gestured toward the book Tom still carried in his hand. He was reading the back cover, or what was left of it, while they walked. She said, "You can borrow *Murder in Mesopotamia* if you want."

"Was this copy discovered there?" Tom said, holding up the well-worn item barely held together by decades of taping—and re-taping.

"Agatha Christie is fun," Betty assured him as the three headed toward the Penthouse Suite. She'd read the book three times herself. Next to the sweetness of anything remotely chocolate, reading was Betty's most treasured addiction.

The security chief shook his head and handed the book back to Tillie. "I don't think I want to read about murder right now. It would be too much like going to work."

Tom's comment brought Betty back to the moment. "I've never been on this floor before," she said.

"Few people have. It consists of only four suites. Each about twenty-four-hundred square feet. And each features a living room, kitchen, three bedrooms and four baths."

"The suites are bigger than my house," Betty gasped, knowing the first thing she'd do if she won the lottery would be to reserve a penthouse. As they reached the last suite Betty asked, "You said no one is registered for this suite?"

Tom answered, "That's what makes this even odder than it already is. The front desk received a complaint of screams coming from inside the suite. That call was made from a wireless cell phone, so we have no idea who called. When we sent security to check it they discovered…well, you'll see."

He opened the door and the three stepped inside a small corridor. At the end of the hallway, Betty saw Severson standing in the center of the living room. Three other policemen were in the room, as well as two security guards. The sheriff nodded to Tom in recognition but continued speaking into his phone.

Tom paused in front of a small door and waited.

Tillie leaned against the wall and whispered, "I get nauseous at the sight of blood. Catch me if I pass out."

Tom asked, "Are you sure you can do this, Tillie?"

She nodded. "Probably. But for the first time in my life I wish was wearing Depends instead of a thong."

Betty mumbled, "Trust me. You'll wish that more and more as you get older."

After clicking off his phone, Severson walked over to the three.

"I'm assuming Tom told you why I wanted you here," he said.

Tillie chuckled nervously. She said, "Well, you know what happens when you assume, Sheriff? It makes an asshole out of you and…"

Betty jabbed her elbow into Tillie's side.

"Ouch!" Tillie cried.

"Tom told us, Sheriff," Betty offered.

Severson opened the door to the hallway bathroom but gave Betty instructions. "Make sure you don't touch anything."

She stepped gingerly inside the doorway. If it weren't for the blood splattered across the white marble tile, mirrors and shiny fixtures, the room was stunning. It included a walk-in shower, a whirlpool for four, and a European-style bidet sitting next to what Betty knew was a remote controlled toilet. She'd seen the commodes at high-end Home Shows. She couldn't imagine that they had actually been installed anywhere. Still, it was a brilliant idea, undoubtedly invented by a woman. A married woman.

She noticed the mirror over the double sinks had the most blood on it. The copper red stains only heightened the fact that the mirror also served as a trendy LCD television monitor that could be turned on or off. Whoever left the blood also left the television blaring inside the mirror, the channel turned to CNN.

Betty's business card sat in the middle of the vanity, inside what looked like a bloody Rorschach test. Someone had scribbled on the card in ink. Even without her glasses, Betty could recognize the name. It was Tillie's.

Sitting next to the splotch of blood was something else that was familiar: A knife that looked exactly like the one used to kill Farsi. Betty stepped backward out of the room.

Tillie leaned her head in, managing to keep her eyes mostly shut. She pulled back and shivered.

The sheriff led the two women to the living room. "Take a seat," he said, pointing to the oversized tan leather sectional that seemed to circle half the room. They sat down but Tom remained standing.

The sheriff walked over to grab his clipboard. As he did, one of the policemen cordoned off the bathroom by placing a big yellow X made from crime scene tape across its doorway.

Tillie muttered, "Shouldn't we grab some of that crime scene ribbon and start wearing it across our chests?"

Betty gave a nervous laugh.

Tillie added, "Like some psycho beauty pageant?"

"This is all so weird," Betty whispered. "One actual murder and the suggestion of another, both connected to Take A Chance."

"Both of them connected to *me*, you mean—the felon," Tillie sighed.

"Not to you," Betty reminded her. "Everything's pointing at Take A Chance Tours. You're not even an employee. You come with the bus we rent."

Tillie looked up to see if Severson was listening. He wasn't. She whispered, "When you're an ex-con, you're connected to any crime within spitting distance. A lot of cops like to take the easy way out and finger the usual suspect."

Betty reached over and squeezed her hand. "Everything will be fine."

Tillie took a deep breath and rested her head on Betty's shoulder. "Thanks. I needed to hear that."

"Hear what?" Severson asked, sitting down on the sofa perpendicular to the women.

Betty let go of Tillie's hand and answered curtly, "That the Cubs will win the World Series."

Severson answered sarcastically, "Well, I'm glad to see you're not taking the possibility of a second murder too seriously."

Betty bit her lip.

Severson looked at her severely. "You have any idea why your business card was in the bathroom? Or why someone wrote Tillie's name on it?"

Betty answered, "No. Perhaps, someone just wanted to remember our driver's name."

"Any idea whose blood it's soaked in?" he asked.

"Not a clue, Sheriff," Betty answered honestly.

Severson glared at Tillie. "What about you?"

Betty answered for her friend, "She doesn't."

"I was talking to Tillie," he said, pointing at the driver.

Betty could see Severson was growing more agitated. His pen pressed into the notepaper so hard Betty thought it would go straight through his clipboard. But she understood. One murder was one too many to investigate, and two would have been overwhelming.

Severson said, "Obviously, someone wanted us to discover your card."

"I agree," Betty responded.

"How easy are your cards to come by?" he asked.

"They're stapled inside our brochures. The brochures are spread across the entire city of Chicago. They're also mailed to every casino or senior group in the Midwest. That card could have been picked up by anyone in a five-state area."

Severson's eyebrow arched quizzically. "Still, doesn't it seem odd to you that one of them ended up inside a suite where no one is registered?"

Betty squared her shoulders and replied, "Of course, it does. If I were you, I'd be thinking the same thing. But I can guarantee you that Tillie, Lori and I are not involved in any way."

"Is there anyone else at Take A Chance that might be?" he asked, glancing up as the door opened and Lori swept inside.

Her niece headed toward the young sheriff and positioned her body directly in front of him, hands at her waist, legs spread wide, resting firmly on her stilettos. Her breathing was deep enough to move her cleavage up and down, as if her breasts were on a joy ride all by themselves. Severson's facial expression changed from a tough cop attitude to a puddle of adolescent desire.

In a disgusted tone Lori said, "Gloria Morgan is the only employee we have. And as long as the victim can't outrun her and her cane, she's your killer."

The sheriff was speechless. But that didn't surprise Betty. She knew that at twenty-four years of age, Severson's brain was in a constant battle with his testosterone. This time his cerebral cortex lost out to boobs, stilettos, and long blonde hair.

Lori turned around and sat down across from him, crossing her legs in the process. "Actually, Sheriff," she added "Gloria wouldn't hurt a fly." Lori turned toward the two women and asked, "Are the rumors true? Was someone else murdered?"

Betty answered, "Not that we know. Where did you hear that?"

"Where do you think? Hannah. She told me she heard it from a number of other riders."

Severson said, "We haven't discovered a body yet, but there is blood splattered throughout the bathroom. In fact, your aunt's business card was found in the middle of it. Tillie's name was scribbled on the card, as well."

Severson reached into his jacket and pulled out a small digital camera. He fiddled with the buttons and scrolled through the pictures that popped onto the camera's screen. He searched until he found the one he wanted. He held it out so Lori could see the screen. The image displayed was that of the bloody bathroom.

Lori squirmed at the photograph and mumbled, "My God."

The sheriff said softly, "I'm sorry to have to show you that." Then, as if remembering he had an investigation to lead, his testosterone retreated and his authoritarian demeanor returned. His voice was stern as he addressed the trio.

"Either someone associated with your company is responsible for the murder or one of you is being framed. There has to be a damn good reason for your card to be in this suite. I don't believe in coincidence," he announced.

Betty bit her tongue. She kept reminding herself over and over that the young man in front of her was in charge. The case was not hers to solve. And he would resent her if she acted like she was his equal.

"Do you have any other questions for us?" Betty asked, glancing at her watch. "I need to check on my people. After all, I am here on business."

"So am I," he reminded her. "I'll need your employee's contact information."

Betty reached over and took his clipboard from him. Reluctantly she wrote Gloria's home telephone number on the pad. There was no telling what her jabbering co-worker would tell Severson.

"Can we go?" Tillie asked as soon as Betty handed the clipboard back. "The bingo session starts soon and I bought a forty-dollar package."

Severson's eyes moved to Lori. "Do you need to leave as well?"

Lori slowly uncrossed her legs and stood up. The sheriff averted his stare as she did. Towering over him, she answered, "If you have no further questions, then yes."

He nodded. "I want to be able to reach each of you. Does everyone own a cell phone?"

The three women wrote down their cell numbers. Betty knew the first number he would be calling would be Lori's.

Chapter 14

"Oh-69, Oh-69," the caller announced, his husky voice reaching into the far corners of the packed bingo hall. It was a little past two in the afternoon and all five hundred seats were filled. The majority of the players used a traditional ink dauber to stamp the numbers on their paper cards. Others used a hand-held portable electronic bingo machine. Even something simple as bingo had become high-tech.

A thin, raspy voice echoed throughout the vast hall in response. "Bingo!"

Groans of disappointment rippled through crowd. Betty recognized the nicotine-drenched tone. She turned around and located the winner—Hannah.

"Thank God, no one else has called Bing . . ." Tillie began to say but was interrupted by the sound of another "Bingo" being yelled out, followed by two more simultaneous screams of the five letter word. Hannah glared at her fellow winners, interlopers of her four hundred dollar jackpot.

If looks could kill, Betty thought, but then dismissed the observation. At the moment, the last thing she wanted to think about was death. All she wanted was to play a few mind-numbing games. If humanly possible, she wanted to block out any thoughts of Farsi, knives, bloody business cards, and the irritating fact that she hadn't been to sleep in over thirty-six hours.

She needed to zone out, if only for a little while. Otherwise, she wouldn't be able to function rationally. As sleep deprived as she was, she could only keep awake by tapping into an adrenaline rush created by anxiety, caffeine, and sugar.

A floor attendant stood next to Hannah to verify the numbers. The attendant read out loud the numbers Hannah had marked off on her bingo card: "B-14, I-23, N-41, G-46, Oh…69."

"That's a good bingo," the announcer called. A wave of disappointment and curse words crashed across the rows of people. The attendant headed toward the other winners to verify their numbers as well.

Tillie shook Betty's shoulder and said, "Look at Hannah go!"

Hannah was up from her 'lucky seat' and doing 'the happy dance' while simultaneously waving four purple-haired miniature troll dolls in the air. The crowd broke into applause but Hannah didn't smile in return. Smiling was something she rarely did, even when she won. By dancing, she was merely following her rules of superstition.

The happy dance and troll dolls were Hannah's personal edge on winning. She did the jig no matter how small the bingo.

"There's at least a dozen more dolls on the table in front of her," Betty noted.

"I can't believe she thinks trolls are lucky," Tillie said as she lined up seven tiny plastic figurines in front of her. "Doesn't she know only leprechauns bring good luck?"

"Or four-leaf clovers," Betty added, pointing at the large plastic green clovers upon which Tillie's leprechauns sat.

Throughout the vast hall, talismans were placed on tables in front of players. The amulets ranged from trolls, stuffed animals and gemstones, to pictures of grandkids or dream houses. The numerous waitresses, who passed out free beverages, were often the beneficiaries of such widely held beliefs. Seasoned gamblers knew the nicer they were to a casino employee, the nicer the gambling gods would be to them.

"The next game will be a postage stamp," the caller announced as the winning card pattern flashed on the giant LED screen behind him. The winning card would need a block of four numbers in one of the card's four corners called.

Betty looked to the stage as the balls began to roll inside the large wired cage, pushing against each other as if they were struggling to be the one chosen. Not unlike the gamblers themselves, thought Betty. Finally, a numbered white ball shot down the channel and into the caller's hand. The crowd immediately fell silent, waiting reverently to hear the first number called.

"G-53," the caller bellowed. The number flashed on the oversized LED screen behind him.

"Louder," yelled a man from the back of the room.

"Louder," griped a few other players from the front table as well. For many of the seniors in the room, the call could never be loud enough.

"G-53," the caller repeated one more time. I-23 was the next ball to roll down the chute.

"Woo hoo! I-23 is my lucky number," the woman seated behind Betty yelled with glee.

Betty looked at the three bingo cards laid out in front of her. The last number called was not lucky for her. In fact, none of the numbers called so far had been. But, try as she might, not even the sounds of the caller could block out the fact that someone was working hard to frame her or Tillie for murder.

She looked at her wristwatch. She'd planned on playing only a few games. Besides a bit of stress-relief, she'd shown up to help corral her riders, pass out their pre-paid game vouchers and try to make her clients feel as if they were still one big, happy family. Betty leaned toward Tillie. "I'm out of here. Can you take care of anything that might pop up?"

"Sure enough" Tillie assured her. "And I have smelling salts in my purse, in case Hannah hits the big one."

Betty liked Tillie's idea. Hannah winning the big one, a $50,000 cover-all, would be sweet. She'd at least stop pestering them for a little while. Or until she came-to.

Betty scurried out of the bingo hall, and into the corridor toward the gleaming brass and glass front doors of the casino. She'd possessed the foresight to bring her parka and knew that taking a walk outdoors would help to clear her thoughts. As soon as she stepped outside, the frigid arctic air pierced her lungs. She zipped up her jacket and started down the cleared pathway.

The resort was located in the center of the reservation. The tribe's maintenance crew continually cleared the parking lots, sidewalks and roads. A guest could easily walk for miles in the winter wonderland and never leave tribal property.

Betty stopped briefly to reach into her pocket. She pulled out her silver iPod. The tiny device contained over 100 hundred albums as well as 17 audio books—all of them mysteries. She chose to listen to the soundtrack of *The Pirates of the Caribbean* with the volume turned low so she could still think her own thoughts and not be caught up in the music.

Betty enjoyed listening to a film score even more than watching the movie itself. She was self-observant enough to know that the music made her feel slightly heroic or even a bit terrified at moments, depending upon the composer's intention. Oftentimes, when she listened to the Pirate's score, she'd find herself thinking that all she really wanted out of life was to command a ship and head out to sea. Of course, if she clicked on the music of *Jurassic Park*, commanding a sea-faring vessel lost out to the appeal of taking on a T-rex or two. And battling a charging, ticked-off dinosaur was something she was used to since Hannah became a regular on her tours.

Passing the corner of the hotel, Betty checked out the employee parking lot located at the side of the building. It was the same lot where dozens of tour busses were parked. In the far corner, the Take A Chance bus sat alone, roped off by yet more yellow crime scene tape.

Betty shoved her gloved hands further into her pockets and hastened her pace. There was much to think about, and it all originated with Farsi. She still hadn't figured out how someone was able to get inside the locked restroom to kill Farsi. There was always the chance that the killer knew the combination to the spare key box. But then how could that same killer force a knife deep into Farsi's back without anyone hearing? And how did that someone lock the door again from the inside once Farsi was stabbed?

Considering his enormous size, it surprised her that Farsi could fit into the tiny cubicle at all, much less a second individual. The miniscule restrooms were a constant complaint from plus-sized passengers.

The small skylight did offer the possibility of outside access.

Well, if the murderer was a ten-year old. The opening was extremely narrow and positioned directly above the toilet. The skylight acted as both ventilation and as an emergency window, if necessary. But it too had been locked tight.

The roar of an engine revving and the subsequent blaring of a car horn brought Betty out of her ruminations. She looked up just as Tours by Tina passed. The pesky tour owner waved from inside the bus. Betty waved back, even though she knew Tina wasn't pleased to see her.

Tina looked at Take a Chance Tours as competition, but so did all the other tour operators. When the Midwest casinos first opened, tour companies specializing in the casino industry multiplied like rabbits on Viagra. Then, when the recession took hold, only the strong survived. Tours by Tina was one of them. Consequently, Tina hated any newcomers like Take A Chance Tours.

A few flakes of snow brushed against Betty's cheeks. The weatherman predicted more snow to fall in the afternoon and evening. She and Tillie would have to keep an eye on the forecast. They were scheduled to leave Moose Bay in twenty-four hours.

She decided to circle around to the back of the resort. As she walked, she listened to her music and considered what she knew about the murder.

First of all, even Farsi's name was fraudulent. Whoever killed him had to be very clever. Farsi was carrying two million dollars—a huge amount of money. She assumed the sheriff was checking to see if the bills were counterfeit. Because of the high tech equipment available to even the most common of counterfeiters, it took an expert nowadays to determine the validity of genuine currency.

The one thing she didn't understand was why the money hadn't been taken when Farsi was dead. If someone were clever enough to slay him in a locked bathroom, wouldn't they be able to manipulate a simple lock on an under-carriage luggage compartment?

And why would they keep trying to make a connection to Take A Chance? Her plasma-decorated business card found in a bathroom was hardly an accident. Perhaps it was merely a ploy, an attempt to point the sheriff in the wrong direction. Or perhaps someone had a grudge against her, Lori, or Tillie.

Unless a Chicago Public Library patron was still ticked off about paying a late fee, her office worker Gloria was hardly a target for revenge.

As Betty reached the end of the employee parking lot, with its hundred cars and dozens of tour busses, she saw the private motor coach belonging to Boris the Baffler. It would have been hard not to notice it. The purple vehicle was accented with gold lettering and silver stars and featured an image of a reclining Boris, hand on cheek while his body was positioned in seductive repose.

Like many entertainers, Boris probably spent half of his life on the road. The decked-out transport was his home on wheels. Betty knew a lot of stars refused hotel accommodations, preferring instead to stay in elaborate motorhomes.

So, it wasn't too much of a surprise when the door to Boris' bus opened, and the performer himself stepped out. But what she saw next caused her knees to buckle.

"*Ogawa*?" she muttered as the elderly gentleman followed Boris down the stairs. Ogawa's cane was held in mid-air and it looked like he was shaking it at Boris. He was also yelling but Betty couldn't discern what he was saying.

"Mr. Ogawa?" she yelled over the roar of a passing engine. For the briefest of moments, she could swear the old man turned her way and glared at her in rage. But, in that same split-second the universe decided to smack her upside the head, causing her world to turn dark as her legs flew willy-nilly into the air. Almost instantly, her body crashed backwards onto the asphalt as an avalanche of snow buried her alive. It not only stopped her calling out for help. It stopped her from breathing.

Chapter 15

Speaking with a heavy Minnesota accent, a lilting voice bellowed, "Lady, are you okay?"

Betty's eyelids struggled to open underneath the weight of the snow while her eyelashes turned into icicles. As she opened her mouth to breathe, she gagged on an incoming deluge of flakes. She forced herself to sit upright as she brushed mounds of snow, slush, and ice from her torso and face.

"Wh-What happened?"

"You fell backwards into a big pile of plowed snow, you did," said the Viking-like woman standing directly above her.

A twinge of pain shot through Betty's back. "How did that happen? One minute I was fine and the next minute everything went dark and . . ."

The woman interrupted her with a comforting tone, "Now, now, there's no reason to be concerned. All you did was slip on black ice, you betcha. Done that a hundred times myself, growing up here in Minnesota like I did."

"I fell?" Betty asked, surprised. She glanced sideways at the road. It was true, a thin layer of ice coated the asphalt. But she had been walking carefully, her walking shoes gripping the road.

"Yeah, sure. Good thing, I was out for my daily one-mile run. I'm on a diet, you know. Gotta lose this weight or lose my job. I'm a gym teacher. Principal says I'm not a good example for the kids. Hooey is what I say. Here, let me help you up." The woman grabbed both of Betty's hands and yanked her to an upright, standing position.

Betty yelped in pain, her left ankle stinging. She smiled graciously at the woman whose Nordic features glistened with sweat while her blonde pigtails bounced about in the breeze. Her bulbous, potato shaped nose was as red as Rudolph's.

"You got a headache or anything?" the woman asked.

Betty shook her head. "I think I'm okay. The snow must have cushioned my fall."

The woman answered, "Yah, you betcha it did. You looked like a snow angel for a moment there, your arms all flapping about." Her eyes were warm and inviting.

Betty glanced over toward the parking lot. Boris and Mr. Ogawa were nowhere to be seen. If they had witnessed her fall, neither had come to her rescue. She didn't know about Boris, but that seemed odd behavior for the kindly Ogawa. Immediately, she became concerned for his well-being.

"Let me walk you back to the hotel. You shouldn't be out here alone," the woman insisted, placing a strong arm around Betty's shoulder.

Betty declined the woman's assistance. She felt she needed to check on Ogawa, to see if everything was all right with him. She had no choice but to head to Boris' trailer.

"I'm fine, really. And there's something I need to do," Betty said, staring at the entertainer's bus.

The woman must have noticed Betty's interest, and gestured toward the vehicle. She said, "I can go with you to that there bus, if you want. I've nothing else to do but lose another twenty on those blasted machines."

Betty answered, "No, that's okay. But, thank you. Thank you very much."

"Okay, then. Promise me, you'll be careful." The woman took off jogging toward the hotel.

"I will," Betty yelled out as the woman pulled a cell phone from her rear pocket. I hope I didn't make her late for something, thought Betty. Good deeds like hers should be rewarded by the universe, not punished.

Betty started walking toward the bus, carefully doing what she now thought of as The Minnesota Shuffle—sliding a bit on icy patches. Still, it took her only a few minutes to reach her destination.

The first thing she noticed was the motorhome's vanity

plate—*Baffler 777*. The bus was licensed in Nevada. Betty had been inside dozens of conversion buses. The deluxe models were always featured at conventions for the travel industry. Lori and she would always make the same corny joke—when they won the lottery they'd buy one to save money on hotels.

The unspoken punch line was that a conversion bus's starting price was usually half a million. It would take a lot of nights on the road to justify spending that kind of money. The end price on the conversion coaches was limitless, depending upon the needs of the entertainer. She'd be surprised if Boris hadn't paid a million bucks for his rig.

But that was a lot of money for any entertainer to spend for comfort, especially one who wasn't an internationally known celebrity. Plus, she'd heard many complaints about the dwindling salaries in the entertainment world. Many of the once-famous and/or now-nearly-dead aging rock stars were working for next to nothing to see their names in lights one more time—or simply to pay the bills. Even Ringo Starr played a casino in Wisconsin.

As soon as Betty reached the bus, she climbed up the metal steps and peered through the sliver of glass in the doorway. She could only make out the driver's seat as she reached over and pushed the doorbell.

No one answered. She pounded on the door. She waited a few seconds and then jiggled the door handle. To her surprise, it wasn't locked. The door swung open and she gingerly stepped inside, completely forgetting her promise to the Nordic Giantess that she'd be careful. She realized there was certainly nothing careful about entering someone's home uninvited.

"Hello?" she said in a hushed tone. Then called, "Anyone home? Hello? Mr. Baffler?"

There was no response. She peered down the center aisle. On the left side of the aisle, a plush sofa filled the space. Across from it sat two red swivel chairs. A small foldable table rested between the two chairs. Betty realized it could probably fold up and out, and would easily seat four. The furniture on The Jetsons wasn't as clever as the furniture designed for luxury motor coaches.

She walked down the dark aisle. "Hello?"

Though it was daylight the interior had the feel of dusk. Tapestry curtains covered the windows and blocked out most of the sun. She could barely make out the images in the framed photos of Boris on the walls. In every photo, the mentalist struck an elaborate pose that suggested glamour, mystery, and possible gender hopping. Vintage advertising posters from the turn of the century completed the artwork hanging in the room. Colorful images of contortionists who rivaled the flexibility of pretzels or ominous looking magicians in action seemed to leap off the walls.

Betty continued slowly down the center of the coach, past the kitchen area, to the back wall, where a closed door was situated in the center. Behind it, Betty assumed, was the bedroom.

She lifted her hand to knock on the door and held her breath in anticipation. She discovered she didn't have to worry about what lie ahead: it was the loud and angry voice coming from behind her that she needed to be concerned about.

"What do you think you're doing?" the man's voice sounded off the paneled walls.

The voice was so powerful that it shook the motorhome in its wake. She spun around to see Boris standing directly behind her. Sputtering, she said, "Please, don't be alarmed. I realize I shouldn't be in here, but..."

"Then why *are* you in here?" he demanded, his muscular arms positioned at his sides, his large hands balled into fists. He looked like a gladiator posed for attack.

"I was worried about Mr. Ogawa." Betty slowed her words, hoping he would buy into her excuse for trespassing.

"Ogawa?" Boris questioned, and then relaxed his stance. "You mean the old man that was here a few minutes ago?"

Betty nodded, relieved. "He's one of my clients. I saw him coming down your steps. I called his name right before I fell on the ice and hit my head. I must have blacked out for a few seconds because when I awoke. . ."

"You're with the casino?" Boris asked, his tone softening.

"I'm a tour operator. Mr. Ogawa is our oldest rider. I'm worried about him slipping on the ice," she lied. The fact Ogawa might fall hadn't crossed her mind. What had crossed her mind was the fact Ogawa had been enraged when she saw him.

"I was afraid for him too, that's why I insisted on escorting him back to the hotel, list or no list," Boris told her.

Betty instantly regretted having such a vivid imagination. She'd turned a perfectly innocent scenario into something suspect. She realized it when Boris mentioned a list. Boris must be telling the truth.

She asked, "You mean Mr. Ogawa's list of eighty-eight things to do before he dies?"

Boris smiled. "Ogawa asked me to help him with number sixty-six, learning to pull a rabbit out of a hat."

"And did you?"

Boris shrugged. "I told him I was a mentalist, not a magician. Besides, I'm fresh out of rabbits."

Betty laughed.

"Is that why Mr. Ogawa was so agitated?" she asked. "I could hear him yelling as he walked down the steps. That surprised me. He's always so sweet and . . ."

Boris interrupted, "The old guy's in his eighties, but he's still a guy. He was upset because I thought he needed help walking. Even the elderly can be macho, Miss . . ."

She held out her hand. "Betty Chance. I'm sorry I invaded your privacy. But, when there wasn't an answer at the door, I . . ."

"Don't apologize" he said as he slowly released her hand. "I would have done the same thing." He then reached over and touched a button next to her. The wall partially opened. The integrated refrigerator door that flowed seamlessly into the woodwork had been hidden from site. He removed a Champagne bottle and grabbed two crystal flute glasses from an overhead cabinet.

"Mr. Baffler, I..."

"Please, call me Boris."

"Mr. Baff...I'm sorry...I mean, Boris. I can see you're expecting company. I'll just be on my way." She turned to leave.

"You're right, I am expecting company," Boris said.

She took a step toward the door of the motorhome.

"But Betty," he continued "It's you."

Betty stopped. She turned back to see Boris smiling at full-wattage, cradling a bottle of *Dom Perignon* in his hands as if it were a newborn.

"Boris, I don't have time to . . ."

He interrupted her. "We've met before, haven't we?" He set the glasses on the counter. He uncorked the bottle and began to fill each flute.

Betty nodded. "Yes, in the casino when you made your rather grand entrance."

He looked embarrassed. "I know it's hokey, but it attracts people to the show."

Then he did something that surprised Betty. He began to move his eyes slowly up and down her body, as if memorizing every inch. Betty shivered and realized it wasn't from fear or the Minnesota temperature. Boris' powers were more than that of a master mentalist. They were sexually compelling as well.

He placed a glass of the chilled imported bubbly in her hand.

"I don't have much time," she said.

"Ah, but there's always time for champagne," he said and lightly clinked her glass. A single, perfect note rose from the crystal glasses and hung in the air.

Betty didn't know what shocked her more—the fact that the bedecked, bejeweled and over-the-top Boris was attempting to seduce her, or that she was totally enjoying it.

Chapter 16

Rivers of black mascara created dark crevices in Lori's once creamy foundation. Grey eye shadow caked around the edges of her lids gave her a diseased look. For a change Lori didn't appear beautiful. In fact, she looked downright ugly. Her reflection in the bathroom mirror suggested she'd been on a bender for a solid month. And she felt worse than she looked.

She fell back against the wall and slid down onto the marble floor. Her knees folded upwards. She grabbed onto them and began to rock back and forth. Since her first panic attack in her teens, she'd always found secluded places to hide. Closets, bathrooms, the back seat of a car, these were among her preferred places to isolate until she could breathe again. Small, enclosed spaces helped make her feel protected.

A familiar voice drifted through the cracks and crevices. Lori could hear Tillie calling out her name while knocking on the hotel room's door.

"Lori?" Tillie called. "Lori, are you in there?"

Lori didn't answer. She couldn't. Not yet. She didn't want to take the chance that Tillie would figure out what was going on with her at the moment. There was no way she'd let Tillie know she was in the midst of a full-blown panic attack. If Tillie knew she'd run to Betty for help.

That was something Lori couldn't let happen. Even Betty didn't know Lori suffered from panic attacks.

If Betty had an inkling, she'd ask questions. Lori wasn't ready to explain her anxiety. Or that she was not only broke but near bankruptcy. Not until she figured out a way to repay Take A Chance Tours. Besides, the attacks lasted only a few minutes. She could wait them out. She always had.

"Lori?" Tillie called out once again, as she knocked on the corridor door. When silence followed, Lori breathed a sigh of relief. Tillie must have given up.

"Thank God," Lori uttered, as if each breath could easily be her last.

Her first panic attack occurred at eleven years of age, a few hours after her mother announced her father had disappeared without a trace. She felt her chest cave inward, shattering her heart into a million pieces as if made from cheap crystal. She knew she would never see him again.

Although young, she was mature enough to keep it a secret. Her mother was dealing with enough already. Her episodes continued sporadically and then suddenly stopped on the first anniversary of her father's disappearance. It wasn't until her mother was diagnosed with cancer four years later that they returned. The same pattern repeated itself with the attacks mysteriously ceasing exactly one year after her mother's death. They didn't start again until she began "borrowing money" from Take A Chance Tours.

The petty cash box in the office normally held hundreds of dollars. The money was on hand to pay for an afternoon pizza, or to provide change to clients who paid for their trip in cash.

Whenever Lori borrowed any money she promised herself she would replace it the very next morning. She was filled with good intentions, often saintly in nature. She even vowed to return more money than she took.

Lori didn't bother to tell her aunt or Gloria about the overnight loans because they were, after all, no big deal. The women wouldn't notice the money was missing. Or if they did, Lori could easily come up with an excuse. She'd say she wanted to buy office supplies on the way home, or take a client to dinner.

It didn't matter, really. She was confident she'd replace the borrowed cash with her winnings from gambling. Or, at least with a credit card advance. When her credit cards maxed out, her panic attacks returned.

Now, sitting inside a hotel bathroom in the late afternoon, it felt like her worst fear was coming true. Her chest once again felt like it was collapsing under pressure. Sweat began to seep through her clothing. Her breaths arrived in quick fire succession.

But once again, the miracle occurred. The thousand pound weight slowly lifted from her chest and her tremors subsided.

She pulled herself up off the cold, tiled floor. She leaned against the vanity and stared into the mirror. Her color was coming back. Her breathing stabilized. She was fine.

She forced herself out of the bathroom and fell onto the bed. She remained prone, wondering if she could find a fix to her financial problems.

Gambling. Her real problem wasn't that she had lost money. The real problem was that she hadn't won any. Winning at poker was the only way she knew of to pay off her debts. Once she'd won enough she'd never look at a card again.

"*Damn Gillette*," she said out loud as she stood up. She probably wouldn't have gambled at the casino if it weren't for him. She knew that this time, *this* particular reckless binge wasn't her fault. She'd been an innocent by-stander.

She returned to the bathroom and picked up a jar of face cream. She unscrewed the wide cap and gently applied the cream to her face. As her fingers moved across her cheeks, she reflected upon the last hour.

Playing cards with Gillette had flipped on that switch inside of her that was so hard to control. An hour after she left him at the poker table, she'd found herself seated in the High Limits Slots area.

Mistakenly, she'd sat in front of a twenty-five dollar slot instead of a five-dollar machine. Although she realized what she had done she was too transfixed by the lure of winning to change machines. She slipped in a fifty-dollar bill and waited as her brain went into hyper drive.

What harm could there be in losing another fifty bucks? I've spent more than that on face lotion. And remember what they say, the bigger the bet, the bigger the win.

She hit the Play Max credit button and the wheel spun around until one red seven, and one white seven appeared, followed by a blank space. Her Ulysses S. Grant was history. She threw in another fifty in case the gods were on her side and merely testing her. The wheel spun again and three single bars appeared. In a matter of seconds her second fifty-dollar investment had yielded five hundred bucks in return.

Thirty minutes later, after a roller coaster ride of spectacular ups and devastating downs, Lori lost another $1500, the same amount she'd received from cashing a check forty minutes earlier. Unless she could come up with a way to cover it, her check would bounce.

Lori could still feel the pain as that last hopeless spin registered a loss. She removed the final bit of make-up from her face and stood there, trying to let it sink into her denying skull that she didn't have a dime to her name. If she were starving to death, Lori couldn't afford a Happy Meal at McDonalds.

The phone's ring startled her and she rushed into the other room and picked up the receiver.

"Hi there." Lori answered, trying to sound cheery and upbeat. If she pulled this off she should be awarded an Oscar for Best Performance.

"I miss you," a low, deep tone echoed. It was Gillette.

Instantly, she felt rage at the man who had led her astray earlier. She said, "Tony, I can't see you. I..."

He interrupted, "What about dinner? You have to eat."

She hesitated. Gillette would be willing to stake her again. She could win it all back. Every dollar. When she did, she'd never gamble again. Her anger started to dissipate. Tony was actually an ally.

Somehow, for a brief moment, sanity returned to Lori and she knew better than to flirt with temptation.

"I have plans with Aunt Betty," she told him, grateful it was true. Gillette was too dangerous to be around. Not only was he sweep-any-woman-off-her-feet-while-getting-her-to-drop-her-panties handsome, his lifestyle centered on the one thing in her life she desperately needed to control.

He continued his plea. "What about dessert?"

Lori felt her resolve weaken. She said, "I can't. Our tour has been given tickets to see Boris the Baffler's show. I need to be there."

"Midnight?" he suggested.

He'd never give up. Gillette was the top dog in any arena he chose to romp in.

"I . . ." she hesitated.

He counterattacked. "Midnight in the poker room, then. I'll stake you five grand."

She could actually feel her heart come to a complete stop before it started again. She managed to say, "You're kidding."

"I never kid about gambling."

It would be wrong to accept, she thought. Very wrong. She didn't even know the man. "Alright," she answered, putting a seal on whatever deal he was proposing.

Tony hung up abruptly. There was no good bye, no fond farewell my princess. Gillette was already acting as if he were in control.

I'll call him back. I'll cancel, she thought a millisecond before a floodgate of possibilities opened in her mind and rational thinking ended.

It could be fun. I need fun. Maybe I'll even win a little. Maybe I'll win a lot. Besides, he wants to do it. It's not like I asked him. And if I win, that could solve a lot of problems. It was his idea. It's not like it's my money, or Take A Chance Tour's money or . . .

The phone rang again.

It's probably Gillette calling back, she decided. She'd tell him no, tell him she'd changed her mind. She picked up the receiver.

"Listen Tony, I really don't think I . . ."

"Lori, is that you?" the voice asked, wavering.

"Gloria?" Lori said, surprised to hear her employee's voice on the other end.

"Uh-huh," Gloria answered in a small, trembling voice.

Lori's throat went dry. "What is it?"

Gloria said, "I can't get ahold of your aunt. She's not answering her phone."

The woman was speaking in a very slow and precise manner. That fact alone told Lori something was very wrong.

Lori asked, "What happened?"

"Someone broke into the office. We've been robbed."

Chapter 17

Two glasses of champagne and one hour of mutual flirtation later, Betty hustled through the hotel lobby. She was still bewildered and bemused from her time spent with Boris. Her plan now was to grab a quick nap. Even a half hour would keep her going until bedtime. She only hoped that if she did sleep, she didn't dream of The Baffler.

Betty wasn't exactly sure why she found the flamboyant mentalist so damned charming and, she had to admit it to herself, hot. She'd always laughed at her mom's friends and their tales of being turned on by Liberace. Betty now realized that she should have been more understanding. The women were barely out of their teens in the1950s when the word gay only meant happy. And decades later she too was attracted to a man of questionable sexuality. Boris did act straight, but it was the word "act" that bothered her.

Maybe her being celibate returned her to a 1950's naiveté? Or maybe she'd become a refurbished virgin? After all, they refurbished computers, so why not . . .

A thought struck her. Did the Baffler use mind control on her? Could that be why she suddenly found herself desiring something other than an afternoon of crème-filled Ho Hos?

How could she be attracted to Boris to begin with? For one thing, he one thing, he was at least twenty years younger. For another, he wore guyliner. Men in makeup did not usually tickle her sexual fancy. She grew up on South Side Chicago where a man was considered a sissy if he ate with a fork. If he needed to stir his cup of black—and only black—coffee he was expected to do it with a tire iron. She was just about to press the elevator button when she heard Tillie's voice.

"Hold the elevator!" Tillie stopped the door from closing with her outstretched hand and stepped inside. Through a wad of chewing gum she asked, "Where have you been? I've been looking everywhere for you."

Betty decided against mentioning she'd been drinking with Boris. Somehow, it didn't seem right for her to take time off to indulge in bad behavior. "What's up?" Betty asked, as the elevator rose. If Tillie wanted to chat, they could do it on the way to her room. After that, Tillie would have to leave. Only a shower and a quick nap were on her agenda.

Tillie waved three crisp hundred-dollar bills in the air before folding them into fourths. She pulled aside the neckline of her blouse and slipped the money deep inside her bra.

"I won three hundred bucks at bingo! I told you that Irish leprechauns kick Norwegian troll butts," Tillie said proudly.

"Good for you!" Betty cheered. "By the way, has the sheriff called you with any new information?"

"Nope. And in case you're wondering, I couldn't find Lori either. The two of you disappeared off the face of the earth. I called both of your cells a dozen times."

The elevator stopped and they stepped into the corridor. Betty said, "I didn't hear my phone ring even once."

She unzipped her bag and poked around the bottom. Then she reached into her pockets. Her phone was missing.

Tillie suggested, "Check your bra. That's where I've lost mine, though once I forgot I had slipped it inside my underwear."

Betty didn't ask Tillie how she could forget that, or how she could sit down with a phone in her panties. Betty didn't bother to check inside her brassiere. Unlike Tillie's ample storage space, her bosom couldn't hide a quarter, much less the small cans of hairspray she'd seen Tillie pull from her cleavage. To Betty, being a plus size woman with miniscule breasts was a lesson in spiritual enlightenment. It reminded her daily that life could be so unfair.

Betty said, "Dammit, losing that phone is a disaster."

"Maybe it's in your room?" Tillie asked, gesturing down the hallway.

"Maybe," Betty answered. It might be frozen inside the huge snow bank she'd fallen into earlier, thought Betty. Or perhaps she'd left it in Boris' bus.

"You don't have any idea where you left it?" Tillie asked.

"A few places," she admitted. She knew she'd be too embarrassed to return to Boris' place. He would think she was looking for more than a phone to hold in her hands.

"Let's look in your room, first. I'll help you search," Tillie offered.

As soon as they opened Betty's door, she had an idea. "Call my cell."

Tillie flipped opened her cell phone and hit speed dial. The phone started ringing on Tillie's end, but neither heard a ring coming from anywhere in the hotel room.

"I'm not hearing . . ." Tillie paused, and then sang the words, "*First I was afraid, I was petrified…*" Betty's ring tone was the Gloria Gaynor hit.

Betty said, "Start looking around. It could be here with the ringer turned off. I'll check the bathroom. Would you mind looking under the bed?"

"No problem." Tillie headed toward the bed. Betty took an immediate right into the bathroom. Just for the heck of it, she pulled back the shower curtain and checked out the tub. She looked under the counter as well. She looked inside of the waste paper basket and the pockets of her terry cloth robe that hung on the back of the door.

"Nothing under the bed!" Tillie yelled from the other room. "Want me to check the dresser drawers?"

"Sure, I have nothing to hide," Betty said stepping back into the bedroom. She watched as her friend began to rummage through the top drawer.

Tillie turned around and gave her a quizzical look. "Are you sure about that?" Tillie held up a pair of sheer black thongs, embroidered with tiny red hearts.

Betty's cheeks flushed pink. "There was a sale at the big woman's store."

"Big *sexy* woman's store you mean." Tillie tossed it back into the dresser. "Like they say, it's always the ones you least suspect." She closed the drawer.

Betty searched the nightstand, then pulled it away from the wall. Except for electrical cords plugged into sockets, there was nothing behind it.

"I knew it!" Tillie announced proudly, holding the door to the mini-bar door wide open.

"My cell phone is inside the fridge?" Betty asked, shocked. She'd discovered missing items in a lot of places, but that seemed odd even for her.

"No, there's no phone but there's no chocolate either. As soon as I saw the truffles in my room, I knew you'd break down and pay the six bucks for the ones in yours!"

"My addiction's that obvious?" Betty asked.

"Are you kidding, me? You'd stuff your Thanksgiving turkey with Godiva if you could," Tillie teased.

"Actually, I have," Betty admitted. "It was called *Mole Poblano.* I had it one Thanksgiving in a casino outside of Tucson. It's this great Mexican turkey dish made with melted chocolate and hot chilies."

"Really? Turkey and chocolate together? I've never heard of that. But then, the fanciest Mexican restaurant I go to is Taco Bell," said Tillie.

The two continued to search. The bed was already made. Betty could tell that nothing was lying beneath the spread. She checked underneath the four king-sized pillows. Then she did a quick peek into the armoire and announced anxiously, "I guess it's not here."

"Maybe you should call the cell phone company and cancel your account?" Tillie suggested, sitting down on the bed.

"You're right. Can you look up the number on the Internet while I shower?" Betty asked, heading toward the bathroom. Her time with Tillie had eaten up any chance for a nap, but at least she could be clean for her clients, if not fully awake.

"Look it up, how?" Tillie asked, looking around the room.

"Use my laptop to..." Betty stopped in her tracks. She swirled around and saw that her slim black laptop was no longer sitting on the desk. Her heart sank. Her computer was missing as well.

If someone had access to her computer then they had access to all of her financial records, including the Take A Chance files she'd downloaded before the trip began. Her laptop was not password protected. She'd never gotten around to entering a password although it would have taken only a few seconds to do so. Now, it was too late.

Betty picked up the room phone to dial the front desk when she heard Lori's frantic voice calling out her name. Betty dropped the receiver and rushed to open the door.

Lori barged in, talking full speed. "Aunt Betty! I have some very bad news!"

Tillie gasped, a look of fresh horror on her face. "Don't tell me they've found another body?"

"No. There's been a robbery," Lori said, walking to the edge of the bed, her arms folded across her stomach as if she were in pain. She sat down next to Tillie. She hadn't taken time to put on make-up or even brush her hair. Betty had never seen Lori look as frazzled or act as flustered.

"Are you talking about my laptop being stolen?" Betty asked, confused that Lori knew about the theft before she did.

It took a moment for Lori to answer. "No, I'm talking about our office being robbed."

Dazed by Lori's announcement, Betty plopped down onto the edge of the bed. She grabbed her niece's hand and said, "Tell me about it."

"Gloria called. Someone robbed the office this afternoon."

Betty's immediate concern was for her employee's safety. "Was Gloria hurt?" she asked.

Lori shook her head. "She was downstairs at the coffee shop when it happened."

"What was taken? The cashbox?" Betty asked, wondering briefly if Gloria remembered to lock the office door. She'd forgotten to do so in the past.

Lori answered, "That was untouched. Only two things were taken. One was our desktop computer."

"And the other thing?" Betty asked.

Lori paused before admitting, "A trip file."

"Which trip?" Betty asked, even though she already knew what Lori's answer would be.

"The one we're on."

Chapter 18

Let me get this straight." Severson leaned back in the conference room chair, his hands linked behind his head. "Your cell phone is missing. Your laptop was stolen from your hotel room. And around the same time your Chicago office was broken into and your office computer taken which just happened to contain the file pertaining to the trip you're on." He paused. "Is that about right?"

Betty fidgeted as she sat across from the sheriff. She said, "I don't know if it was *exactly* the same time, but darn close. Our assistant was out of the office on her coffee break when it happened."

"Did she leave the office unlocked the same way Tillie left the bus unlocked?" Severson taunted.

Betty admitted, "I don't know. Sometimes, Gloria forgets things. But, it's never caused a problem until now."

Severson shook his head in disgust. "Does anyone from Chicago ever bother to lock a door?"

Betty didn't respond. The two were alone in the conference room the sheriff had deemed his temporary on-site office. His men were upstairs in her hotel room, going over it inch-by-inch, looking for any shred of evidence.

She had dispatched Tillie and Lori to check up on any passengers they could find. Taking care of her clients was something Betty was used to doing by herself. The guilt of neglecting them on this trip was nagging at her. She didn't have time to answer idiotic questions from a stupid man-child.

Severson jotted down a few notes and asked, "Did the stolen file contain information about the tour you're currently on?"

Betty reached for the carafe of coffee sitting on the tabletop. She refilled her cup as well as the sheriff's. If acting like a girly-girl secretary would get him to treat her with respect, she'd do it.

She answered, "Fortunately, the file's information is on the CD I burned for you earlier. All we have to do is figure out why my office and hotel room were broken into at the same time. Obviously, whoever took my laptop from my room is connected to someone back in Chicago."

Severson sat with a smug look on his face. "We?"

Betty knew she'd taken a leap of faith to include the term *we* in regards to the investigation. She said, "I know I can help you. We can go over the information together. If there's anything that looks suspicious or out of place, I can . . ."

"Solve the mystery? Like some sort of Angela Lansbury?" he interrupted right before a half-grin emerged.

Betty couldn't tell if he was being sarcastic or not. He appeared ready to accept her offer of help.

He removed his arms from behind his head and pointed his finger accusingly at her whenever he used the word *you*. "I know *you* like working a case and that *you* think of yourself as an amateur detective."

"Why do you think that?" Betty asked.

"Your son called me this morning."

"Codey called you?"

"He told me you and your husband would . . ."

"Ex-husband," she corrected.

Severson continued, "...work his unsolved cases together when you were married. I guess even the Chicago Police department considers you something of a . . ." He paused.

She grimaced at what word could have been said about her constant involvement. "Buttinsky?" she asked.

"Expert at crime analysis," Severson answered. For the first time, his remark sounded like a compliment rather than an accusation.

She relaxed and leaned back in the comfortable swivel chair. "My son would say that, but I'm not sure that my ex would completely agree. I couldn't figure out he'd been sleeping around since day one of our marriage. I think that proves I'm not the great amateur detective I thought I was."

Severson smiled gently. "Maybe you didn't figure anything out because you didn't think there was anything to figure out."

"You're right, I didn't" she said. One of Betty's biggest flaws was in trusting the people she loved unconditionally.

"Well," Severson said thoughtfully, "a spouse shouldn't have to."

Betty looked at the Sheriff who seemed to grow a little older before her eyes.

The sheriff turned his attention back to the case. "There must be a connection to Take a Chance."

Betty realized that, without saying so, Severson had just accepted her offer of help. Or at the very least, admitted she was no longer an adversary.

Severson reached into his attaché case and pulled out a stack of papers. They were the printed version of the documents Betty had given to him on the CD. He started sifting through the items. "There has to be some sort of incriminating evidence in this file, or it wouldn't have been stolen."

"Or there's a third possibility." Betty suggested, pausing to ensure he wanted her to continue.

"What's that?" he asked.

"The murderer is trying to throw us off track. He, or she, knows we will spend a lot of time investigating the data in this file."

"Time that could be spent investigating other leads" he said, finishing her thought. The sheriff nodded his head in understanding. "Could be. By the way, is anyone connected with Take A Chance involved in any sort of criminal activity or have a criminal background?"

Betty wondered if he was still testing her. "You mean a criminal background other than Tillie's? I assume you already know everything about her felony conviction."

"I mean anything of late. I'm looking for an activity that wouldn't be on the books."

Betty answered, "Not that I know of. To be honest, even though we've become friends, Tillie and I don't socialize outside of work. But, I'm sure she'd never do anything that would land her back in prison."

"How long has Tillie been an employee?"

"Technically, Tillie doesn't work for us. She works for the bus company we contract with. If I ask her, however, Tillie will do favors for me while on tour—like track down a passenger. I don't pay her a salary but I tip her very well. The only employees at Take A Chance are Lori, Gloria and myself."

"What about Lori? Any dark secrets lurking in her background?"

For a change, Severson didn't blush when he mentioned Lori's name.

Betty grinned. "Her one continual act of lawlessness is speeding. But, my niece usually charms her way out of any ticket."

Severson tapped his pen methodically on the tabletop. "What about the people the three of you associate with? Are any of them experiencing problems? Drugs? Gambling? Money issues?"

Betty shook her head. "Not only are the three of us boringly normal, but so are our friends."

"Even Gloria?"

"Well, she did tell me she would like to kill every single patron who failed to return their library books, but other than that she's pretty normal."

"Still, you don't spend every single moment with Tillie, Lori or Gloria," he reminded her. "There's no way you can know what a person is up to behind closed doors."

"That's true," Betty answered.

"Let's examine this file," he said, dividing the papers into three stacks.

One stack contained the filled-out information forms for the trip. The second contained Betty's cheat sheet on each client. The third stack provided the accounting information, including individual costs and forms of payment.

The sheriff said, "We need to analyze each bit of information on each of the passengers."

Betty noted the "We" and smiled to herself.

"Let's look at their method of payment," he continued. "Their likes or dislikes..."

Betty nodded. She knew they couldn't disregard any bit of information. A single flake of evidence could lead to an avalanche of proof.

"...where they live in proximity to each other, etcetera."

Betty stood up and walked to the large presentation board on the wall. Grabbing a black dry erase marker from the aluminum tray she turned to the sheriff. "Where do you want to start?"

"Let's begin with the ones who are related."

"Well, we have five married couples," Betty said, as she listed their names on the board. "Four of the couples have traveled with us before."

"Put an asterisk next to the new riders," Severson suggested.

Betty followed his direction. While continuing to write she said, "There's a mother and daughter who are repeat customers, as well as a new mother and son. We also have a grandfather and grandson. The grandfather told me it's the boy's eighteenth birthday today."

She drew asterisks next to their names and continued, "There are three sisters as well as a pair of sister-in-laws." Betty placed the marker back in the metal tray. "As far as I know, no one else is related."

"Tell me what you can about the new riders," the sheriff instructed.

Betty glanced at her watch. It was already past four-thirty. She was scheduled to meet a few of her clients for dinner at six before heading to the showroom by seven. She'd have loved to return to her room for the shower she still hadn't been able to take. There was no telling what her make-up or hair looked like. Still, finding the killer was more important than smearing on lip-gloss.

"Group the new riders into similar likes and dislikes," Severson suggested.

Betty connected the riders who preferred poker tournaments. Slot machine aficionados were on their own, as well as bingo players. In her time as a tour host, she'd found most gamblers habitually stayed with their game of choice throughout the entire trip.

She wrote a "CC" next to their name if they'd used a credit card for payment, a check mark if they paid with a check, or a dollar sign if they paid in cash.

"Did any of them mail in a cash payment?" Severson asked.

"No," Betty answered. "A cash client has to come into the office and prepay for the trip or they're not guaranteed a spot."

"How many people paid in cash?"

She tallied up the figures. "Seven."

"You sound surprised. Is that a lot?"

"It's more than normal. Usually, two or three pay in cash. Hannah is always one of them."

Severson asked, "Besides Farsi, how many of the new riders paid cash?"

"All of them," Betty answered.

She studied the five names: three men and two women. She racked her brain to discover a commonality among the group. She noticed a higher number of male riders than the norm. Females usually outnumbered the men two to one.

She focused again on newbies and the fact that one of new riders had been Farsi. Except for Mr. Ogawa, none of the men listed had been friendly toward her or Tillie. In fact they'd been distant and cold. She realized something else, something she hadn't noticed before although it had been right there all along blocking her view.

"Well, Sheriff Severson," she said, turning around to face him, a small smile emerging. "I just realized one more lie my husband told me."

"What do you mean?" he asked intently.

"Size does matter."

Chapter 19

"Is this machine taken?" Tillie asked cheerfully as she sat down in front of a Wheel of Fortune slot. She'd recognized the man next to her as one of her passengers. She announced, "I love this machine. Every time Pat Sajak's face pops up on the screen, I get excited. What a hunk!"

The man didn't acknowledge her comment. Tillie carried on anyway, "I identify with Vanna, her loving rhinestones and such. I don't mean to brag, but I know I could do her job. I'm real good at pointing things out that need to be pointed out."

The man just grunted.

Tillie feigned surprise. "You rode on my bus, didn't you? Maybe you don't recognize me? I'm Tillie, your driver."

"I know who you are," he said in a slightly agitated voice, his pale thick fingers continuing to work the machines.

Probably unfriendly due to a losing streak, figured Tillie. Gamblers were like that. Though he didn't seem keen on her attention, Tillie believed it was her duty to converse with him a bit longer. Later, after returning home, the sixty-some-year old would remember a sexy woman flirted with him. He'd immediately re-book.

Tillie continued to chat and spin the wheels. On her last attempt, she netted a nine-cent profit.

She pressed the cash out button and announced, "I always quit when I'm ahead." She plucked the ticket from the slot and scrambled out of the seat. "Don't forget, we have comp tickets for the seven o'clock show."

His response was a grunt followed by a belch. Tillie scooted away as fast as she could, afraid of which orifice would next offer a greeting. *Men!* She grumbled, as she searched for more passengers. She noticed Lori heading toward Hannah. Hannah was shoving one bill after another into the machine. At the end of the row was another passenger. He too was enormous. His wide body easily spread across two chairs. One of his trunk-like legs stretched down the aisle and the other was scrunched between the machine and chairs.

Tillie slid into the chair nearest him. "You rode with us from Chicago, didn't you?" she asked, her voice as bubbly as the cacophony of the surrounding machines. "I'm Tillie, your driver."

"Slevitch," he muttered, never letting his eyes leave the video poker machine. He continued pushing the button with a finger that could double as a corn dog.

The man was playing one quarter at a time. If he hit a royal flush, he'd only win two hundred bucks, instead of the $24,000 progressive if he'd bet five quarters at a time. Either he was broke or he wanted what Tillie wanted, to lose his money as slowly as possible.

She asked sweetly, "Have any luck, yet?"

He rasped, "There's no such thing as luck."

"Really? I thought all gamblers believed in that four-letter word."

Slevitch growled out, "I don't. There's only one thing that counts. Mathematics. It takes strategy to play the odds."

He picked up his ice-filled drink. Tillie could smell the gin on his breath when he spoke. She noticed an accent but couldn't place it. The man who had boarded the bus could be from anywhere in the world. Tillie herself was half-Polish, as well as Irish.

Tillie asked, "Mathematics? Like in two plus two kind of math?"

He crunched on a piece of ice. "It's more complicated than that."

She sighed. "Well, no wonder I'm not a good gambler. Unless I have a calculator, I can't add one plus one, much less two."

For the first time he laughed. As he did, he reached up and pressed the deal button. Five cards appeared on the screen, three of clubs, seven of spades, five of hearts, and a pair of queens. He pressed the hold button in front of the queens and discarded the rest.

She leaned over and whispered, "You're not one of those card counters I've heard about, are you?"

His smirk told Tillie that he was amazed by her lack of intelligence. He hit the deal button and three new cards appeared: seven of hearts, four of clubs and another queen. The royal triple netted him an eight-buck win.

"You can't count cards on a video slot," he told her, hitting the deal button once more. This time when he reached up, the sleeve on his suit jacket edged down a bit. Tillie glanced at his wristwatch to see the time. What she saw half-hidden beneath his watchband, made her recoil. Instinctively, she wanted to bolt.

Instead, she took three deep breaths. Her prison counselor had taught her to do mindful breathing when her emotions overtook her reasoning. In the joint, being afraid was a daily occurrence. If she didn't handle her emotions, she'd pay the price. And in the joint, that price could be death.

It's just a tattoo, she reminded herself blocking out the image of the ink beneath the timepiece, *nothing more. It could mean anything.* She had over a dozen tats herself and none of them meant anything more than one too many Pina Coladas.

To be honest, she wasn't one hundred percent sure what she saw on the hairy wrist. The inked image that peeked out a bit from underneath Slevitch's watchband was partially hidden by dark fuzz. She could have been mistaken.

Against her better judgment, she decided to find out for sure. She looked around to see if anyone was watching. Oddly enough, a big, brassy blonde woman, ten machines away, was giving her a dirty look. Tillie wondered briefly if the woman was Slevitch's wife. Then she remembered seeing him ride alone on the bus.

Tillie pushed her torso toward Slevitch, placed her hands inside her waistband and pulled her blouse down, revealing more of her cleavage. She could feel Slevitch's eyes leering. It would be hard for him not to notice. Tillie had positioned herself so that her breasts were almost resting on top of his hold button.

Without touching Tillie, Slevitch managed to maneuver his finger to the deal button. As he did, his sleeve slipped upward. Tillie stared at the 18k gold Cartier watch once again. Although the timepiece covered most of the inked image, she could clearly make out most of the tattoo beneath it. The smudged inked tat was exactly like those done in prison. They were created with urine, soot and a Bic pen. Every gang had their own symbol. Tillie recognized the one that marred Slevitch's wrist.

She mumbled, "I guess I'm done gambling for the day," and jumped up, staring down at his wrist as she did. Slevitch must have noticed her gaze because he immediately placed his other hand over his watch.

She continued babbling nervously. "Nice looking watch. I saw that same watch on the Home Shopping Network for only three payments of $29.95. I would've bought it for my boyfriend, if I could've decided which boyfriend to buy it for."

She waved a quick goodbye and fled to the end of the slot area and fell against a wall. Her stomach clinched in pain, and sweat began to form on her forehead. Slevitch's tattoo matched the skin art of the women in prison who prided themselves on being Tillie's enemies. Before Tillie was released, she'd heard the gang had put a price tag on her life.

She wanted to run and find Betty, to tell her about the man's tattoo. But she didn't know if she should. *What was she going to say? That she thought the Take A Chance paying passenger was an ex-con? And that he was sent there to kill her for some petty, jailhouse grudge?*

Her thinking was out of control. Slevitch had done nothing wrong to her. And if he were an ex-con, so what? The tattoo could have been just a coincidence. It's not like a gang held a trademark on symbols.

Tillie shook her head in self-disgust. If she'd learned anything in prison, it was that a stool pigeon was the lowest form of life. Besides, maybe Slevitch was only guilty of having bad taste in tats, like the angry ex-husbands who tattooed their ex-wives' faces on their butt cheeks.

Whatever his reason, Tillie decided she wasn't going to start spreading rumors. Not yet. She wasn't going to do anything until she figured out why the woman who gave her a dirty look when she spoke to Slevitch was now shooting her a look that could kill. And more importantly, why the woman looked so damn familiar.

Lori knew there'd be hell to pay if she asked this particular client for a favor but she decided to do it anyway.

"Can I bum a cigarette?" Lori asked, standing directly behind the woman as she gambled at a slot machine.

"You're smoking again?" Hannah chided, pausing to take another drag from her non-filtered stick of tobacco. "I thought you quit! At your age, you shouldn't smoke!" Hannah crushed the remains of her cigarette into an ashtray.

"And you?" Lori asked.

"At my age, it doesn't much matter," Hannah remarked. Watching the final remnants of cigarette smoke escape from Hannah's mouth, Lori instantly recalled the nickname her aunt had given Hannah the Dragon Lady of Calumet City.

"I'm just feeling a little antsy," Lori admitted.

Hannah handed Lori a yellow plastic lighter and yanked a cigarette from her pack. "Is the fact that a man was killed on your tour getting to you?" Hannah asked.

Lori lit up and inhaled deeply. It had been eleven months since her last puff. The old habit felt new again. It felt wonderful.

"Kind of," Lori muttered, knowing the murder was only one of the many reasons her world seemed to be falling apart.

"Wanna know why?" Hannah asked, although it sounded more like a statement. "Because you're young, that's why. You're not used to people dying. At my age, you get used to seeing your friends drop like flies."

Lori nodded. Farsi's death did trouble her. But her inability to stop gambling scared her even more. As she remembered the amount she'd already lost at Moose Bay, a sound came from deep inside her that was a combination of a groan and a cry for help. Fortunately, the only one that heard it was Hannah.

Hannah informed her, "If that's your stomach I hear growling it's because of that damn international buffet. You can't trust anyone to wash hands these days. It's like the whole world is the third world, if you know what I mean."

"My stomach's fine, Hannah," Lori answered, looking around for other clients she could chat up. At least visiting with clients kept her away from the tables. "Thank you for the cigarette."

"You won't be thanking me when you get lung cancer," Hannah warned.

"That's true," Lori said, turning to walk away.

"Lori, wait a minute," Hannah said in a tone that was both strange and unfamiliar for Hannah. It sounded caring.

"I've been thinking about this murder thing, plus about the ride up here," she said to Lori.

Lori sat down on the swivel stool next to her. "Do you know something?"

"It's not what I know but what I observed. Just because I have cataracts, doesn't mean I can't see what's going on."

"What is it?" Lori asked, feeling herself grow impatient. If Hannah knew anything, Lori would need to let Betty, or the sheriff, know as soon as possible.

"On the bus ride here, it wasn't only Farsi that was quiet, but other people as well. There were at least two other grumpy men on board. That's just not right. Nobody's unhappy on their way to a casino."

Lori had to agree.

Hannah continued, "I don't like sour pusses. The role of curmudgeon belongs to me and no one else!"

Lori had no idea that Hannah was so self-aware. Perhaps her Aunt Betty was right. Maybe Hannah just wanted attention after all.

"Do you remember who the riders were?" Lori asked.

"One of them was a really big man. He wore a Chicago Bears jacket the entire ride. He never once took it off, though the temperature was hotter than Hades."

Lori knew the temperature in the bus was always kept on high. There were too many complaints from the senior passengers if it wasn't. "What specifically did you see that was odd?" Lori asked.

"The two men didn't play Bingo on the bus. Farsi didn't either. That made no sense to me. The bingo games are free to play and the prizes are cash. What gambler in his right mind would turn down those odds?"

"Not many," Lori agreed.

Hannah whispered, "There's something else. I've been playing almost nonstop since we got here and I haven't hit a single jackpot."

"But there are a lot of trips when you don't win," Lori reminded her.

"True, but not when it's like this."

"Like what?" Lori asked.

"Like it's heaven on earth and there's nothing but winning jackpots and free cocktails."

"Come again?" Lori asked.

"Have you gambled since we've been here?" Hannah asked.

Lori felt her cheeks flush. "Only a little."

"Slots?" Hannah asked.

Lori shook her head. "Poker."

"Well, maybe that's why you haven't heard anything."

"Heard what?" Lori asked.

"The sounds of jackpots being hit. I've heard at least a dozen and personally seen seven or eight. And all of them for $1,999.00."

"Really?" Lori asked, knowing that wasn't an unusual amount to win. One dollar more and the IRS would have to be notified of the win.

"No telling how many other jackpots have been won. Doesn't that seem odd to you?"

Lori agreed. "It does."

Hannah rubbed out her cigarette in the ashtray and immediately lit up another before stating, "Like I said, there's something fishy going on in Minnesota. And it stinks."

Chapter 20

Betty slid into the plush seat between Tillie and Lori just as the house lights dimmed.

"Did all of our people show up for tickets?" Lori asked, scanning the main level of the theater. The auditorium was completely packed. Only the balcony seats were empty.

Betty held up a single ticket in her hand. She said, "Everyone except Mr. Ogawa."

Lori suggested, "Maybe he's on a winning streak?"

Betty shook her head. "I hope so. Learning to gamble was on his list of 88 Things To Do before he dies."

Tillie said, "What's to learn? You slip a buck into a machine and press the play button. Presto – you're a gambler. It doesn't take a pocket scientist to play a slot machine."

"Or a *rocket* scientist either," Betty affirmed sitting back into the stadium-styled seating.

Music filled the auditorium while a laser light show of red, white and blue beams zigzagged across the stage. The score from *Chariots of Fire* rose to a deafening pitch. Suddenly, fireworks exploded onstage as a purple fog emerged from the sidelines. Two Las Vegas style showgirls danced across the stage.

The duo wore large, white feathered headdresses that fanned out three feet on each side. Their ensemble was a skimpy flesh colored bikini, covered completely in diamond rhinestones. Their bottoms were adorned with three-foot tail feathers. Their bikini tops barely covered their multiple assets. The two glided gracefully in four-inch high heels and posed dead center on the stage. They positioned their arms in a dramatic fashion and pointed toward the empty space between the two of them.

Tillie leaned over. "Do you think they're real?"

Betty asked, "Their diamonds?"

Tillie answered, "Their boobs."

The man behind them must have heard Tillie's comment because he leaned forward and said, "Who cares?"

The showgirls did a half turn. Their barely covered rear ends became visible to the audience.

"Oops," Tillie said and pointed toward the women. "I guess no one's invented silicone butts, yet. Even with feathers, their rear ends are as flat as a pancake."

The man crouched forward one more time and whispered. "Like I said, who cares?"

Betty had to agree. Ass or no ass, the women were gorgeous.

White smoke began to swirl around the showgirls' feet and raced to the ceiling in a torrent, completely shrouding the young women in its wake. A large explosion boomed and the white fog seemed to separate. Boris rose dramatically from the bowels of the stage and now stood between the two showgirls. There was another explosion and one of the girls jumped into the air with fright. With his right hand, Boris reached out and caught the heavy headdress as it slipped suddenly off the leaping showgirl's head.

The audience burst into a round of applause. Boris grinned and gallantly replaced the heavy headwear back on the young woman. The two women ran off stage, holding onto their headdresses with both hands as their pink tail feathers fanned up and down.

Boris said, with a flourish and a bow, "Welcome to Boris The Baffler."

The audience began to applaud again but Boris held his palm upward, signaling them to stop. He said, "Please, there's no need to show your appreciation." He smiled. "You See? I already know what you're thinking."

Chuckles, as well as moans, rippled across the crowd. Betty realized that Boris' charm captivated the audience as quickly as it had captivated her only a few hours earlier.

The showgirls ran back on stage. This time they were dressed in navy blue janitor jumpsuits cut into short shorts and halter-tops. Red baseball caps and stilettos completed their sensational look. They began to set up a row of five metal chairs, center stage.

Boris looked upwards and spoke to the sound booth at the back of the balcony. "Bring up the house lights, please."

As the lights lit up the room Boris said, "Keep the lights up for the rest of the show. I've nothing to hide, although I know a lot of you think I do." He peered out over the crowd. "I would like five volunteers from the audience. Raise your hands if you'd like to be chosen."

Tillie jumped up and waved her hands wildly in the air. At least twenty others did the same.

With one hand on his forehead, Boris' eyes scanned the audience. He selected four other people to join him before his eyes caught Tillie's. He gestured for her to come onstage.

Although she was the last to be chosen, Tillie was the first to make it onstage. "Should I sit down?" she asked, as she stood next to Boris.

Boris sighed playfully, as if he were eternally bored with his job of being a mind reader and said, "I knew you would ask that." Tillie plopped herself on the first chair. The other four—a man and three women—soon followed.

From her seat in the audience, Betty recognized the male volunteer. It was Slevitch, one of the men of size she'd suggested the sheriff investigate. Slevitch was one of Betty's new passengers who paid in cash. He was also one of the men that she'd asked Severson to investigate. She pointed out that all of her new riders, including the now dead Farsi, were people of enormous size. In fact, they actually looked as if they could be related.

As far as she knew, the sheriff hadn't been able to find Slevitch to question him. Slevitch hadn't shown up for his scheduled interview with the sheriff's department either. Yet, here he was, volunteering to be part of the Baffler's show. And more surprising was seeing Tillie's reaction when he worked his way onstage. Tillie seemed to recoil slightly, as if she were terrified.

Boris' voice boomed across the theater as he handed a stack of index cards to each of the showgirls. "My lovely assistants, Maddie and Heather, will hand each of the volunteers an index card. But first, I'd like the girls to memorize what is written on the cards."

The two dancers quickly scanned each of the cards.

Boris asked, "What three words are written on only four of the cards?"

"Tell the truth," the pair said in unison.

"And what three words are written on the other card?" Boris demanded.

"Tell only lies!" they announced.

"Shuffle them and then give one to each of our volunteers, face down," he instructed. "I would like each of you seated to refrain from looking at the card that is given to you until I tell you to do so."

When the two showgirls passed out the final one, Boris turned to the audience and said, "Because we are in a casino, I am assuming most of you know what a *tell* is."

His statement was met with "You betcha" and nodding of heads.

Boris continued, "For those who don't, every human being has a tell, a small change in their behavior that is easily detected when they tell a lie. It can be a twitch of the neck, a pulling of the ear, or one eyebrow that raises a millimeter at the most. These actions are not noticeable to most people, but are easily noticed by those trained in this art as I have been."

Boris began pacing back and forth on the stage. "Being able to read minds isn't magic. For instance, today I surprised a man in the casino by telling him he was a retired plumber. He failed to remember his union emblem was embroidered on his overalls. I shocked another woman when I read her mind. She was thinking that I," Boris paused for dramatic effect, "was dressed like Liberace. As if I hadn't heard that before."

The auditorium burst into applause while Betty thought, *well that explains that*, knowing she was the woman he was referencing.

Boris continued. "Reading minds is merely a skill passed down through the centuries from one generation of shaman to another."

A man in the front row yelled, "Teach me how to read the dealer's mind! I'm already down three hundred bucks."

Boris responded with a smirk. "Actually you're already down three *thousand* big ones."

The crowd erupted into laughter and when it quieted, the man added meekly, "Why'd you have to say that? My wife had no idea."

Immediately, the woman to his left hit him in the head with her gold spangled purse.

The crowd roared again and Boris offered the man words of comfort. "Don't worry. You're going to win $20,000 this very weekend."

The man jumped up and ran out of the auditorium toward the casino. His wife followed in hot pursuit.

The audience clapped loudly. Boris added, "Alas, I failed to let him know that his win will be when he's playing Monopoly with his grandkids. But don't worry. He'll be ahead by the time he leaves the casino—by three dollars and seventy-seven cents."

Betty grinned. She didn't know how much of Boris' act was staged beforehand, but it was certainly entertaining.

Boris turned away from the volunteers. "I want each of you to read the card my assistants have handed to you. Then, turn it over so I cannot see which card you have. However, do not show any emotion or reaction to what is on your card. Maintain your best poker face at all times."

Each of the five participants read their cards. Betty could tell they were doing their best to follow Boris' instructions. Even Tillie sat stone-faced and erect. In fact, she'd been that way ever since Slevitch walked onto the stage.

Boris said, "By merely watching the volunteer's facial expressions while holding their hands, I will be able to tell who is lying to me, no matter how good a liar they might think they are."

Boris turned to one of the senior ladies. He reached down and took each of her hands in one of his. "What is your name, dear?"

"Beverly England."

"And what do you do for a living, Mrs. England?"

"I'm retired. I live on Social Security, a small investment portfolio," and then with a hint of embarrassment, "and jackpots from penny slots."

Boris chuckled. "And your favorite movie star is?"

"Why, Harrison Ford, of course. The sexiest man alive!"

Quick laughter shot up from the crowd.

Boris leaned over and took a deep whiff. "Why, Mrs. England, you've had a very large margarita for Happy Hour."

"I've had three," came her honest response.

"I know," Boris said, patting her shoulder. "I was being a gentleman."

Boris stepped over to the next participant, a large, redheaded woman. He took her hands in his and asked, "What is your name?"

"My name is Kelly O'Sullivan," the middle aged redhead said proudly in a heavy Irish brogue. "I'm on vacation from the sweetest of motherlands, Ireland herself."

Although the accent was completely different, Betty recognized the woman's voice. Kelly O'Sullivan was the same woman who had rescued her from the snow bank. Except when the woman befriended her, Kelly O'Sullivan spoke with a Minnesota accent and her hair was blonde.

Briefly, Betty wondered if she'd hit her head harder than she thought on the snow-covered concrete. It was then Betty noticed Boris' *tell.* His normally warm eyes glazed over in ice as he stared at the redheaded woman. He gave her the same, hardened look that he'd shot at the retired flamenco dancer earlier.

In a stern monotone, he asked, "And what do you do for a living?"

There was a slight hesitation before the woman answered. "I work in a laundry. Nothing comes into me doors that doesn't go out clean as a leprechaun's whistle."

Boris dropped her hands abruptly and moved in front of the next volunteer, Tillie. His demeanor instantly changed and he became friendly. He smiled as he placed Tillie's hands in his. He asked, "What is your name, sweetheart?"

"Tillie," she answered.

"And your favorite activity is…?"

Tillie's mouth dropped opened immediately and she quickly shut it, placing one of her hands over her lips. Even from where she sat,

Betty could see that Tillie was blushing.

Boris responded gently, "Tillie, we're all adults here. It's okay for you tell everyone that your favorite activity is sex."

Tillie rolled her eyes in defeat. "Whatever."

A dozen men gave Tillie a standing ovation.

"And your second favorite?"

"Oh that's easy, scrapbooking." Tillie beamed and then added, "Of course I don't keep a scrapbook about sex."

After the crowd's laughter died down Boris said, "Actually, I think you should. Now, what do you do for work?"

"I drive a tour bus. Plus, on the side, I sell a wonderful line of make-up." Tillie leaned toward the audience. "I always have free samples, ladies."

Boris turned to step toward the lone gentleman on stage; he reached out his hand as a loud clap of thunder roared throughout the hall. Boris spun around quickly and stared up at the sound booth. Betty realized whatever just happened, shouldn't have.

There was another clap of thunder and smoke flew across the stage while laser light beams dashed randomly and strobe lights pulsated. Finally, there was a loud pop. It was the sort of pop Betty had heard at shooting ranges. The sort of pop that filled the air with the smell of burnt, rotting eggs. The smell of gunfire.

Immediately, Slevitch fell out of his chair, his large body crumpling to the floor. Even from where she sat, Betty could see the front of his tan shirt was beginning to turn crimson.

To stop from screaming, Betty put her hands to her lips. This wasn't part of Boris the Baffler's act.

Chapter 21

Audience members fled up the aisles and out of the auditorium. Only a few brave souls including Betty and Lori, stayed behind, transfixed by what was happening onstage. Two of the show's volunteers remained frozen in their chairs. The showgirls had dashed away the moment Slevitch hit the floor. Boris stood in the center of the stage, his eyes scanning the theater, undoubtedly looking for the attacker. If he was a true mentalist, his skills weren't working very well.

On stage Tillie knelt next to Slevitch. He was still alive. His arm shook as he reached up and grabbed Tillie's hand. He mouthed a few words and then immediately let go. His arm fell to the floor. Slevitch was dead.

Tillie lifted herself up slowly and backed a few paces from the body. The woman who said her name was Kelly O'Sullivan placed her hands on Tillie's shoulders. As she did, she positioned her lips near Tillie's ear and whispered something. Betty watched as the bus driver's eyes widened.

Tillie's hands grasped at her stomach, as if in pain. The woman known as O'Sullivan pulled Tillie to a chair and forced her to sit. Then she glanced at the stairs where security guards were already blocking anyone from leaving the stage.

Betty's focus darted between the stage and the balcony. She wanted to keep an eye on Tillie, yet she was on the lookout for another shot as well. She assumed the bullet came from the upper level. As far as she could tell, except for the lone soundman in the booth, no one was up there.

"Should we grab Tillie and run for it?" Lori asked as she clutched Betty's sleeve.

Before Betty could answer Tom Songbird rushed into the auditorium, pushing his way down the aisle. Severson was close behind, along with several of his men. The sheriff leapt onto the stage and knelt next to the splayed body. He placed two of his fingers on the man's neck.

"We need to get Tillie off that stage," Lori said abruptly and dashed out of her row. She was halfway down the aisle when Betty managed to catch her. She stopped Lori and pulled her back into a row of seats.

"We can't," Betty informed her, knowing the sheriff would certainly question their motives for getting Tillie away from the crime scene. Even if it were only a coincidence, a person connected to Take A Chance Tours was once again standing next to a corpse.

"The sheriff's in charge," Betty reminded Lori. "He's the one who gets to tell her when to leave. Not us."

"He'll listen to me," Lori said, her breath becoming more rapid.

Betty said, "Not this time."

Lori relented and sat in a seat. Betty sat next to her and turned her attention to the O'Sullivan woman who was standing at the back of the stage. She watched as the redhead paced in small circles, her hands balled into fists. The woman was mumbling to herself as she occasionally stared at the balcony. Betty realized that Kelly O'Sullivan—or whatever her name was—figured the shot originated from the second level. Just like Betty did.

It was ironic to Betty that the same woman she thought of as a hero earlier was now someone who frightened her. And it was even odder that the woman had spoken to her in a Minnesota accent yet chattered on stage in perfect brogue Irish. And there was no doubt in Betty's mind that the woman was also the retired flamenco dancer who'd hit a jackpot earlier.

Just who are you, Lady? And what are you up to? Betty wondered, as she sat in the chair, her forefinger tapping thoughtfully up and down against her lip.

It took every bit of self-control for Betty to stay put. She too wanted to yank Tillie out of the theater. She could only begin to imagine what the driver was feeling. If the bullet had strayed only a foot to the right, Tillie's chest would have been the one that was ripped apart.

The sheriff turned to one of his men and yelled angrily, "Check everyone's ID in this room. Get their names and get them out of here."

The deputy jumped off the stage. One by one, he interviewed the few audience members that were left. It took him only a few minutes to reach Betty and Lori.

Betty was just about to hand him her driver's license when the officer said, "I know who the two of you are. You both can leave."

"Thank you," Betty said.

As soon as Betty and Lori exited the theater she saw that Severson's men were interviewing people. It surprised her that one of the men being questioned was Mr. Ogawa. He hadn't even been at the show, yet he seemed to know what happened. When it came to murder, news traveled at warp speed.

Ogawa was pointing at her as he spoke. She assumed he was telling the officer he was one of her riders. Or perhaps he was telling the policeman that he was able to cross another item from his *88 Things To Do* list: seeing a man shot to death.

Betty shivered at her own dark humor and started to walk out of the lobby when Lori put her arm on her shoulder and stopped her. "Aunt Betty?"

Betty's ears perked up. Lori almost never used the "A" word unless she was either worried, afraid, or the bearer of bad news.

"What is it?" Betty asked, as Lori stepped in front of her.

Lori's face was stern. "Maybe we should cut this trip short. We could head back home tonight."

Betty shrugged, despairingly. "We can't. We're scheduled to be here until tomorrow afternoon at two. Besides, we still don't have a bus to take us back. We can't ask senior citizens to hitchhike to Chicago."

"We could charter a plane," Lori suggested. "It would cost a fortune but considering what our clients have been through . . ."

"Most of our clients won't set foot in a plane. Why do you think they travel by bus?"

Lori's shoulders momentarily collapsed, as if she could no longer carry the weight of the world. She said, "I just—well—this tour doesn't seem to be working out for anyone. I mean...people keep dying! I just thought if we left now, we'd . . ."

Betty placed her arm around Lori. "I can't leave early, Lori, but if you'd like, go home. I can handle this. I'm sure Tom would arrange a private plane for you . . ." Betty stopped talking as Mr. Ogawa walked up to them.

She studied the thin, balding, grey haired man, his body bent over, held up by a cane. Betty was extremely worried about him. Stress could kill a senior almost as quickly as a heart attack.

"Are you all right, Mr. Ogawa?" she asked.

"Oh yes. I am fine, thank you very much," he said, looking up, a serious look on his face. "May I ask a question, Miss Betty?"

Even in the midst of chaos, Ogawa was as polite as ever.

"Of course." She smiled back. If only all of her clients were as pleasant as Ogawa.

"I have never been on a gambling tour before. Do all of the tours include the sort of things that have been happening on this one?"

Betty shook her head. "Not at all. Usually, the only excitement is finding out its Seafood Night at the buffet."

"I see," Ogawa said, before admitting timidly, "perhaps this is my fault after all."

"How so?" Betty asked.

"It was the last thing on my list, number eighty-eight. 'Have the most exciting day of your life—even if it involves death,'" Ogawa said sadly, and then added, "But I meant my own death, Miss Betty, not anyone else's."

Betty swallowed hard. She felt so sad for the kindly old gentleman. She could tell he actually felt guilty. "Mr. Ogawa, there's no way you could have caused the murders."

"Oh, but there is. If I had shown up perhaps the shooter would have shot me instead of Mr. Slevitch. I would have volunteered. To be onstage is also on my list and I've yet to accomplish it."

Betty was surprised Ogawa knew the man's name. She said, "Mr. Ogawa, no one on Take A Chance Tours had anything to do with Slevitch's murder."

"I wouldn't be so sure," a voice boomed behind her.

Betty twirled around to see Sheriff Severson holding a Ziploc bag in the air. Even a novice in the art of crime could tell that what he was holding up was evidence.

Normally, she'd be fascinated to see what he'd gathered as evidence. But this time she wasn't. Inside the plastic bag was one of her business cards covered with blood. And again Tillie's name was on it.

Chapter 22

The ice cubes clinked against the cocktail glass as Betty walked across her hotel room. A splash of rum and coke spilled onto the beige carpeting while a few droplets managed to leap into the air and land on the front of Betty's blouse. In her other hand she carried two beers. Tillie grabbed the non-alcoholic one, while Lori reached for the Heineken.

Betty plopped into an overstuffed chair and sifted through her purse. She pulled out a package of Lucky Strike Lights. There was only one cigarette left. She placed the empty pack on the table next to her.

Lori shifted uncomfortably on the edge of the bed. She said, "Are you sure you want to do that? It's been years since you . . ."

Betty interrupted, "I'm not going to light it. It just helps when I am stressed to know I can."

Her favorite brand of smokes had been discontinued the same year her marriage ended. She took it as a sign from the universe—*time to get rid of bad habits, even if you were married to one.*

Betty caught Tillie's surprised expression and explained, "I didn't smoke until I met Larry. It was his idea for me to start. He said it made me look sexy. But the minute I found out he'd been . . ." Betty paused. She didn't want to use the words 'screwing his brains out' or 'a lying scumbag' while Lori was in the room. Larry was still her uncle. Betty finished, "…seeing someone else, I quit. Besides, I only smoked because he did."

Tillie, however, did not hold back. She said, "Too bad you didn't screw everything that moved, because he did."

Betty chuckled. Tillie's spirit may have been broken a few hours earlier by seeing a man die in front of her, but she was back in full form. Betty responded, "If I had to do it all over again, maybe I would have had a few one-day stands. The UPS men were unbelievably hot."

"Yep," Tillie said, raising her beer in a toast. "Nothing like a man in uniform. Or better yet, out of it!" She took a swig.

"Why did you want us to get together?" Lori asked, one leg bouncing nervously up and down against the other.

Betty could tell Lori wanted leave. Maybe Lori just needed to be alone. Betty knew her niece tended to isolate herself when overwhelmed with life. But considering what had happened, being alone wasn't wise.

Betty said, "There's safety in numbers, Lori. I think we should spend the night together."

Lori responded solemnly, "There were over five hundred people at Boris' show and that didn't turn out to be so safe."

"True," Betty relented. "Maybe we can use this time wisely. We can put our heads together and figure out why Take A Chance is connected to every single murder scene."

Tillie said, "The killer is probably shifting the blame to us on purpose. You're an easy target, just like I am. Farsi was stabbed on your bus."

Lori piped in, "And if they are trying to frame one of you, it could be the reason your business cards keep popping up around dead people."

Betty swirled the cubes around in her glass. She said, "I can't be framed because I can't be convicted. Wouldn't I need a reason to kill someone? I don't have one."

Tillie said, "Some people kill just because they can."

Betty had to agree. Psychopaths were more common than she'd like to think. She leaned forward and said, "That's true, but I'm not a serial killer or a nutcase. My instinct is telling me the reason someone is planting my card with Tillie's name scribbled on it is because of a personal vendetta of some kind."

Tillie responded, "Are you sure it's not one of your competitors? Maybe someone who wants to take over your business?"

Both Lori and Betty burst into laughter.

Betty said, "Thanks for that, Tillie. I needed a laugh. After our measly wages are paid, Take A Chance's profit this year will be around four thousand bucks. Someone would have to be insane to want to take over our company."

Tillie shrugged her shoulders and leaned back on the bed. "Well, if it's not the company they're after, then it's one of us. We all know I'm an ex-con, so that certainly makes me a suspect. But take a gander at Lori. There's nothing wrong with her. How could anyone possibly want to frame her? She's not only perfect physically, her personality's flawless."

"At least the sheriff thinks so," Betty said as she smiled at Lori, who didn't return the gesture.

"I'm hardly perfect," Lori shot back, her body noticeably tensing up. "I use a lot of makeup to get this look. And trust me, my personality is not what you think it is."

"At least no one hates you," Tillie said. "I can name at least a dozen people that detest me, and that's just relatives."

Betty swore she saw tears well up in Lori's eyes right before she mumbled, "No, my relatives don't hate me. Yet."

"Okay, kiddo." Betty jumped up and grabbed the bottle from Lori's hand. "No more beer for you!"

"Like I said, I'm not perfect," Lori said, smiling weakly.

Betty asked, "What about you, Tillie? Is there any way you're connected? Even by accident?"

Tillie played with her empty bottle before tossing it a good five feet. It landed perfectly inside the wastebasket. "Nope, not me, not my friends, and not even the ex-cons I still write to," she answered abruptly.

Betty stated, "I wanted to ask you about the Irish woman on stage with you. There's something about her that's very odd."

Tillie stopped smiling. She said, "Go on."

Betty continued. "She's the one who pulled me from the snow bank when I fell. Except when she yanked me up she spoke with a Minnesota accent, and not an Irish brogue. She also claimed to be a gym teacher, not a laundry worker like she told Boris. And I'm pretty sure she also pretended to be Spanish yesterday."

Tillie's face went ashen. When she didn't respond, Betty asked, "What did she whisper to you onstage?"

Betty couldn't tell if Tillie was embarrassed or starting to hyperventilate. Her breathing became labored. Tillie stood up and her eyes turned to ice. She replied in a monotone, "Listen, officially I've been off the clock for hours. It's been a long day. I'm going to my room."

Betty pleaded, "Tillie, I didn't mean to . . ."

Tillie held her hand up. "You were fine. I've just hit the wall, that's all." She walked to the door and unlocked it.

"Tillie, I . . ." Betty said, standing up.

Tillie turned around. "Trust me, you don't want to know what she said to me."

"I do want to know," Betty replied.

Tillie shook her head in despair. She answered, "It was the same thing I heard in prison day after day. Whenever one of the eastern Europeans gang members wanted to terrorize anyone, they'd whisper five little words.

"What were they, Tillie?"

"Why don't you believe me when I tell you it's better you don't know?"

"What are the five words?" Betty demanded. But before she could stop Tillie, her driver threw open the door and bolted.

Tillie raced down the stairwell and reached the first floor landing in a matter of minutes. Sweat beaded on her face. Her make-up turned clammy. She opened the stairwell door and stepped into the hotel lobby.

Tillie knew Betty would be worried, but she desperately needed time to think. She had to decide if it was worth taking the chance of being killed to do the right thing. She made it as far as the glass doors of the hotel entrance when she heard her name being called.

"Tillie!"

Tillie groaned. Even without turning around she knew who was calling out to her.

Her gut told her to run and not stop until she reached the Arctic Circle. When she did, she'd never look back again. But she repressed her desires and swirled around. "Yes, Sheriff?"

"I've left you three messages," he stated.

"I haven't been to my room and, and—maybe my cell battery is dead? You know the old joke about a single girl and her batteries?" Tillie hoped to sound funny. But she sounded pathetic, instead. Her best bet was to try to give the sheriff what he wanted—respect. Her demeanor turned serious. "What do you want, Sheriff?"

His face tightened. "Did Slevitch hand you something right before he died?"

Tillie bit into her lower lip. "I don't know what you're talking about," she lied.

"Mr. Ogawa told my Deputy he saw the victim place something in your hand when you were onstage kneeling next to him."

She instinctively tightened her hand into a fist, as if she were getting ready to defend herself. Instead, she forced herself to stretch out her fingers as wide as possible. She began to silently count to ten. Immediately, her body started to relax just the way her anger management counselor said it would.

"Ogawa?" she questioned. "He wasn't even at the show. Besides, isn't he like two hundred years old or something? Can he even see that far? I thought all seniors have cataracts by that age."

"Evidently not. He said you slipped the paper into your pocket. He said it looked like a note, or a business card."

"That's crazy! Don't you think I'd tell you?" she asked.

"You do realize it's against the law to lie to an officer…?"

Tillie interrupted, "Sheriff, do you see the clothes I'm wearing? It's the same outfit I had on stage. It doesn't even have pockets."

Tillie lifted her shirt at the bottom and turned around slightly, pushing out her ample rump outwards for emphasis. "Wanna search?" she mocked.

The sheriff's boyish look returned. But this time it was red from rage, not embarrassment. He demanded, "Why would Ogawa lie?"

Tillie answered in a huff. "He was probably having a senior moment. He might have seen a shadow, or a flicker of a ring, or whatever. Who knows?"

Severson adjusted his belt and pushed his gun further into its holster. "From now on, if I leave you a message, call me ASAP" he said abruptly, and then added, "For some reason, I'm not buying your story, McFinn."

"Why not?" Tillie asked.

"Because once a con, always a con."

Chapter 23

It was the perfect flirty dress—cotton candy pink with thin spaghetti straps that could break apart at any minute. The vintage find was not too short and not too long. A shiny lime green ribbon wrapped twice around Lori's small waist and tied in a bow in the front. The full skirt, made puffy from Lori's favorite inherited 50s petticoat, swished hello with every step. In her pink leather pumps, Lori's fashion statement demanded: *Look at me, world, I'm here*.

It was a little past midnight and Lori was wide-awake. Her aunt had almost collapsed from exhaustion and finally went to bed. She'd fallen asleep within moments. With Betty's first soft snore, Lori had sneaked out of the room and back to her own. A quick shower, fresh makeup, and a change of fashion did wonders for her attitude.

Besides, her gut was telling her a winning streak was heading her way. She failed to remember that every time she gambled and lost she felt the same way. But this time she convinced herself it would be different. It would solve problems, not create them.

"Wow, great dress," a young man said between puffs on his cigarette as she walked through the casino.

Lori smiled back at him. "Thank you."

She was in a good mood, an incredibly happy mood, a manic one in fact. It was a little after midnight and she was on her way to the high limit poker room to meet Tony.

As she walked the aisles, the sounds of the slot machines became a symphony of hope to her. It was unlike the sounds she heard the machines emit when she felt despair. Sometimes, after a big loss the electronic imitations of dropping coins came at her like bullets, tearing her apart. But now, in the happy mood she was in, the slot tones sounded as pure as Julie Andrews' voice.

She maneuvered her way through the late night crowd. She passed the penny, nickel, quarter, dollar, and five-dollar machines. Eventually she worked her way to the row of twenty-five dollar slots. Behind the pricey one-arm bandits was the entrance to the high stakes poker room.

The guard, standing next to the doorway, greeted her. "Good evening, Miss."

"Good evening," Lori said in return as she walked into the sequestered room. Although any casino guest could enter the walnut paneled sanctuary, very few did. The hundred dollar minimum buy-in intimidated even die-hard players.

There were only two tables in the room, and only one seat was available. It was next to Tony.

She slipped in beside him. There were four other men seated around the green felt-top oval table. The fact that there were only males at the table was good, Lori decided. The general consensus among the majority of men was that females couldn't play poker worth a damn. She would use this to her advantage.

"Hi there," she said in her naturally low and sultry voice. She leaned over to brush Tony's shoulder with her own.

Tony smiled back and said, "That's some dress you're wearing."

Flipping her hair back with the tip of her hand she asked, "Think it'll bring me luck?"

A seventy-something-year-old man seated at the end quipped, "That dress could bring you more than that."

"Not with you sport," another player responded, setting down his beer. "Not unless the drink you have in your hand is liquid Viagra."

"A martini is Viagra," the old man snapped back.

"Not four of them in a row," the other player taunted.

Both Tony and Lori laughed. She was glad to see that Tony didn't mind the fact that other men flirted with her. He could have acted jealous, but instead he looked content, like a cat about to devour a very pink canary.

A waitress who managed to show more cleavage than Lori, bent over and whispered, "Beverage?"

Lori responded, "Perrier, please."

"Same here," Tony said and tipped the woman with a chip.

"Thanks," the waitress gushed, grinning as she pocketed the hundred dollar chip.

Tony slid five stacks of black chips toward Lori. She didn't bother to count them. She knew there would be ten chips in each stack, each worth a hundred dollars.

Lori nervously lifted her fingernail to her lip to bite it but quickly lowered her hand. *Stay cool*, she reminded herself as her demeanor changed back to Ice Princess. As the first card was dealt, each of the players adopted their game face. The four presidents carved into Mount Rushmore were more animated than the men sitting at Lori's table.

As the cards were dealt, the witty repartee disappeared, along with any hint of sexual innuendo. Profanity, no matter how bad the loss or how exhilarating the win was not allowed while playing cards at most casinos. The game was a ballet of quiet etiquette and hidden desires. It was no wonder Lori felt at home seated behind a stack of chips.

The rules of poker had been easy for her to learn. The game was divided into hands where the object was to eventually achieve a certain combination of cards. Some combinations were easy to get, others almost impossible.

But it was the nature of the game that intrigued her. Lori understood from her first day of playing poker that she wasn't playing cards—she was playing people. They were the ones she had to beat, not the random shuffle of the deck.

To survive in the game, she'd learned how to read tells, gestures, and attitudes of the gamers around her. She understood that if there were any real mentalists in the world, it was the ones sitting around an oval table knowing who among them held a Royal Flush.

It took only a few minutes for Tony to win the first game. A Four of a Kind made it easy for him. The second game was won by him as well, and then another.

"Good job," Lori gushed after his third win, happy for him as he gathered more chips, yet unhappy for herself. Her stack was already dwindling in number.

"Thanks," he said, paying little attention to what she said. He was deep into his zone of concentration.

The martini drinker next to him didn't notice Tony's solitary demeanor. Instead, he growled, "Well, at least I can tell my grandkids I lost their inheritance to Tony Gillette."

As expected, Tony kept on winning. But Lori surprised everyone by calling an all-in on the tenth game and raking in a mound of chips as her prize.

"I'm out," one of the men said, shooting her a look of shock and awe. "You're a lot smarter than you look, Lady."

She didn't take offense. She'd just taken $2,000 off the man. "Thanks but I'm just movie star dumb—and lucky," she admitted playfully and readied her chips for the next bet.

During the next hour of play, a few players came and went. Tony and Lori remained firmly in their seats, sipping water as the others chugged down their free booze.

Tony continued to take the majority of the hands. Lori managed to win a few. She was riding high when two men in dark suits walked up to the table. One of the burly giants placed a large hand on Tony's shoulder and gripped it tightly. He said loud enough for everyone at the table to hear, "Please come with us, Mr. Gillette."

Tony stiffened. He didn't ask why they wanted him to follow. He set his cards on the table downside. "Is there a problem?" he asked, through gritted teeth, his granite-like face showing no emotion.

"Please, follow us," the giant repeated. Lori noticed that two more suited men had appeared in the doorway. They were all wearing the same stern expressions.

Grabbing his chips, Tony stood up abruptly. He glanced at Lori, and in a brief change of attitude said, "Have fun."

He turned and proceeded out of the room, the gang of men following closely behind.

"What the...?" One of the men exclaimed, stopping in mid-sentence to drink a large portion of his vodka on rocks.

"You think he was cheating? Maybe card counting?" a young man seated next to Lori on her left, asked. He looked up at the dozen or so eyes in the skies. "Man, oh man, if he was, he is so screwed."

The martini drinker retorted in disgust, "Of course he wasn't counting cards. He's Tony Gillette, for Pete's sake. And don't you know you're not supposed to swear at a table?"

"Screwed isn't a swear word," the young man said, and then must have realized it would be better for him to apologize. "Sorry," he mumbled.

You think you're sorry, now? Just wait till I'm done playing you, you'll be more than screwed. You'll be broke! Lori thought in retaliation. Tony was obviously in some sort of trouble, and the punk next to her had made light of it.

Abruptly, another player took the side of the young man by adding, "Just because someone's a champion, don't mean he can't be a cheater."

It was then that three words drifted into Lori's mind about Tony that she'd never thought she'd imagine: *Or a murderer.*

Disgusted with herself, Lori quickly forced that thought from developing any further. She had absolutely no reason to think that Tony was connected to either Farsi or Slevitch's death. Besides, she didn't want to think about *that* right now. She couldn't. Right now she only wanted to think about winning.

As the next card was dealt Lori's concerns disappeared. Instead of being worried about Tony, she concentrated on the game. When she saw the three Aces she'd been dealt, she knew the fates were on her side.

For the next six hours, she didn't think of Tony once. At 7:00 A.M., when she finally left the table, she was holding in her hands what the others once held: their money.

Chapter 24

I*t is so cold –Polar bears are buying fur coats.*

It is so cold –my lawyer's putting his hands in his own pocket.

Every Rodney Dangerfield one liner she'd ever heard about being cold jumped into Betty's brain. If nothing else, at least she'd freeze to death with a grin on her face. It was nine in the morning and Betty was standing in twelve-degree weather waiting for Tillie. According to the irritatingly happy weather woman on the local channel, the wind chill stood at twenty-two below zero.

She pushed her gloved hands further into the pockets of her hooded parka. A red wool muffler covered most of her face. How she'd carry on a conversation outdoors was beyond her comprehension. But when she called Tillie's room a few minutes earlier, Tillie refused to speak to her, either on the phone or indoors.

Betty felt Tillie was being paranoid, but her fears could turn out to be justified. Casinos were known to go to any measure to protect their interests.

"Hey," came a voice cutting through the thick, frigid air. "Cold enough for ya?"

Betty turned and saw that Tillie hadn't bothered to wear a muffler. The Cubs cap her friend had on provided minimal protection against the piercing wind. At least Tillie's faux rabbit fur jacket looked warm.

"Could be colder, ya know," Betty shot back.

The interchange of over-the-top Minnesota dialect had been their favorite in-joke on the drive north. The women were die-hard fans of the movie *Fargo.* Despite the film's title, the movie was set primarily in Minnesota, not North Dakota. Betty and Tillie had perfected their Minnesota tongue all the way from Chicago to Moose Bay.

Tillie increased her speed. Her short, muscular legs sped down the sidewalk. Betty struggled to keep up, mumbling through her scarf,

"How far are we walking?"

"I'm thinking Florida," Tillie answered.

Betty lowered her muffler and said, "Okay, but we're stopping in St Louis for a pee break."

They walked in silence for a while, their path following the sidewalk that circled the property. Only two other people were outside—a lone jogger and a maintenance man operating a snow blower.

After a few minutes Tillie said, "Remember the woman who was on stage with me last night?"

"The once flamenco dancer slash Viking blonde slash Irish redhead?" Betty asked, rolling her eyeballs upward to make sure they hadn't frozen in place.

Tillie said, "She and I met in prison years ago."

"Tell me about her."

"Her real name is Rose. She was always larger than life, even when she weighed a hundred pounds less than she does now. Her weight gain is the reason I didn't immediately recognize her," Tillie admitted, her breath escaping with every word and hanging in midair like comic-strip dialogue.

"Get out of here!" Betty said, suddenly feeling empathy for the woman. Gaining a hundred pounds could make anyone go bananas. She, if no one else, could understand that. Still, exchanging binge eating for binge killing was hardly the answer. Weight Watchers is usually the preferred choice.

Tillie admitted, "I thought she looked familiar. But, I couldn't place her."

The two women walked down the plowed sidewalk, watching their steps as they negotiated patches of ice. Betty kept quiet. Tillie's memories were obviously painful for her. The best thing to do would be to let her friend open up at her own pace.

After a dozen yards Tillie said, "I didn't know her very well. She was the leader of a Serbian gang. Their main enemies were the Croatian prisoners who also did their fair share of ass kicking. As did the Irish, Italian, Baptist, Jewish and Aryan gangs."

"What gang did you belong to?"

Tillie chuckled. "The musical theater gang. Now that's a guaranteed way to get your butt kicked in the pen."

"Or in high school" Betty added.

"Anyways, that's how I met Rose," Tillie explained, pulling her bill cap a bit farther down on her forehead.

"She was part of the theater group?" Betty asked, realizing that could explain the woman's penchant for impersonation. That or she suffered from multiple personality disorder.

Tillie said, "No, but she wanted to be. When we held auditions for *West Side Story,* Rose stormed in and demanded we give her the lead. She claimed she was born into a family of brilliant actors."

"Did she get the part? If so, I'm guessing it was as Tony and not Maria," Betty said, wondering if someone could freeze to death while both talking and walking. She watched as cars carefully navigated the parking lanes and plowed roads.

Tillie said, "We told her she couldn't carry a tune and offered her a job with the stage crew. That infuriated her and she vowed to get even."

"Seems petty" Betty questioned.

"In prison, petty can seem pretty big."

"Did she?" Betty asked as ice began to form on her eyelashes. "Get even?"

Tillie said, "The night of the performance, the set caught fire. The inmate who played Maria was seriously burned. No one could prove it, but we decided the arsonist was Rose."

Betty figured if Rose took the chance of killing someone by arson she'd just as likely try to murder again. Betty asked, "Do you think she's trying to frame you because you didn't cast her? Wouldn't that make her a total psychopath?" She replaced the knitted scarf back over her mouth.

Tillie shrugged. "Trust me, all actors are crazy. But actually, I may be just a convenient fall guy for her. It could just be a coincidence that we're both here at the same time. Or, who knows? Maybe she planned it. I've been your driver on other trips. It's likely that I would be your driver again."

The two reached the area where Betty had fallen the day before. Betty said, "It was right around here that I slipped."

"Are you sure you slipped?" Tillie asked.

"Sure, I remember being near this part when I . . ."

Tillie interrupted, "No, I mean, are you sure it was your fault? Rose was known for sneaking up on inmates and knocking them out from behind. Her trademark was flinging a coin-filled sock to the back of the head."

To be honest, Betty couldn't be sure what happened. She asked, "Why would Rose attack *me*?"

Tillie shrugged. "Who knows? Maybe it was because you're my friend. Or Rose thinks you know something. Rose is half-psycho and half-bitch."

Betty wrapped her arms tighter around her torso. She said, "I still don't have a clue as to why people keep getting killed."

"I might," Tillie said as she lifted her jacket collar high around her bare neck. "Do you want to know what Rose whispered to me onstage?"

Betty nodded, small clouds bursting through her chilled lips.

"'If you sing, you die'. In prison, that was the Serbian gang's warning about going to the cops." Tillie shivered.

"Why didn't you tell me last night when I asked?" Betty asked.

"I didn't want to get you involved or put you in danger. I keep forgetting that because we're friends you already are." Then Tillie asked hopefully, "We'll always be friends, right Betty? No matter what?"

Betty placed her gloved hand on Tillie's shoulder for reassurance. In a lighthearted tone, she quipped, "Like I've said before, 'buds for life.'" But she knew Tillie would take her answer seriously, just as Betty did with their friendship.

Betty glanced back at the casino hotel in the distance. In the cold and wind it felt like the picturesque entrance was three thousand miles away. She said, "Both Slevitch and Rose were Serbian. Do you think they were related?"

Tillie answered, "I think they might have been married."

Betty replied skeptically, "If he was her husband, she didn't seem too upset when he was killed right in front of her."

Tillie waved off her answer. She said, "From what I hear about marriage, a lot of wives wouldn't be upset if their husbands were killed."

Betty stopped walking and suddenly announced, "Wait a minute! I just remembered Tom said Farsi was Serbian. It can't be a coincidence they are all at Moose Bay at the same time."

Tillie responded, "I agree. And didn't you say Tom thinks there's something fishy about the progressive jackpot win. Thirteen million could help erase a lot of spousal guilt."

Betty knew it was the right time to ask about Slevitch's last moments on earth. She grabbed Tillie's wrist. "What were Slevitch's last words?"

Tillie stopped walking and wrapped her arms around her body tightly as if holding herself for comfort. "He muttered the word 'Boris' and then said 'look inside'."

"'Boris' and 'Look inside'" Betty repeated solemnly, a bit confused. She had no idea what she was expecting. Maybe a confession of guilt?

"Does that make any sense?" Betty asked.

"Actually it makes total sense, considering what he handed me," Tillie said as she reached into her pocket. "I didn't know what he gave me at first because it was wrapped up in a slip of paper." She pulled out a brass key.

Betty asked, "Is that a house key?"

"No, it unlocks a bus." Tillie lifted her hand and pointed her gloved finger at the purple and white bus with the words *Boris The Baffler* plastered across the side. She said, "That bus."

Betty's heart raced. Just yesterday its owner tried unsuccessfully to charm her Tuesday panties off. Now that entire romantic episode had turned into something sinister. She asked, "What are you going to do with the key?"

Tillie answered cynically. "Use it, of course."

"You should give it to the police," Betty said, as a wind gust played havoc with her outerwear. Her moist breath was creating an ice wall on the inside of her muffler. *How do people live in Minnesota?* she wondered.

Tillie continued, "I can't. What if there's evidence in the bus that connects Boris to the murder? Or me or you?"

Reluctantly Betty realized she'd have to admit her little dalliance of the day before. She said sheepishly, "Well, you won't be the first person from Take A Chance to break into his bus."

Tillie gave her a quizzical look.

Betty explained how yesterday she'd seen Ogawa and Boris arguing on the stairs, right before she fell on the ice. She told how she'd entered the vehicle uninvited and that Boris had shown up. That he readily accepted her explanation of concern about her oldest rider, Ogawa. She was telling Tillie about the champagne and the disco ball hanging over Boris' bed when Tillie stopped her abruptly.

"You were in Boris' bedroom?"

Embarrassed Betty muttered, "The door to the bedroom was open. I only peeked inside."

Tillie exclaimed, "Betty Chance! In all the time I've known you, you've never flirted with a single man—or a married one. Does this mean you're finally over that idiotic ex-husband of yours and moving on?"

Betty half-smiled. "Looks like I'm over that idiot ex and searching out other idiots." Betty glanced at the bus. "When are we going to use the key? Now?" she asked, wondering if she'd have the nerve to actually go through with Tillie's plan.

Tillie shook her head and turned around, heading back to the hotel. She said, "During Boris' afternoon matinee."

Betty shuffled alongside her. She said, "None of this seems real to me."

Tillie brushed a few snowflakes off her faux fur. She said, "You got that right. Including the bit you told me about Ogawa."

"Which bit?" Betty asked.

Tillie answered, "You said Ogawa showed up at Boris' door, begging for help in learning how to pull a rabbit out of a hat."

"What's odd about that?"

"Remember when you asked me to check on passengers? When I found Ogawa, he was showing someone a card trick."

Betty said, "Well, anyone can learn a few party tricks."

Tillie said, "That's what Ogawa said to me when I told him I was impressed. But one of the other passengers blurted out that Ogawa was the finest magician in all of Belgrade."

"Belgrade? That's in Serbia, isn't it? Ogawa told me he was from Budapest."

Tillie smirked. "Well that's funny, because I heard him tell someone else he was from Krakow and his father was Japanese."

Betty made a quick decision about Ogawa and his little list of things to do. She said, "I guess there's one more thing Ogawa needs to put on his list before he dies."

"What's that?" Tillie asked.

"Learn to tell the friggin' truth."

Chapter 25

At one-thirty in the afternoon Lori headed toward the Hungry Moose Buffet, her hips moving with a cha-cha beat. She was in a wonderful mood. Only seven hours earlier she'd left the poker table $29,000 ahead. Lori couldn't have been happier if she'd won a million bucks.

"Lori," Tony's voice echoed from behind her.

She spun around and shot a Cheshire cat grin at the man who'd helped turn her losing streak around. She was actually surprised to see him walking around free. The last time she saw him he was being escorted by a security force.

"Thank you for staking me," she said, assuming he'd already heard what happened after he left the poker table.

As soon as he reached her he kissed her on the top of her head. He answered, "You're welcome."

Lori fought the urge to instinctively pull away. In reality, she barely knew the man. But for now, forced manners prevailed. She continued, "I would have called your room, but I was worried I'd wake you up. Plus, I didn't exactly know what happened to you after you left."

"You mean after I was forced to leave," he said with a half grin.

"Can I ask what that was all about?" she asked, knowing she was overstepping boundaries. Still, she had watched her date being led away by Men in Black.

"A misunderstanding; nothing more. Sometimes the security underlings get carried away when their boss calls someone in for a chat."

"Tom Songbird?"

Tony nodded. "It's nothing I can get into right now, but if you're worried I can guarantee you I'm one of the good guys."

She nodded as if she completely believed him. In fact, the opposite was true. Too many things had happened on this trip for her to trust anyone.

Lori reached into her purse and pulled out a white envelope. It was stuffed with five thousand dollars. She handed the money to Tony but he held up his palm to reject it. Lori asked, "Are you sure you don't want a cut of my winnings? After all, you're the one who staked me."

He said, "Watching you play is my payback." He slipped his original investment inside his custom-made suit jacket. Even at noon, Tony Gillette was dressed to kill.

They walked together down the hallway as Lori searched for her aunt. Betty had left her a message to meet her in the buffet. Unfortunately, Lori had overslept.

Tony placed his arm around her waist as they walked, and said, "My sources tell me you played like a champion."

Lori flinched. Tony must have felt it and pulled his arm away. She hoped her little action reminded him her affections couldn't be bought, not even for gambling money. She wasn't *that* addicted, she thought. With a jolt she realized once again she referred to herself as an addict.

She pushed the negative thought out of her mind. She'd focus on being positive about her skill as a gambler. "I did play well," Lori said. "In fact, the best I've ever played. After the first few losing hands were dealt, it all turned around in my favor. I couldn't catch a bad card, though maybe it was just luck."

"Poker isn't about luck. It's about skill, which you certainly have."

"Thank you," Lori said quietly. She knew Tony's compliment was sincere. She didn't know him well, but by now she knew he'd never joke about gambling. It wasn't merely a game. It was his livelihood. His life.

After her early morning's astounding win, she now found herself fantasizing about becoming a professional player. It'd certainly solve her little problem of not being able to stop gambling. She wouldn't have to stop. If it was the way she earned a living, who could criticize her habit? If she could muster up a bit more self-control, being a pro would solve all of her problems.

As Tony spoke his next words, Lori wondered if he could read minds like Boris claimed to do.

"Have you ever considered going pro?" Tony asked.

She admitted, "Not until this morning."

"You'd be very good. Plus with your looks, the television networks would be crawling all over each other to get to you."

Lori shrugged her shoulders in modesty. "There are a lot of attractive professional female poker players."

"None of them can compare to you. And with my coaching, there's no telling how far you'd go."

"It's tempting, but I already have a job."

"You just called what you do to earn money a job. Wouldn't you like a career that is a passion? And one that pays a fantastic amount of money?" Tony asked, tempting her more than he knew.

Lori loved running Take A Chance Tours, and adored working with her aunt. But, the little known fact that she kept borrowing from the company's funds was putting both her and her aunt at financial risk. That terrified her. At least if she was self-employed, the only one she could destroy would be herself.

He stepped in front of her and came to a stop. Tony said, "I'll be here until the tournament on Saturday. Is there a chance you could stay?"

"I'm sorry, no. I have to help my aunt. We're scheduled to leave tomorrow, and we still don't have transportation scheduled. After all she's been through I don't think I should leave her."

"Are you sure? I'd really like you to stay," he urged.

"So would I," said another voice that came directly behind her.

Tony's face turned to stone and his eyes glared over Lori's shoulders.

She turned. Severson was standing stoically, practicing his alpha male stance. His legs wide apart, his shoulders squared, and his thumbs rested inside his belt. He looked as if he would draw his pistol at any given moment.

"And just why do you want me to stay, Sheriff?" Lori asked, her voice dripping with sarcasm. "Are you asking me out on a date?"

Severson responded with the same sarcastic tone. "There are two dead bodies connected to your tour company. Remember?"

Lori sputtered back with anger. "I didn't have anything to do with that."

Tony interrupted, "Sheriff, unless you arrest her, you can't force her to stay. I'm confident my team of highly-paid attorneys would agree with me."

Severson responded, "I didn't say I would force her to stay, just that I'd like it if she did. Just like you would like it, except for a very different reason."

"I doubt that, Sheriff." Tony laughed.

Severson shot Tony a look of disdain. "Miss Barnes, I need to talk to you alone."

Lori leaned over and kissed Tony on the cheek. "Thank you again for everything. I'll get ahold of you before I leave Moose Bay."

Tony brushed her long hair from her eyes and then walked away.

Severson placed his arm on Lori's shoulder as he led her toward the hotel elevator. As soon as they were inside Lori held her finger near the control panel, positioning herself to be the one who pressed the button. She asked, "Are we going up?"

Severson shook his head. "No, Lady, you're going down."

Tillie pushed the half eaten piece of chocolate cake as far away as she could. "If I want to keep my brain working, I'd better not have too much sugar."

Betty nodded, looking at the six different deserts she'd laid out in front of her. She'd only taken a bit of each, but she wasn't being wasteful. The casino wouldn't mind. They understood that sampling was part of the process of writing a review. It was as if Betty were a revered sommelier whose nod of approval would bring a round of applause at any five-star restaurant.

She jotted down a few notes in her small leather bound notebook, writing each word carefully. Something had changed in Betty the moment she decided to write a blog. Writing about food, as well as eating it, had become her passion. She was determined her writing would be as good as any cuisine she tasted. She began to see food as a thing of beauty, and not a secret hiding place for her emotions. Her lifelong guilt about enjoying even a miniscule bit of sweetness evaporated. How could she scribble about paper thin discs of dark chocolate sitting atop Jasmine blossom ice cream and not fall in love?

Betty glanced at her watch. "I'm a bit concerned that Lori didn't show up."

"You didn't want her to come with us, did you?" Tillie asked, thinking it would be better if Lori were not part of the Great Baffler Bus Break-In.

Betty shook her head "No, not at all. But since the three of us usually have all of our meals together when we're on tour, I didn't want to do anything out of the ordinary that might attract attention.

Tillie asked, "Do you want me to look for her?"

Betty said, "No, there's no time."

Betty checked her watch. It would be two o'clock by the time they'd finished their meal, the exact time that Boris would be on stage. When they left the buffet, the two women would walk past the show room to make sure the matinee was in full swing. Then they'd hurry to Boris' motor coach.

Betty was feeling a time crunch in more ways than one. Take A Chance Tours was scheduled to leave in twenty-four hours. She still had to find time to do her daily blog posting, as well finish her review of the buffet. She knew her readers wouldn't mind if she were late in blogging, but her advertisers wouldn't be as forgiving.

Betty put her notebook into her shoulder-strap purse. The bag was secure enough that if she had to run for it, it wouldn't get in her way. She was wearing running shoes instead of flats and a lightweight jacket with leather gloves within the pocket. And the basic staple of her daily wardrobe—black elastic waist pants—would be easy to run in. Surprisingly, it had taken her more time than she'd thought to choose an outfit. She wasn't exactly sure what the current fashion trend was for breaking and entering.

Betty shifted about uneasily in her chair. "It's almost time."

"That it is," Tillie said, sounding anxious.

"Are we sure about this?" Betty asked for what seemed like the millionth time since they'd decided Boris' bus had to be searched.

"We have no choice." Tillie said, a trace of doubt in her voice.

She reached over and took a huge bite of chocolate cake. "For energy."

Betty reached over and stabbed the remaining piece.

"We're going to need it," she said.

The two women headed out of the room.

"It's this way," Severson said, pointing down the long, brightly-lit tiled hallway.

Without even asking, Lori knew where they were heading. They were going into the bowels of the casino. Or at least that's what Tom Songbird had called it.

It was the area far below the casino and hotel that made everything possible. Ground level and above was designed for guests and gambling. Underground were the kitchens, laundries, heating and cooling systems and, of course, the main event of the moment—the surveillance room.

Lori relaxed a bit when she saw Tom Songbird waiting for them to arrive. As soon as they reached him, Tom placed his outstretched finger on the keypad and spoke, "Thomas Edison Songbird."

The door to the room slid open and Lori and the sheriff followed him inside.

Lori looked around and uttered, "Wow! I've seen this type of room in movies, but it's way more impressive in person."

Six employees were seated at desks, surrounded by sixty wall monitors. Tom had told her that Moose Bay had over sixteen hundred cameras situated around the property. Every square inch of the casino and hotel, except for bathrooms or guest rooms, was captured on camera.

"This way." Tom said, leading them to the far end of the room. A single monitor, attached to a digital VCR sat on the largest desk in the room. He picked up the remote and hit the start button.

Lori watched as the image of a hotel corridor popped up on the screen.

Severson said, "That's the hallway in front of the penthouse suite where the blood was discovered in the bathroom. The video you're watching was taken fifteen minutes before the anonymous call concerning screams inside the suite."

Lori asked, "Have you had that blood tested yet? Was it human?"

"That's not important, right now. Look," Severson said, his finger pointing toward the screen.

On it, a woman dressed in a bulky black hoodie, black spandex pants, and red high heels stopped in front of the penthouse door. Although the image was crystal clear, Lori couldn't be sure who the woman was. The woman's head was tilted downward. The part of her face that wasn't covered by her hoodie was hidden behind large sunglasses. But, when she reached up to adjust her sunglasses the sleeve on her hoodie slipped down her arm.

"There!" Severson yelled, and Songbird stopped the tape. Songbird zoomed in on the image in front of him until only the woman's wrist filled the screen.

Lori swallowed hard and realized why she had been called into the room. The lady in question was wearing the same bracelet Tillie always wore.

"We want you to verify the woman is Tillie," the sheriff said.

"I, I can't be sure," Lori stuttered. "She dresses like her. I mean, Tillie certainly has her own sense of style. And the bracelet is the same kind that Tillie wears."

"Next image," Severson instructed.

Tom hit the fast-forward button. He stopped within a matter of seconds. The monitor displayed a view of the same woman right outside another hotel door. Lori recognized the room number. It was Betty's.

"This image was taken around the same time your aunt's laptop and cell phone were stolen," Tom informed her. "There's something else we want you to see."

Songbird fast-forwarded to a picture of Mr. Ogawa walking down another hallway.

"Why are you showing me Mr. Ogawa?" she asked, still shaken from seeing what looked like Tillie breaking into hotel rooms.

"Keep watching the tape," Severson demanded.

Lori watched Ogawa walk slowly down the hallway using his cane as support. Then she heard a loud pop. Lori knew that sound. It was the sound of a gun being fired. Obviously, Ogawa recognized the sound as well.

As soon as he heard it, Ogawa's entire demeanor changed. He immediately straightened up in a pose of perfect posture while his face tensed. His body did a quick 360, surveying the entire area with his eyes as he pulled a handgun out of his pocket. When he determined there was nothing to fear, he slipped the gun back into his jacket and assumed his frail, bent posture. He again proceeded to shuffle down the hallway. Lori realized for the briefest of moments, Ogawa appeared to be thirty years younger.

"He's been lying about his age!" Lori exclaimed, acknowledging the incredible performance she'd just witnessed.

Songbird nodded. "Looks that way. We've determined that the pop sound came from a couple of kids lighting firecrackers in their hotel room. But it was loud enough to snap Ogawa out of performance mode."

The tape continued rolling. Lori watched as the frail Ogawa reached the elevators. Even from behind Lori could recognize his hunched back, baggy clothes, and a rear end that was flatter than a...

"Wait a minute!" she yelled. "Rewind back to the image of the woman at the door, the one you think is Tillie."

Songbird rewound the tape and pressed freeze.

Lori instructed, "Zoom in on the woman's butt."

Without questioning Songbird did as she asked. The image of the woman's rear end filled the screen.

Lori said, "I know that butt, and it's not Tillie's. Tillie is always saying the only thing God gave her bigger than her mouth is her butt. That butt is as flat as a pancake, as flat as Ogawa's, and as flat as Boris the Baffler's showgirls."

Chapter 26

"We only have forty-seven minutes left," Betty said anxiously, standing on the steps of Boris' luxury coach.

Tillie unlocked the front door and the two women stepped inside the bus. Tillie asked, "You're wearing gloves, right?"

"Sure am," Betty said. "But remember, there's still a chance the cops could find a strand of our hair or something."

Tillie smirked. "*Please*, that forensic crap is for television. No police department can afford to investigate hair follicles for a B&E. Just remember your promise that you'll take the rap for both of us. It'll be your first offense. You'll get off with community service. But me?"

Betty repeated Tillie's earlier explanation of what would happen to her. "You'll be screwed, and not in a good way."

"Let's get this over with. I'll take this side." Tillie pointed toward the gleaming kitchen area and small flip-up dining table.

Betty began to search her side, which included an eight-foot couch, two swivel chairs, and cabinets.

Tillie slid open a door under the small stainless sink.

"Nothing unusual," she announced while shifting through a bucket of cleaning supplies. She closed the door and began rummaging through the side drawers.

Betty removed the leather couch cushions. She reached deep into the side of the couch. She called out, "Jackpot!"

Tillie swung around on her knees. "What did you find?"

Betty looked embarrassed as she held up a coin. "Sorry. That's what Codey and I would yell when either of us found a quarter in the sofa."

Tillie sighed. "My family didn't yell anything. We'd just tackle each other for it."

The two women continued working as quickly as possible. Betty rushed through the small built-in drawers under the couch while Tillie riffled thorough the rest of the kitchen.

Opening a drawer Tillie uttered, "Wow!" She held up a shimmering fork. "Boris' silverware is real, as in sterling. His eating utensils are worth more than my car."

"His crystal is just as fine," Betty responded.

"I bet his sheets have a thread count of a million." Tillie said, "Oh, I forgot you already know that."

"Tillie! I only peeked inside his bedroom."

"Uh huh," Tillie answered in exaggerated disbelief.

Betty shut the drawers. Her eyes roamed to the framed photos on the walls. There were at least three-dozen. All of them were vintage black and white snapshots of carnival performers. Boris had told her they were of his family.

She checked her wristwatch. "It's been twelve minutes and we haven't found a thing."

"You found twenty-five cents. By the way, did you put it back?"

Betty's face flushed. "Heck, no. I went into automatic and slipped it in my pocket. It seemed like the right thing to do because that's what I've always done."

Tillie replied, "And now you should be able to understand how a criminal thinks. It's doing what seems like the right thing to do at the moment, even though you know it's wrong."

"Like stealing Tampax," Betty responded.

"Like stealing Tampax," Tillie confirmed.

Betty opened a closet door. Inside were shelves of men's shoes, but it was the items on the top shelf that piqued her interest. Stacks of men's inserts were piled high. She held one up in the air.

"Look at this. I had no idea Boris wore lifts."

Tillie walked over, grabbed a shoe out of the closet and studied its sole. "This shoe alone would add four inches to his height."

"And the insert another three," Betty said, peering inside. "I guess he's not tall. In fact, he's kind of short."

Betty said, "Do you realize that everyone, are pretending to be someone they're not?"

Tillie opened the bathroom door. She stepped inside and said, "There's nothing in here that I can see."

Betty pushed back the expandable door to the bedroom. She and Tillie squeezed inside. The room was only big enough for a full-sized side bed with two small nightstands on each side. Like the rest of the bus, the walls were paneled in teak. Maroon curtains hung across the top half of the back wall.

Tillie pointed to the drapes and said, "I could use those after a night shift. Not a drop of golden sun gets through." She looked up. "But I don't need *that*," she said as she pointed her index finger to the center of the ceiling. "Not unless I decide to become kinkier than I already am."

Betty was shocked. She hadn't noticed the small web cam on her previous visit. She'd never been as thankful in her life that she'd turned down sex with a beautiful man.

Betty gestured toward the six framed headshots of Boris that lined the walls, each one featuring a different pose and costume. "I guess Boris doesn't have an issue with self-esteem."

Tillie answered, "Sure he does. That's why he has a half-a-dozen pictures of himself. He has one of those Neapolitan complexes, because he's little."

"Napoleon," Betty said, correcting Tillie's misspeak, but not feeling the need to explain further.

"Yeah, him too," Tillie said, not noticing the correction. "Even with that stupid hat of his, Napoleon was still looking at belly button lint twenty-four seven."

Tillie paused before adding, "This bed is weird."

"Looks nice to me."

"I'm talking about the way it's positioned." Tillie cocked her head. "Most people insist the bed be placed parallel to the road. That way the sleeper doesn't get tossed around as much when the driver hits a pothole."

Betty shrugged. "Maybe the bed's too long to be turned the other way."

Tillie took a quick glance around the room. "I'll be damned."

She swung around and yanked the drapes open. Instead of a window, they covered a solid wall.

"Where's the window?" Tillie asked. She began placing one foot in front of the other and walked toward the front of the bus. As soon as she reached the end she yelled back to Betty, "Fifty-two! It's only fifty-two feet!"

"What are you talking about?" Betty yelled back.

Tillie raced back to Betty's side. She said, "I figure my clunkers are about a foot each in length. According to my fake Blahniks, this bus interior is fifty-two feet long. There's eight feet of bus missing."

"But how could . . .?"

Tillie interrupted, "I know buses, Betty. Trust me, this one is sixty-feet long. I check out every bus I see. And there is a rear window on this motor coach. I've seen it."

"Where is it?"

Tillie said, "Behind the solid wall the drapes were hiding. The back window is inside a secret room."

"Get out!"

"No, really! I'm positive there's a secret room." Tillie spread her gloved hands wide and placed them on the back wall. She began methodically feeling up and down on the wall. She asked, "Do you see anything that could be a button or a switch? Something that could open a secret door or entryway?"

"No."

"Then go through the drawers," Tillie instructed. "It could open by remote control."

Betty rushed to the nightstand and pulled out the drawer. As the contents fell onto the bed, she jumped back quickly into the air as a handgun bounced upon the mattress.

"God, I'm sorry. If this thing had gone off you..."

Tillie interrupted her. "We don't have time for apologies. Give me that thing."

Betty reluctantly handed the gun to her. Tillie clicked on the safety but instead of handing it back, Tillie slipped the gun inside one of the pockets of her coat and zipped it shut.

"Tillie, I don't think you..."

"Keep looking for a door. We're running out of time."

Reluctantly, Betty returned to her search, concerned that the former felon she knew as a friend was in possession of a weapon. If Tillie were found with a gun, she'd definitely end up back in jail.

Betty rummaged through the drawer, announcing each of her finds to Tillie. "One tube of chap stick, two bottles of lotion. Oh, ick! Six packages of condoms, a boxed DVD, and oh ick again, double ick!"

Tillie turned around. "What did you find?"

"The DVD's an adult DVD," Betty admitted.

"Big deal," Tillie answered.

"That's the problem. It is a big deal. Now, I know why Boris was attracted to me. I'm a fetish!" Betty held the DVD up in the air so Tillie could read the title.

"*Big Old Mommas Gone Wild,*" Tillie read out loud before adding, "I wonder if there's a series called *Redheaded Bus Drivers I'd Like To...*"

"Okay, back to work!" Betty interrupted and glanced at her watch. "The show's over in eighteen minutes."

"Check out the other areas in the bus for switches, or a remote," Tillie instructed.

Betty rushed to the front and pressed every button and switch she could find, also jiggling the thermostat, pushing every number on the microwave, and working the TV remote in the living area. Nothing did anything except what it was supposed to do.

"Wait a minute!" Tillie yelled from the back room and rushed to Betty's side.

"I'm smaller than you, right?"

"Give or take eighty pounds."

"Go to the bedroom and wait for me."

Betty watched as Tillie scrambled off the bus. She raced to the bedroom. Whatever Tillie had in mind was important.

Betty's heart skipped a beat. She didn't know if she was excited or terrified. She'd always wanted to be a cop, to be one of the good guys chasing down the bad. She just didn't envision doing it as a fifty-five-year-old tour operator.

"Betty? Can you hear me?" Tillie's voice was coming through the back wall.

"Yes!"

"I think I found the switch to the secret room," Tillie yelled. Within seconds the door on the back wall slid open. Tillie stood in the middle of the once hidden room. Breathless, she said, "Not only did I find the switch back here to open the wall up, but I figured out the entrance to this secret room is located in the luggage compartment underneath the coach. That's how I got into this room. I entered through the luggage compartment. I'm small enough to fit."

"But not Boris, Rose, or Slevitch."

"Or Farsi, or anyone else of size. Bottom line, whoever could squeeze through the luggage compartment was in control of the room."

"And that alone could tick off a plus-sized crony."

"Enough to kill?"

"Maybe. Take a gander at what's hidden back here."

Tillie stepped aside and Betty entered the tiny room.

A countertop rested along the backside of the room. In the center sat a computer along with inkjet printer and a paper cutter. The shelves above the counter were divided into sections, filled with bottles of brown and green liquids, reams of paper, and what appeared to be stacks of blank plastic cards. A blow dryer sat next to them.

"Look at that thing," Tillie said, pointing toward the elaborate ceiling exhaust fan.

"That's pretty fancy for a bus."

"Not if you're using chemicals."

"You think Boris is a counterfeiter?" Betty asked, wondering why she bothered asking the obvious.

Tillie said, "They're *all* counterfeiters. This isn't a one-man job. See the sink? Remember how Rose claimed to work at a Laundromat? And how Boris glared at her?"

Betty's face lit up in recognition. "Boris was furious at Rose for admitting onstage what they were up to! Not only are they counterfeiters, but they're laundering money."

"Not exactly," Tillie said. "I think Rose was complaining about having to wash *new* currency to make it look old. See the chemicals and the sink?"

Betty asked, "You know how this counterfeiting thing works?"

"Counterfeiting was one of the trades I learned in jail, just in case my sobriety didn't work out. I called it my 13th step. It's actually pretty easy to do. Any kid with a thirty-dollar ink jet can turn five bucks into a fortune."

Betty said, "Until he gets caught."

Tillie responded, "Most people get caught because they're stupid. Boris and his gang aren't dumb. Look at what they're making." Tillie pulled out a printed piece of paper from the printer feed. She showed Betty the front and flipped it around to show the back of it. "Three perfect looking five-dollar bills on one sheet."

"Fifteen dollars that cost pennies to make," Betty said in understanding.

"Look around you." Tillie used her index finger to count the reams. She stopped at twenty-four. "Five hundred sheets multiplied by twenty-four equals 12,000 sheets."

Betty did a quick mental calculation. "At fifteen dollars on one sheet, that's $180,000 in fake bills. Just think what they would have if they'd printed a hundred dollar bill."

Tillie answered, "They wouldn't. They're too smart. Who checks a five-dollar bill? You walk into a store with a hundred, odds are the clerk will hold it up to a light. But paying with a crummy old Abe Lincoln? Who gives a crap?"

Betty held a printed sheet of bills in the air. "Honest Abe, indeed," she said. Then asked, "How do they get the bills to look old?"

"They're dipped in iodine and whatever else they come up with. Look at the date on the bill." Tillie handed Betty the sheet.

"1988," Betty read aloud.

"That's because after that the feds have all sorts of do-dads to check any new currency. Like a security strip hidden in the paper next to Abe's face. Look at the packaging on one of the unopened reams of paper. Tell me who makes it."

Betty slipped a ream from one of the shelving units. "I can't tell. The printing on the packaging is foreign."

"Exactly. This paper was probably made in China or Iran. The paper you buy at Office Max is made in the good old USA from wood pulp. The stuff Boris is using is made from cotton fiber, just like the paper the Feds use."

"You do know a lot about this," Betty said in awe.

"Prison 101."

"So you're saying that if a clerk touches one of their counterfeit bills, it feels right?" Betty asked.

"And looks okay," Tillie nodded. "That's where Rose comes in. The chemicals she uses makes the bills feel and look old. But that's not all that's going on." Tillie picked up one of the thin black cards. "Can you guess what they're doing with this?"

"They're counterfeiting credit cards?" Betty asked, looking around for a machine of some sort that would emboss the cards.

"Not credit cards. The plastic is too thin for that, but not thin enough for a microchip. Inside one of these suckers is a chip strong enough to override a slot machine's computer once it's slipped inside the ticket-in, ticket-out slot."

"Hannah claimed there were too many jackpots being won," Betty recalled.

Tillie added, "Including one for thirteen million dollars."

Betty scanned the room once more. "There's enough evidence here to put Boris away for eternity. We've got to find the sheriff."

"I agree. You head out the front and I'll leave the same way I came in, through the luggage compartment."

"But, it'll be quicker to use the front door."

"I want everything to look normal, in case Boris gets back here before we do," Tillie insisted.

Betty stepped out of the room and watched as Tillie pressed a switch. The wall slid shut and Tillie disappeared from sight.

As Betty turned to leave she heard a small whirring sound and looked up. The web cam that she and Tillie thought was for bedroom games was following her every step. Betty raced outside and down the slippery steps. According to her wristwatch, the matinee was over in a matter of minutes.

"Hurry up!" Betty cried, waiting for Tillie to emerge from the compartment underneath the bus.

She waited only a few seconds more before she went blank.

Chapter 27

Aunt Betty! Wake up!"

Someone was shaking Betty's shoulders like they were a sack of Idahos. For the briefest of moments she hoped it was only a bad dream, one that included a hand grenade detonating inside her head. A shock of icy cold startled Betty awake. Kneeling above her was Lori, who was holding a second handful of snow poised to be tossed into Betty's face.

Betty asked, "Did I fall again?"

"Not unless you tripped on a stuffed sock," Lori said, holding up a bulging athletic sock tied tightly at the top with a pink ribbon.

Betty pulled herself into an upright position and looked around, still confused. She mumbled, "Tillie?"

Lori misunderstood what her aunt was asking. "It wasn't Tillie who did this. I was halfway across the parking lot when I saw that Irish woman and Ogawa running towards you. You know, the one who was on stage when Slevitch was killed?"

"She's Serbian, not Irish. And her name isn't Kelly, it's Rose," Betty informed her, as she stood upright.

Lori said, "Well, whoever she is, she struck you across the back of your head with this sock filled with pennies. You went down immediately."

"You said Ogawa was running?" Betty rubbed her forehead. If she was going to continue being an amateur detective, she'd better start carrying aspirin.

"Like a fifty-year old athlete," Lori answered.

Ogawa probably took lessons from Kevin Spacey's performance in *The Usual Suspects*—or the other way around. In a flash Betty realized Boris' tour bus is was no longer there. It was missing. And so was Tillie.

"Did you see Tillie get *off* the bus?" Betty asked.

Lori answered, "No. All I saw was Rose and Ogawa jumping on. They drove that way." Lori pointed her finger northward.

Betty could see the purple and white vehicle as it sped past cars and maneuvered around snow blowers. She pointed at the speeding motor coach. "Tillie's inside the secret room. We've got to stop it."

Lori's gaze took on a look of concern. "Secret room? Aunt Betty, are you feeling okay?"

"Yes," Betty answered, although the inside of her head whirled like a Maytag on rinse. "Trust me, there's a secret room in that bus and Tillie is inside it."

"I'll call Severson," Lori responded as she opened her purse to find her cell.

"Call him from there," Betty pointed toward the roped-off Take A Chance bus. "We don't have a second to lose."

"But..."

"We have to follow Ogawa now!" Betty said, already sprinting toward the bus.

For the first time in her life Betty's extra weight acted as propulsion, forcing her body forward at break-neck speed. She could tell her niece was struggling to keep up. Within a minute, Betty was at the side of the Take A Chance bus and yanking yellow crime scene tape off its door.

Betty lowered herself onto the frigid asphalt and reached underneath the frame. She felt around for a few seconds and announced, "I know Tillie keeps a spare key somewhere down here." She pulled out a small black metal box. "Here it is!"

Sounding surprised, Lori said, "I have a magnetic box like that for my car. She has one for a friggin' bus?"

"It's a south side Chicago thing," Betty said as she slid open the top of the little container. She removed a key and opened the door. "Moms make their daughters hide a key in case their boyfriend wants more than a kiss. And Tillie will always be, no matter how tough she thinks she is, a South Side Girly-Girl."

Betty didn't bother to pull down the steps, but instead hoisted herself up and onto the landing.

Lori followed her, while managing to look inside her purse. As she began to rummage through her pockets, she groaned, "I don't have my phone!"

"We'll use the phone on the bus to call the dispatcher." Betty held the ignition key out to Lori. "You take the wheel."

Lori stared at the maze of pedals in front of her. "I can't. I've never driven a manual transmission."

Betty said, "Okay, I'll drive."

"You've driven a stick?" Lori asked.

"Once," Betty answered, sliding into the driver's seat.

"Once?"

"When I was sixteen" Betty said, slipping the key into the ignition.

Lori stood next to her. She grabbed the vertical bar.

Betty started the engine, pushed the clutch pedal down, shifted into first and stepped on the gas. The bus took off with a jolt that tossed Lori back onto the front seat.

The windshield was dirty causing Betty to squint to see through it. She fiddled with buttons and levers and managed to turn the windshield wipers on. Another switch splashed washer fluid over the entire window. But the frigid weather outside made the wiper fluid freeze almost instantly. Blowing snow also played havoc with her limited vision. If the wind gusts picked up speed, she'd soon be dealing with driving in a blizzard.

Lori pointed toward the stoplight a quarter mile away. "Ogawa's bus is stopped behind an RV at the casino entrance."

Betty could see half a dozen news reporters and their trucks stationed along the shoulders of the road up ahead. She knew there was no way Ogawa could get around them safely. She might be able to catch up with him after all.

Betty shifted into a higher gear, and pressed her foot hard against the gas pedal. The Take A Chance bus leapt over a concrete curb. She deftly guided the vehicle back onto the road.

"Sorry," she said.

Lori shouted, "The light's turned green. Ogawa's turning left."

"They're heading to the freeway," Betty said, worried. The expressway was only five miles away.

"I'll bet they try to make it to Canada," Lori added, right before her aunt scraped the sides of both a parked Volvo and a rusted pick-up.

"Crap," Betty mumbled, gripping the steering wheel even tighter. She shifted gears. The sound of clunks and squeals rattled the air. The engine revved like a motorcycle driven by a teenager on his first ride.

"I hate stick shifts," she muttered.

"Canada's what? A few hours from here?" Lori asked, standing up. She used one hand to hold onto the vertical bar again, and her other to pick up the phone receiver from the instrument board.

"Yeah, but the wilderness area starts way before the border. That means they'll be able to drive on dirt roads that weave through the woods. They'll be able to sneak across the border before anyone can find them."

Lori kept pushing buttons. "How does this stupid thing . . .?" She blurted, "Watch out!"

Betty didn't flinch. She drove straight through the red stoplight. Somehow she managed to turn left in the process without tipping the bus over. But she did knockdown a road sign or two.

Betty exhaled a "whew" and mumbled another, "Sorry."

"Stop apologizing," Lori stated, sitting down in the front seat and snapping a seat belt around her. "Because I have a feeling you'll be doing it every other minute."

Betty felt the tires skid on a patch of black ice and the bus sliding toward the snow banks along the side of the road. She was able to steer the vehicle back onto the road before a collision with a passing car. But the swerving motion must have frightened the other driver. He lost control of his dark green Chevy Blazer and careened into a powdery ditch.

In her rearview mirror Betty caught a glimpse of the upset driver giving her a one-finger salute through his rolled-down window.

Lori said, "Should I try to figure out how to contact the dispatcher again?"

"Forget about it," Betty told her.

"But, we've got to let the police..."

"Trust me, we just sideswiped two parked cars in a casino parking lot, ran an SUV off the road and took out a few road signs, and we did it all in front of a news crew. The police have already been called."

"Are you sure?"

Suddenly, out of nowhere, a silver Porsche appeared on her left. As it sped by, Betty read the license plate, *Baffler 2*.

Boris was at the wheel.

She glanced at the speedometer. The speed limit on the narrow and curvy country road was thirty-five mph. Boris had to be driving sixty. She was already going fifty-five. And Boris' bus was going faster than she was.

As if reading her mind Lori asked, "How fast can this thing go?"

"Let's find out," Betty answered, and pushed the pedal to the floor.

Betty saw that Lori was hanging onto her seat for dear life, yet she was more concerned for Tillie. There was no telling what was happening to her friend. If she were still trapped inside the luggage compartment, she was undoubtedly being tossed around like a guppy in a hurricane. But if Rose and Ogawa had already discovered Tillie inside the bus there was no telling what could be happening to her.

Betty watched as Boris' Porsche flew over a hill while driving in the wrong lane. She waited to hear the chilling sound of an impact. There was nothing. Three seconds later, a Dodge Caravan came over the same hill in the same lane that Boris had used. Amazingly, he avoided killing the horrified family in the passing mini-van.

Betty stared straight ahead, wondering what would happen next. She announced, "If there are police cars in the area, Severson will ask them to set up a roadblock, probably at the freeway entrance, or further down the road.

Lori turned to look behind her and said, "I think Tom told me the town only has two units."

"Then Severson will call in the State troopers," Betty assured her.

"What happens if they set up a road block and..."

Betty finished her sentence for her, "And Ogawa decides *not* to stop?"

Lori asked, "Do you think he would do that? That would put all of their lives at risk, including his."

Betty answered, "To be honest, I don't see why he wouldn't."

She realized Ogawa would be facing two counts of murder as well as charges of counterfeiting and casino tampering. He'd truly be old and stooped before he was eligible for parole.

Lori pointed to the bus in front of them and asked, "What's that?"

Betty stared straight ahead as the wind tossed snowflakes around the prairie landscape like confetti at a Macy's Thanksgiving Day Parade. "What's what?" Betty asked, not noticing what Lori was referring to.

"There! That thing hanging out of the side window of Boris's bus. Is it a flag or something? Do you think they want to surrender?" Lori asked.

Suddenly, the *thing* flew away from whomever or whatever was holding it. The wind propelled it straight back and toward the Take A Chance bus. At the speed they were going, if it was something harder than clothing, it would have crashed through the window killing them both. But it was only fabric. Still, it terrified the two of them.

"My god," Betty gasped, barely able to keep the bus under control as she stared at the large piece of cloth that covered a large part of the windshield. Dark, red liquid oozed from the fabric and smeared across the glass as the wiper struggled to fling it off.

It took a moment before Betty could admit what she saw in front of her.

"That's Tillie's shirt."

Chapter 28

The Baffler's motor coach careened down the icy highway as the Take A Chance tour bus followed in high-speed pursuit.

"That blouse cost me twenty-seven dollars!" Tillie yelled at Rose, who still hung partially out of the window as Ogawa drove. For a change, Ogawa was acting his age, his real age. The man had to be in his early sixties, not eighties like he claimed.

"I wanted to make a point," Rose answered, pulling herself back inside the bus.

"What point? That you don't appreciate fine fashion?" Tillie growled.

Rose snarled back. "That the next thing I toss out on the highway will be you, if you don't shut up."

Tillie bit down on her own lip to stop from saying what she wanted to say. Instead, she counted slowly to ten before she spoke out loud. "They're going to catch you."

"No, they won't!" Rose retorted. "Don't you think we know what we're doing? We've rehearsed our getaway a dozen times."

"This isn't penitentiary theater, Rose. The sheriff won't be shooting blanks. His bullets are going to be real."

"So are ours," Rose replied in a practiced monotone.

"Hey, what happened to your accent?" Tillie asked.

"I'm speaking with an American accent. Notice how my words sound as if they're coming out of my nose instead of my throat? I've perfected the annoying, twangy sound you Americans are so fond of."

"Sounds fine to me," Tillie huffed as the bus slowed momentarily and curved to the right. Tillie could see that Ogawa was entering the freeway ramp, heading north. She said, "I gotta ask, how did you open the door to the secret room? I thought the only way inside was through the luggage compartment."

"You stupid American. My Ogawa can open anything, and he can shut anything as well. Including your mouth," Rose warned.

Tillie fidgeted uncomfortably on the couch. Her hands were bound with a silk belt from one of Boris' robes. Her ankles were tied together as well. Rose had forced her to take off her jacket and blouse. The jacket was still sitting on the couch. The gun Tillie had found in the secret room was still inside the jacket. Her ketchup-covered blouse was somewhere on the road behind them. She was wearing only her spandex pants and a pink lace brassiere, her cleavage fully exposed. Tillie observed Rose was focused completely on Tillie's breasts.

"I didn't know you found women so attractive. Did prison do that to you? Or were you that way before?" Tillie asked.

Rose's hateful glare intensified. "I was looking at your stupid vulture tattoo."

"Vulture? Did you flunk your citizenship test? It's a bald eagle Rose, our national symbol. Really, you ought to be ashamed of yourself for being so stupid."

"Stupid?" Rose yelled. "You call me stupid, you worthless whore!"

"Who are you calling a whore? I may be easy, but I'm not for sale," Tillie hollered back.

"Shut up!" Ogawa demanded from the front. Tillie saw his narrow eyes reflected in the rearview mirror. She watched as his eyes drifted to her chest.

"Stop ogling my boobs, you old perv!" Tillie shouted.

"Oga!" Rose screamed, placing her hands on her hips to emphasize her point. When she did, the bus listed sideways and Rose grabbed onto a cabinet door for support. Through gritted teeth she growled, "I told you if I ever caught you looking at another woman, I'd divorce you! I'm tired of you cheating on me with every slut that comes your way!"

"Hey, I'm not a slut either!" Tillie said, defending herself again. But Rose's jealous outburst made her realize Slevitch hadn't been Rose's husband. Ogawa, who was one-third the size of Rose, had that honor.

Tillie decided to use Rose's jealousy to her advantage. If Rose didn't want her husband staring at Tillie's jiggling boobs, she might demand Tillie put her jacket back on to cover her breasts. Tillie would be that much closer to the handgun that was hidden inside the zipped pocket. Tillie's words rolled off her tongue like honey when she asked Ogawa, "Hey, are you that famous Serbian actor Rose said she married?"

Ogawa didn't answer but Tillie saw a slight smile on his face reflected in the rearview mirror.

Her next words tumbled out in an exaggerated breathless tone. "I think I could be an actress. Some people think I look like an older shorter Marilyn Monroe," she said, inhaling rapidly, her breasts moving up and down like a pair of ripe cantaloupes in a runaway supermarket cart.

Ogawa didn't respond, but Rose did manage to kick her in the shin. "Stop flirting with my husband, you slut," Rose yelled.

"Ouch," Tillie yelled back before adding, "What husband? You just said you were going to divorce him."

"I am," Rose shot back, giving Ogawa the evil eye. "He's dead to me now. But that doesn't mean you're still not a slut."

"Yeah, but at least I'm the slut who broke up your marriage," Tillie snarled.

Tillie said ouch again as Rose kicked her once more.

Tillie needed to get at the gun. If flirting with Ogawa could give her the opportunity, she'd go for it. Or perhaps she could figure another way to get loose. However, she also didn't want Rose to pick up her jacket. The extra weight alone could tip Rose off that something was in the pocket that shouldn't be.

"You look a lot younger than the eighty-eight years you claimed to be," Tillie cooed to Ogawa. "What are you, in your sixties, like Rose?"

Rose responded in a snit. "I'm fifty-four! And I'm constantly told I could pass for thirty-four."

"By who? The little voices inside your head?" Tillie asked.

Rose pulled her foot back in full attack mode, but Ogawa hollered,

"Rose, stop kicking the hostage."

Hostage? Tillie wondered. That's what she was to them? She thought she was only an intruder they'd discovered standing inside their secret room.

Tillie muttered, "Thank you, Mr. Ogawa." After a brief pause, she added, "I was being honest when I said you had me and everyone else fooled. Until I saw you with your shoulders straight and your old man shuffle gone, I had no idea. Even your voice sounds different. Before that, I would have sworn you were an octogenarian. I've got to say, you're one great actor."

"Thank you," he answered, pushing the accelerator down even further.

Good, Tillie thought, *the little man's ego is bigger than his brain*. Tillie knew she could work with that. If nothing else, she could keep the two of them playing *good kidnapper—bad kidnapper* for a while, to keep them distracted.

Tillie continued talking. "If you think you can hold me for a huge ransom, you can't. I'd bring in a hundred dollars, tops. My friends aren't rich and my family wouldn't pay a dime to get me back. In fact, they'd pay you to keep me."

Rose responded in a condescending tone. "We don't need money. We'll use you to negotiate with the police."

"You think they're going to make a deal so I can be let go? The sheriff thinks I'm worthless. Want to know what he said to me? It's something even *you* could understand, Rose. He said 'Once a con, always a con.'"

Ogawa interrupted, "Boris just sped by. Hang out the window Rose, and see if anyone else is following us besides the tour bus. That's as far as I can see."

Rose lowered the window again and hoisted her large body halfway through the window.

Tillie said, "If you open your mouth and pant, you'll look just like a Saint Bernard."

Rose leaned back inside and slapped Tillie then leaned out the window again.

Tillie bent forward and said, "Listen, Ogawa, like I said, the sheriff hates me. I'm positive he'll try to convince a jury that I'm part of your gang."

"What gang?" Ogawa said. "We don't have a gang. We're a family."

Tillie said, "Well, you're not exactly the Brady Bunch."

Ogawa retorted, "We do what we need to do to survive."

"Me too, and I'll do whatever it takes not to go back to prison again," Tillie said. She felt ashamed that what she was saying was true.

"Humph," came the reply from Rose, her upper body still dangling in the frigid air.

Tillie wondered if she leaned hard enough to the left, if she could knock Rose completely out the window. As soon as Tillie edged close to her, Rose pulled back inside.

Rose announced, "There's a bunch of red lights flashing a few miles behind us."

"Damn," Ogawa said, "Rose check the map in the glove box. See if you can find an alternate route."

As Rose searched the glove box for the map, Tillie butted in. "Rose will take too long to find it. Let me help. I've been driving these roads for years. I know them backwards and forwards."

Tillie wasn't exactly telling the truth. She'd never been farther north than Moose Bay. When Ogawa didn't respond, she continued, "Plus, you're only driving sixty. I can go faster, no problem. I'm a professional bus driver."

Rose spat in her face and asked, "Why should we trust you?"

Tillie shook her head, trying to shake off the spittle from her cheek. "Because I'm inside the same speeding death ship you are. If your husband's going to kill us all, I'm part of the us that will be killed."

"My husband is an excellent driver!" Rose blurted out. "Everyone in our family is, especially Boris."

Ah ha! Tillie thought. If Rose and Ogawa were married, Boris was probably their son. The two showgirls might even be their daughters. Boris and the women shared ebony-colored hair and razor sharp cheekbones. Their almond shaped eyes hinted of an oriental night time visitor to some ancestor, generations ago.

But who the heck were Farsi and Slevitch? If they were *family*, why were they disposed of as easily as used Kleenex during flu season?

Tillie continued, "I can tell Ogawa's a good driver, but not in this case. Maneuvering a vehicle of this size at this speed takes practice. Let me help. Besides, I need a job. There's no way in hell anyone else will hire me after a body was found stabbed to death in a bus that I left unlocked."

"It didn't matter if it was locked or unlocked," Rose scoffed. "Oga went through the skylight."

Tillie should have felt relief on hearing that Ogawa didn't enter the bus through doors she had forgotten to lock. She would have thanked him if she wasn't screaming, "Watch out!"

Ogawa steered the bus to the left, missing by mere inches the car parked along the edge of the highway. The man chatting on his cell phone hadn't even noticed he was a millisecond away from becoming road kill.

Gripping the wheel tightly, Ogawa asked, "Are you sure you can grab the wheel safely and take over without tipping us over?"

"No problem. I've done it before," Tillie lied.

Tillie saw Ogawa staring into the side rearview mirror. She could hear sirens gaining on them. She knew the Take A Chance bus was close behind, although she had no idea who was driving. She prayed silently it wasn't Betty. Her friend could probably run into three cars, a truck and a goat while sitting at a stop sign.

"Untie her, Rose," Ogawa demanded.

Rose growled at him. "Are you sure?"

"Do it!" he insisted.

With her nostrils flared, Rose reached down and untied Tillie's hands. Tillie rubbed her wrists for a few seconds before bending over and untying her ankles.

"Stand up," Rose demanded.

Tillie immediately lifted herself and reached for her jacket.

"What do you think you're doing?" Rose snapped.

"I don't want you or your hubby staring at my tits," Tillie explained.

Ogawa demanded, "Let her put it on Rose. It'll draw less attention from truck drivers that pass."

Rose mumbled a few Serbian words while Tillie quickly grabbed her jacket and zipped it up. She could feel the pistol rubbing against her side. With any luck, she'd be able to grab the gun as she drove.

"Get in front," Rose yelled, and pushed her toward the seated Ogawa.

Tillie watched Ogawa deftly push his seat backwards while maintaining control of the bus. Keeping one foot on the gas, he partially stood up and yelled, "Slide!"

She understood what to do. She slid underneath Ogawa, as he lifted his lean torso up and away from the seat. He continued to hold onto the steering wheel. As soon as Tillie's rear hit the seat she grabbed the wheel, Ogawa quickly let go, and Tillie placed her foot on the gas pedal. In a matter of seconds the two had exchanged places.

"Don't do anything stupid," Ogawa demanded.

Tillie knew he was concerned she'd choose to slam on the brakes or crash the bus on purpose, hoping she'd live, even if no one else did.

"I won't," she lied, just as she felt the cylinder of a handgun press into her temple.

Tillie was impressed. Not only was Ogawa a great actor, he was also a master pickpocket.

Chapter 29

Betty clicked on the windshield wipers, causing Tillie's shirt to fly into the air. It landed in a snow-covered median strip on the highway. She was terrified of the driving conditions but grateful the road was recently plowed. From her viewpoint, the entire planet looked as if it were sculpted from snow and ice.

Betty's foot continued to press heavily on the gas pedal as she struggled with shifting. *Clutch up...gas pedal down...clutch up*, she kept repeating. It was the only thing she remembered from Driver's Ed forty years earlier. That, and if the engine sounded like it was about to break in two from grinding, something needed to be done immediately—like shifting, clutching, braking, and mumbling seventeen Hail Mary's.

Lori asked, "Do you think we should slow down to let the cops pass?"

"I'm afraid if I slow down, I'll kill the engine. If they want to pass us, they will." She hoped it were that easy. "Reach into my purse," she instructed. "Grab my iPod and plug it into the speaker. Play anything. It'll help me focus on my driving." A blaring film score would be better to listen to than police sirens. Plus, the powerful, emotional music would reinforce her feelings of being a warrior woman.

Lori did as requested, and as the music started, Betty shouted, "Not that one! Any album but that one." John William's poignant score to *Schindler's List* was not what Betty needed to hear at the moment. She already had enough to cry about, without listening to that.

Lori clicked on *Raiders of the Lost Ark*.

"Perfect!" Betty said. Indiana Jones to the rescue. The first few notes immediately made her feel like she was destined to be Tillie's heroine after all.

Lori lowered the volume and said, "I have to ask you a question."

The bus hit another patch of ice and began to slide into the next lane. Betty hung onto the wheel with all of her strength. She managed to maneuver the bus back into the proper lane.

When she caught her breath Betty answered, "Sure."

Lori's voice sounded angry. "What were you and Tillie thinking? Why were you playing cops and robbers at your age?"

Betty didn't take offense. She knew Lori had a right to be mad at her for doing something so idiotic. "I told you, we were looking for evidence."

"Didn't it cross your mind how dangerous that was? If I did anything like that, you'd skin me alive," Lori protested.

Feeling chagrined, Betty explained, "We weren't going in completely blind. We had a plan."

"Oh, a plan?" Lori answered sarcastically. "Well, that's good to know. How's that plan working for you?"

"Not so great," Betty answered, her eyes focused on the speeding fourteen-ton vehicle in front of her that held her friend captive.

"So, did you find anything in your quest?" Lori asked.

"Like I said before, counterfeiting equipment, plastic strips that can trick a slot machine into paying out. That sort of thing."

"Anything else?"

Betty waited before she answered. It would be painful to tell her niece but she couldn't lie to her anymore. "A handgun."

"Handgun! Was it loaded?"

"Probably."

"Where is it?"

"We're chasing it."

"It's hard to concentrate with you holding a nine-millimeter to the side of my head," Tillie said as pleasantly as she could. Now was not the time to tick Ogawa off, not with a Glock in his hand.

"Funny, you didn't think it would be hard to concentrate when this little goodie was nestled in your pocket," Ogawa reminded her.

While keeping her eyes on the road for patches of ice, passing cars, possible stray wildlife like deer or moose, Tillie said, "I gotta say, you're one hell of a thief, Ogawa. I didn't feel a thing when you lifted the gun from me."

Rose piped in from behind. "My Oga can do anything. He's a magician, a singer, a contortionist, a . . ."

"Contortionist?" Tillie interrupted.

Rose puffed up and folded her arms in triumph. "See Oga, I told you she was stupid. She doesn't even know what that is."

Tillie knew what the word meant. It just surprised her she hadn't thought of it before. A contortionist, especially one as small as Ogawa, could have squeezed his upper torso through the tiny skylight and surprise Farsi with a knife in his back.

"Mr. Ogawa, do you do all that weird stuff like dislocating your shoulders to fit into places?" She asked, nonchalantly.

"It's called double-jointed, idiot!" Rose barked.

Tillie envisioned Rose's Oga during the coffee break at Tyler Falls. The rest of her passengers were inside the truck stop. They were loading up on candy treats and tourist trinkets while Ogawa changed from acting like an old man courting death, to a world-class contortionist. As agile as he was, he easily could have climbed onto the top of the bus and used his skills to reach into the crammed space and stab Farsi.

That part was clear to her. What she didn't understand was why he killed Farsi. And Slevitch. Especially if they were part of a family as Ogawa claimed, and not just crooks.

Rose waved her hands frantically and pointed toward the rear of the bus. "They're gaining on us!"

"Faster!" Ogawa demanded.

Tillie glanced at the speedometer. She was already pushing seventy miles an hour in conditions that warranted forty, max. Not only was there ice and snow on the road, the gusts of wind were growing stronger causing snowflakes to frantically swirl in the air. A blizzard was forming right in front of her eyes.

"Look at that!" Rose screamed and pointed toward the other side of the highway, where two speeding highway patrol cars were coming from the opposite direction.

Tillie could hear their piercing blasts as their lights flashed red. At the very last instant, a patrol car swerved around a slow moving snowplow. Tillie knew there was no way the patrol cars could cross the snow covered median. But the fact they were there meant the authorities to the north knew what was going on as well. Ogawa must have realized that little bit of insight as well.

He said, "Get off at the next exit or sooner if you can find a way to do it."

Tillie nodded, knowing there was no way she was going to attempt to play hopscotch on a snow-covered embankment. Not yet, not while there was a chance she could still live. She also didn't want to pull off the road and drive over what looked like white, bare flat tracts of land. In the winter what looked like simple plains could be very misleading. Frozen ground wasn't necessarily hidden beneath. Underneath the snow a half-frozen lake might be waiting. Its thick layer of ice would shatter like crystal under the weight of the bus.

"Where are we heading? Winnipeg?" Tillie asked, keeping her eyes on the road. With every hill she ascended she prayed there wasn't a slow moving anything on the other side. Hitting a deer at the speed she was going could kill them as easily as running into a stalled semi or a parked snowplow.

"Maybe," Ogawa answered, "maybe not."

"We have to go there, Oga. Boris will be waiting for us," Rose reminded him.

Tillie took the opportunity to ask, "Is Boris your son? He looks like you Rose. He's so handsome." Tillie knew Boris didn't look anything like Rose. But what mother wouldn't take that little lie to be the truth?

"I know," Rose answered.

"And the showgirls, your daughters?" Tillie asked.

"My nieces," Rose said her face taking on a concerned look.

Tillie jumped at the chance to chum up to Rose. "Are you worried about them? They're so young. Are you afraid the cops grabbed them before they could get away?"

Rose shook her head. "They know what to do. I'm sure they're safe. But, thank you for asking."

That was the first time Rose had ever thanked Tillie for anything, or been civil to her. For a brief second, Tillie thought she might be able to wheedle herself into the family, after all. She shook her head in disgust at even entertaining the thought for a moment. Larceny may have been in her background, but murder would never be in her future.

Tillie asked coyly, "So was Farsi your brother or cousin?"

Stone cold silence was the only answer to her question. Rose just dropped her head, and Oga's face grew sterner. Tillie continued anyway. "And Slevitch? Was he your relative, too? And are the girls . . ."

"Shut up and drive," Ogawa yelled.

Tillie bit her lip. She'd find out soon enough who everyone was. If she lived, that is.

The terrain was becoming hillier as they advanced farther north. With every incline she braced herself. The speedometer read seventy-one. For the first time in her life, she might push a bus to eighty.

As soon as she reached the next hilltop, Tillie saw the lone man in the distance. Around a mile and a half up the road a patrol car was parked horizontally across the highway. A single patrolman stood on the side of the car, aiming his pistol straight at them.

Tillie instantly analyzed the situation. There was no way she could drive around the car without putting the officer's life in peril. The bus would certainly clip the patrol car and both the car and the man would be catapulted into eternity.

Tillie reached over to shift the gears down when Ogawa screamed, "Don't slow down!"

She cautiously placed her foot lightly on the brake as Ogawa pushed the gun harder into her temple. He demanded, "Turn off the road."

"Where?" Tillie asked straining to see an exit through the frosty window. "I don't see an exit."

Ogawa bellowed, "Turn!"

He placed his free hand on the wheel and began to steer it to the right. Tillie had to go along with his actions. If she tried to yank the wheel back to the left, they'd end up rolling over for sure. Or worse yet, Ogawa could pull the trigger either by accident or not.

"I'll do what you want!" she screamed.

Ogawa released his hand. Tillie could feel the hair on the nape of her neck stand in terror. She took a deep breath and, with all of her strength, turned the steering wheel one hundred and sixty degrees. The bus ran over a bump of some kind and soared in the air for a moment and then landed, continuing upright.

Without losing a beat, Tillie steered down the side of the ditch and then up the other side. As soon as she reached the top, the rear of the bus hit the embankment and fishtailed left, and then right. The bus, still going at a dangerous speed, toppled over. The last thing Tillie saw was her world turn upside down—then going blacker than she could ever have imagined.

Betty and Lori each let out a cry of anguish at the same moment. They'd watched in horror as Boris' bus swerved off the road and tumbled on its side ahead of them. Betty began breaking.

"Tillie..." Betty whispered quietly. At that very moment, two patrols car sped past toward the wreckage. Severson's car was in the lead.

Along the side of the road, the bus was lying like a gigantic, purple and white coffin on wheels. Betty could see the dents and crunches in Boris' smiling, painted image that decorated the entire side. Both State Highway Patrol cars and the local police pulled up alongside the accident. Policemen jumped out of their cars, pulled out their pistols and raced toward the wreckage. News trucks arrived and reporters and cameraman jumped out.

Betty continued her struggle with shifting, clutching and braking as she slowed. She managed to reach the scene without killing the engine and pulled the bus up behind a police cruiser. As soon as she stopped, she opened the door and she and Lori rushed out.

"Tillie will be okay. I know she'll be okay," Lori said as they raced along the highway's shoulder, each of them slipping on the salt and ice as they ran.

"She has to be," Betty answered, knowing that it would be unbearable to think otherwise. When they were within a few yards of the bus, a patrolman rushed up to them, his firearm drawn.

"Stop right there!" he yelled.

Severson heard the command and turned to look. He told the officer "They're okay, you can let them by."

The patrolman lowered his gun and Betty and Lori rushed over to the sheriff.

"Why are you here?" she spat out quickly as her shoes pressed into the crunchy snow that surrounded her feet.

Sheriff Severson grimaced. "I was going to ask you the same thing. What the hell were the two of you thinking, trying to chase down a speeding motor coach?"

"We weren't thinking," Betty admitted. "But I meant, how did you know to follow us so quickly?"

The sheriff answered disgustedly. "We were a few minutes away from apprehending Ogawa when you took off after him. We're planning to arrest him and his gang for murder and counterfeiting, if he's not dead that is."

Lori asked, "You knew about the secret room?"

The sheriff looked at her confused. "Not until you just mentioned. We found a phony bill in one of the slot machines. It had Rose's fingerprints all over it. Then we figured out one of the showgirls was the one who broke into the penthouse suite, trying to frame Tillie."

"Speaking of Tillie," Betty said, pointing toward the crash scene. Two patrolmen had climbed on top of the bus. Incredibly, as the officers managed to yank the door open a hand appeared from inside the bus, clutching and waving a stack of bills in the open air. Betty couldn't tell to whom the fingers belonged. The wiggling fingers could have been Rose, Tillie or even Ogawa.

Relief appeared in the whisks of red hair that were edging upwards out of the doorway. Tillie hoisted herself slowly out of the bus. The two officers guided her to the ground. Limping, and holding one of her arms in obvious pain, Tillie trudged toward the two women.

Betty yelled, "Tillie!"

Tillie responded with a weak smile and then stumbled, appearing to pass out. An officer caught her right before she hit the ground. He wrapped his arms around Tillie's body, lifted her up, and carried her as if she were nothing more than a sleeping child.

Chapter 30

I wasn't in a coma," Tillie said one more time, poking at her plate filled with organic spring greens, almond bits and Mandarin orange slices. "I don't know why you keep saying that." Although her arm was in a sling, and the buffet jam-packed with customers, she'd refused to let Lori or Betty carry her food back to the table for her.

"In our minds, you were," Lori said. "You were passed out for three hours."

"Did you ever think I passed out because the cop next to me was a hunk of burning love?" Tillie suggested, a sly look making her eye lids crinkle.

"Most cops are hunks, even with their love for all things pastry" Betty smiled warmly. It was wonderful to see her friend joking around, considering she'd been involved in a horrific accident only twenty hours earlier.

She asked, "Did the doctor say how long it would be until you can drive again?"

Tillie responded, "It should only be a few weeks. By that time, I'll be off pain killers for my sprained wrist."

Gloria had arranged for a tour bus and driver to take them back to Chicago. Take A Chance Tours would be able to leave right on schedule. In only three hours Betty would be checking off her clients' names on her list and watching them board. "You really are lucky," Betty said, shaking off the image of what could have happened to her friend.

"Incredibly lucky," Lori added, sitting back in her chair.

Betty noticed Lori gazing toward the buffet entrance. Tom Songbird had said he would be joining them.

Tillie nodded. "Luckier than Rose and her poor Oga."

Both had been severely injured in the accident. Rose suffered a broken leg and a cracked pelvis. Because Ogawa had been standing up when the bus crashed, he catapulted through the windshield like a racehorse out of the gate. Although he wasn't killed, he'd never work as a contortionist again, or walk. His spine was severed.

As Tillie lifted her arm to take a sip of coffee, a glimmer of gold sparkled on her wrist.

"You're wearing your bracelet!" Lori said, grabbing a spoonful of New Orleans bread pudding. The last time she'd seen the familiar piece of jewelry it was on Ogawa's wrist in the security tape.

"Tom gave it back to me this morning. He said the cleaning lady found it in the dressing room, the same place she discovered Betty's cell phone and laptop," Tillie stated.

"Ogawa must have stolen it off your wrist without you knowing it," Betty said, shifting her attention to Lori's plate of bread pudding. As far she was concerned, life didn't get any better than eating a concoction made from French bread soaked in eggs, sweet cream butter, and an ocean of Kentucky bourbon.

Tillie said, "That's true. Ogawa could yank teeth from a mule without the mule raising an eyebrow. He's a genius. Too bad he didn't use his talent for good rather than evil."

Betty agreed as she poked at her Tandoori Chicken. The dish was excellent but she'd already sampled five different international cuisines. Now that the murders appeared to be solved, she could finally concentrate on her job. Before she checked out of the hotel, she needed to post a brief review of the Hungry Moose Buffet on her blog, as well as share a few recipes.

Betty asked, "Tillie, did Ogawa or Rose talk about being related to Farsi and Slevitch?"

Tillie shook her head. "Not really, but they did talk about 'family'. The sheriff told me afterwards that he'd discovered Farsi and Slevitch were Ogawa's brothers-in-law."

Betty didn't mention that it was she who informed the sheriff of her hypothesis that Farsi, Slevitch, Rose were related. She'd suggested their propensity for being overweight was genetically connected.

She suggested he check into a few of her other extra-large riders, as well as a few that she'd seen in the casino.

Lori admitted, "It still shocks me that Rose didn't seem to even cringe when her own family member was killed onstage in front of her."

Tillie answered disgustedly, "That's an example of how strongly the Serbian gangs feel about the people who rat on them. Once someone turns they're no longer considered human, even if it was only a few minutes earlier that you would have killed *for* them." Tillie catapulted an almond bit into her mouth. "Did the sheriff say anything about the money?"

"Just that the two million in Farsi's luggage was real, and not counterfeit," Betty replied.

"Still no idea why the money was in his luggage?" Lori asked. "Or why he was killed?"

A baritone voice behind them said, "Farsi was planning on escaping to Canada with the dough." Tom Songbird had walked up without any of them noticing. He slid into a seat next to Lori. "He'd arranged for a rental car through the casino host. He even pre-paid for it."

"Was it Ogawa's money he stole?" Betty asked.

Tom nodded. "Severson told me it was the—quote, unquote—family money. Farsi stole it from their jointly owned safety box. He probably thought no one would miss it because there was another twelve million inside the box."

"So I'm guessing he took what he thought was *his* share?" Betty asked.

Tom said, "Ogawa didn't look at it that way, although both Farsi and Slevitch probably did. Slevitch was furious that Farsi was killed. Slevitch threatened to turn Ogawa in unless he was given the two million to keep quiet. Ogawa killed him, instead."

Betty asked, "How did Severson find all this out?"

Tom reached and grabbed a grape from Lori's plate and tossed it in the air. He caught it in his mouth, swallowed and answered, "Rose."

"Rose sang to the cops?" Tillie asked, her mouth dropping open in shock.

"Like an off-key canary." Tom grinned.

"Why?" Betty asked, also amazed.

"She's basically trying to cut a deal for herself" Tom explained. "She knows Ogawa will spend the rest of his life behind bars so she's trying to save herself a little time by telling everything she knows."

Betty sat back to digest the information from Songbird. There were still a few questions she needed answered.

Songbird must have read her mind. "Remember the bathroom scene? The one that looked like an episode of CSI Moose Bay?" he asked.

"Yes?" Betty said, encouraging him to carry on.

"The showgirls are Rose's nieces. Heather's the one who broke into the penthouse dressed like Tillie, and scattered the blood around the bathroom."

Betty asked, "Did Rose give any reason why the gang tried to frame one of us?"

Tom shook his head. "She just said the two of you were easy targets. I do know they were able to hack into your company's database even before they broke into your office and stole your computer."

"So they already knew that Tillie would be our driver for this trip?" Betty asked.

Tom said, "Looks like it."

Betty continued, "Then why did they have someone steal our desktop and the junket file?"

Tom answered, "Rose said Ogawa was paranoid about Farsi. He was afraid Farsi had given you his real name and address."

Lori asked, "But why wait to kill him on the tour bus? Why not before?"

Tom answered, "Rose said that Ogawa had made a phone call at the truck stop on his cell phone. That's when he learned about the money being taken. One of his family members in Chicago tipped him off."

Betty asked, "You're certain that Ogawa killed Slevitch as well?"

Tom nodded. "Rose claims he did. Shouldn't take too long to confirm it if true."

Lori asked, "Has Boris been apprehended?"

Tom shook his head. "No, and the two girls have disappeared along with him."

Tillie added, "Rose and Ogawa's kids never had a chance at a straight life, did they? I guess the apple just doesn't fall far from the tree, it hits you in the friggin' head if you're standing too damn close."

Betty noticed that Lori was quiet and looked pensive.

"What's the matter Lori?" Betty asked.

Lori pushed her plate away and said quietly, "Tony Gillette wasn't involved in any of this, was he?"

Tom looked confused.

"Your men led him away from the high-stakes table..." Lori began.

"Oh, you're referring to the poker room incident last night," Tom interjected. "I read my men the riot act over that. Tony's done a few favors for me from time to time. He's great at identifying card counting. I wanted him to view a security tape. I forgot to tell my men to say pretty please with sugar on it."

"So he's not in trouble?" Lori asked, suddenly relieved.

"No, not at all." Tom said. "He's accepted my apology. Tony's a first-class guy!"

Betty asked, "What about the thirteen million dollar win? Did Ogawa tamper with it?"

Tom answered, "There's good news and bad news you'll want to know about. The good news is that the headquarters in Nevada validated the win. I thought there was a system error that happened at the same time as the win, but it had nothing to do with the winning spin itself."

"What's the bad news?" Betty asked.

"It concerns someone on your tour," Tom said with a half grin.

Betty's brow furrowed quizzically until Tom explained, "Hannah found out the progressive is being awarded right before your bus leaves."

Betty groaned in exaggerated pain. "I'll bet she'll be standing in the front row, claiming the money should have been hers."

"It gets worse," Tom added.

"How?" Betty asked, not knowing if she really wanted to hear.

"Hannah heard me say the media will be present when we hand the winner the check. She made a point of telling me that during the ceremony she will let the media know the truth."

"What truth?" Betty asked.

"The truth about Take A Chance Tours."

Three hours later, Betty scrambled down the hotel sidewalk wheeling her luggage behind her. Fortunately, Lori had volunteered to welcome the passengers as they boarded the bus. Tillie stood at the side of the bus steps as well, assuring the riders that the new driver was more than qualified to take them back to Chicago. From Betty's viewpoint, it looked as if the bus was almost filled.

"Everyone show up?" Betty asked, as she watched the bellmen jam bag after bag into the luggage compartment.

"Everyone but Hannah—and here she comes." Tillie said, pointing down the sidewalk. Betty turned.

Hannah was moving slowly, her cane cracking angrily against the concrete with every step.

Betty could tell she was still angry about her performance at the news conference only minutes before.

Hannah had shown up at the event as promised. She bullied her way to the front of the crowd. All during the ceremony she kept raising her hand like a schoolgirl begging to be called on. Once the oversized check was presented to the winner, a television camera panned over to her. A budding reporter asked, "Is there something you'd like to say about the multi-million dollar win at Moose Bay?"

Hannah, seeing her face on the monitor of the camera, and probably realizing millions of people would hear what she was going to say, lost her bravado. Instead she said, "It's wonderful," and scurried off.

For Betty, the best thing about the nationally aired sound bite was that Hannah was wearing a Take A Chance Tours t-shirt.

Tillie tapped Betty on the shoulder, and said, "I'm going inside. Maybe I'll use the microphone to tell a few jokes before Road Bingo begins. Who knows? Maybe I'll decide to become a tour host."

"You'd be a great one," Betty replied, watching Tillie walk up the steps.

Betty looked back at her niece, who appeared to be lost in thought as she stared back toward the casino. Betty said, "The sheriff was looking for you earlier. Did he get ahold of you?"

Lori nodded. "He wanted to know if he could give me a call when this entire thing was over."

Betty scoffed, "That could take years."

"Exactly," she smiled. "That's why I told him he could."

"What about Tony Gillette?" Betty questioned, knowing his interest in Lori rivaled the sheriff's.

"Tony's flying into Chicago to take me to dinner on Sunday," Lori smiled before a serious expression took hold. "Aunt Betty, there's something I need to tell you."

"What?" Betty asked, hoping Hannah's slow moving assault toward the bus would give Lori enough time to share what was on her mind.

"This weekend turned out to be pretty good for me at the tables. I did really well at poker. I mean, I love playing poker, maybe too much in fact," Lori admitted, her eyes shifting downward.

Betty waited for Lori to continue, thankful that Hannah, who was still a few yards away, was hard of hearing.

Lori continued, "I'm thinking about taking a shot at becoming a professional poker player. That's one of the reasons Tony is flying in to see me. He wants to become my mentor."

"Lori, that's great," Betty answered. "Remember what I always say? Do what you love and the money will follow."

Lori nodded, but the worried look on her face told her aunt that for whatever reason, the change in careers frightened her. Maybe her niece didn't want to burden Betty with Take A Chance accounting. Betty decided to add, "Besides, what could possibly go wrong? If it doesn't work out, it doesn't work out. And I can take over the accounting for a while. It's no big deal."

The look on Lori's face didn't change. Betty thought her offer to help would have comforted Lori. She said, "Lori, I really don't mind helping you with the company's finances. You're overworked as it is, and I've been thinking for a while about hiring a professional accounting firm. That way you could help me with promotions."

Lori gulped. "A professional accounting firm? It's really no problem for me to handle the money."

Betty smiled warmly. "No. When we get back I insist on hiring a firm to handle our money. It's time we did an audit anyway."

Lori lifted her tear-filled eyes. "Sure, it's time we did that. We should have been doing it all along. But, once we do, I hope you'll always let me be a part of Take A Chance."

"You better be," Hannah called from nearby. "You're the only good thing about the company."

Lori said, "Thanks, Hannah. I needed that." She added diplomatically, "But Aunt Betty and Tillie are just as good as I am, if not better."

"Humph!" Hannah sputtered. She turned her attention to Betty. "Lucky for you, I still have enough money left in my bank account after this crummy trip to go on your next tour!"

"Lucky for me," Betty responded, her fingers crossed behind her back.

Hannah spun on her heels to climb the steps into the bus. She hesitated as she placed her foot on the first step. Betty realized she needed help, and gently placed her hand on Hannah's elbow to give her a lift up. Without uttering a word of rebuke, Hannah accepted Betty's help like she always did at the end of their journey.

Betty looked around at the bustling atmosphere of tour bus departures just as multitudes of new guests were arriving. Over the milling of the crowd, she heard a "Woo-hoo!" from another tour operator. It made her chuckle. It was always exciting to arrive at a casino with a busload of gamblers. For Betty's group, she could feel the contentment of a job well done. The tour had, against all odds, ended smoothly and she could tell that her passengers were pleased.

She watched as a hotel staffer finished placing bags into the luggage compartment and closed the door. He gave the driver a thumbs-up. The tour was officially over and a new one would soon begin.

She buttoned up her coat and thought, "Lucky for all of us."

Buffet Betty's Blog

www.buffetbetty.com

Hungry Moose Buffet: Five Popped Buttons!

In only one hour, our tour bus will leave the Moose Bay Casino. I can tell by your posted comments that most of you are aware of what's happened on this trip. News about murder and mayhem certainly travels at lightning speed across the internet! And if you're wondering if what you've read—murder in a locked bathroom, a murderous passenger disguised as an elderly man, a gang of international counterfeiters—is true? Well, yes it is. But, pretty much when you run a tour company that specializes in casino junkets anything can, and usually does, happen. It's not all jackpots and buffets!

But if you don't mind, I want to be fair to Moose Bay. Forget about the murders and the phony money for a while. Moose Bay is wonderful and I want you to visit as soon as possible. So, let's concentrate on the Hungry Moose Buffet and not the horrible events of the last few days. I want all of you to drive to Moose Bay! Don't worry about driving when there's six feet of snow on the ground. Or the fact that a moose might cross the highway at any given point. Moose Bay is worth the trip. For one thing, the loose slots that they advertise really are loose. I put ten bucks in a multi-progressive and walked away with a crisp twenty dollar bill an hour later. Woo hoo! Ten bucks profit for an hour of fun! Life doesn't get any better than that!

And the food? Fantastic! From locally grown ingredients to international cuisine expertly prepared, I gladly give five popped buttons to the Hungry Moose Buffet at Moose Bay Casino! Following are three recipes I wheedled from their chef for you to enjoy!

PECAN CRUSTED WALLEYE

2 walleye fillets (½ lb. each)
flour seasoned with salt and pepper
1 large egg, slightly beaten
¾ Cup finely chopped pecans
2 Tbsp. butter
2 Tbsp. minced scallion
3 cup all-purpose flour
1 ripe pear, peeled and cut into slices
¼ cup white wine
juice of ½ lemon
¼ cup heavy cream
2 tbsp. bleu cheese

Dredge walleye in flour, shake off excess, dip in egg and coat in pecans. Melt butter and sauté walleye 6 minutes on each side. Transfer fillets to a plate and cover to keep warm.

Drain excess grease. Add scallions and pear. Cook 1 to 2 minutes. Add wine, and cook a few more minutes. Add cream, season with salt and pepper. Add lemon juice. At the last minute, add the bleu cheese and spoon over the fish.

NEW ORLEANS BREAD PUDDING

Bourbon Sauce:
½ cup bread melted butter
1 cup sugar
1 egg
1 cup Kentucky bourbon whiskey

Bread Pudding:
1 loaf of stale French bread, cut into 1-inch squares (6-7 cups)

1 quart milk.
3 eggs, lightly beaten
2 cups sugar
2 Tbsp vanilla
1 cup raisins (soaked overnight in ¼ cup bourbon)
½ teaspoon allspice
1/3 to ½ teaspoon cinnamon
3 Tbsp unsalted butter, melted

Instructions:

Bourbon Sauce:
In a saucepan, melt butter; add sugar and egg, whisking it together. Stir constantly over low heat until the mixture thickens. (Do not allow to simmer because it could curdle.) Whisk in bourbon to taste. Remove from heat. Whisk again before serving. The sauce should be creamy, and smooth.

The Pudding
Preheat oven to 350 degrees F. Soak the bread in milk in a large mixing bowl. Press with hands until well mixed and all the milk absorbed. In a separate bowl, beat eggs, sugar, vanilla and spices together. Gently stir into the bread mixture. Stir the raisins into the mixture.

Pour butter into the bottom of a 9"x13" baking pan. Coat the bottom and the sides of the pan with butter. Pour in the bread mix and bake at 350 degrees for 35-45 minutes, until set. The pudding is done when the edges start browning and pulling away from the edge of the pan. Serve with bourbon whiskey sauce on the side; pour on to taste. Best fresh and eaten the day it is made. Makes 8-10 servings.

MAPLE WALNUT PUMPKIN PIE

Ingredients:

1 (15 ounce) can pumpkin
1 (14 ounce) can sweetened condensed milk
2 eggs
1 teaspoon maple flavoring
½ teaspoon ground cinnamon
½ teaspoon salt
½ teaspoon ginger
¼ teaspoon nutmeg

Walnut Topping:

1 (9 inch) Graham cracker pie crust
½ cup firmly packed brown sugar
1/2 cup all-purpose flour
½ teaspoon ground cinnamon
3 tablespoons butter
½ cup chopped walnuts

Instructions:

Preheat oven to 425 degrees F. In large mixing bowl, combine pumpkin, sweetened condensed milk, eggs, cinnamon, maple flavoring, ginger, nutmeg and salt; mix well. Pour into pie shell. Bake at 425 degrees F for 15 minutes. Reduce oven to 350 degrees F; continue baking 30 minutes. In medium mixing bowl, combine brown sugar, flour and cinnamon; cut-in butter until crumbly. Stir in nuts. Remove pie from oven; top evenly with crumb mixture. Return to oven 10 minutes. Cool. Garnish with chopped walnuts as desired. Store covered in refrigerator.

ABOUT THE AUTHOR: Pat Dennis is the award-winning author of *Hotdish To Die For,* a collection of six mystery short stories where the weapon of choice is hotdish, deadly recipes included. Readers demanding more were rewarded with *Hotdish Haiku*, featuring 50 haiku and recipes from her and other writers. Her short stories and humor appear in many anthologies, including: Anne Frasier's *Deadly Treats*; *Who Died in Here?*; *The Silence of the Loons; Resort to Murder: Fifteen Tales of Murder, Mayhem and Malice From the Land of Minnesota Nice; Once Upon A Crime Anthology*; and *Writes of Spring*. Her works have been published in NPR's *Minnesota Monthly, Woman's World, Hartford Courant, Pioneer Press, Sun Current*, and more. She is the author of the novel, *Stand-Up and Die*. Pat is also a stand-up comedian with over 1,000 performances at comedy clubs, Fortune 500 companies, Women's Expos, and special events. She has appeared on the same venue as Lewis Black, Phyllis Diller, and David Brenner. Visit her at www.patdennis.com. For recipes, contests, and restaurant reviews visit Pat and her alter ego "Betty Chance" at www.buffetbetty.com.

ACKNOWLEDGEMENTS: I am indebted, as always, to my friends and fellow writers: Marilyn Victor, Lance Zarimba, Theresa Weir (aka Anne Frasier), Lori L. Lake, Peter Schneider, Chris Everheart, Gary Bush, Wendy Nelson and Pat Frovarp. And I am in awe of my amazing editor, Nick Dimassis, for not only doing such a brilliant job, but for believing in the book.

CPSIA information can be obtained at www.ICGtesting.com
Printed in the USA
BVOW041708240313

316254BV00001B/51/P